Where the Heart Finds Home

I0695161

VIVIAN BELLE

STERLING RIDGE PRESS LLC

Where the Heart Finds Home © 2025 by Vivian Belle

All rights reserved. No part of this book may be reproduced, distributed, or transmitted in any form or by any means, including photocopying, recording, or other electronic or mechanical methods, without the prior written permission of the author, except in the case of brief quotations embodied in critical reviews and certain other noncommercial uses permitted by copyright law.

This is a work of fiction. Names, characters, places, and incidents either are the product of the author's imagination or are used fictitiously. Any resemblance to actual persons, living or dead, events, or locales is entirely coincidental.

All Scripture quotations, unless otherwise indicated, are taken from the Holy Bible, New International Version®, NIV®. Copyright ©1973, 1978, 1984, 2011 by Biblica, Inc.™ Used by permission of Zondervan. All rights reserved worldwide. The "NIV" and "New International Version" are trademarks registered in the United States Patent and Trademark Office by Biblica, Inc.™

Cover designed by Sterling Ridge Press LLC

Published by: Sterling Ridge Press, LLC www.sterlingridgepress.com

ISBN: 978-1-966093-16-9
Printed in the United States of America

First Edition: March 2025

For permissions, contact: support@vivianbelle.com or visit www.vivianbelle.com

Dedication

To all who have journeyed through wilderness seasons,
who have weathered life's blizzards and still found the courage to hope.
May you discover, as Laura did, that sometimes our most difficult
paths
lead us precisely where we need to be.
And to those still searching for belonging—
may you find the place where your heart can finally rest,
where love takes root and flourishes,
even through life's harshest seasons.
Vivian

About The Author

Vivian Belle is a talented author known for her sweeping **Historical Christian Romance** novels set against the untamed beauty of the American frontier. With a deep love for history and storytelling, she brings to life **resilient heroines, steadfast heroes, and faith-filled journeys** in the vast, rugged landscapes of the past.

Nestled in the **majestic mountains of northern West Virginia,** Vivian finds endless inspiration in the rolling hills, winding rivers, and boundless sky that mirror the spirit of her stories. When she's not writing, she enjoys **kayaking on tranquil waters, hiking through breathtaking mountain trails, and, of course, getting lost in a good book.**

Vivian's novels capture the heart of **faith, love, and perseverance**—where strong women and honorable men overcome life's trials to find hope, home, and happily-ever-after. Whether she's exploring the great outdoors or crafting her next frontier romance, Vivian's passion for adventure and storytelling shines through in every word she writes.

You can find out more about Vivian and her latest releases at www.vivianbelle.com or follow her on social media for updates and behind-the-scenes glimpses of her writing process. Stay connected—you won't want to miss the heartfelt stories of love and family she has in store!

Also by Vivian Belle

Where the Heart Finds Home

Faith on the Frontier

Love in Hopewell Creek

Contents

Chapter 1

Laura Rose Hartley clutched her worn leather satchel against her chest as the stagecoach lurched violently over another rut in the road. The wooden wheels crunched through the gathering snow, each rotation seeming more labored than the last. Outside the small window, Montana's vast landscape had disappeared behind a veil of white, the afternoon light dimming with each passing minute.

"Getting bad out there," muttered the elderly man across from her, his weathered face creased with concern as he peered through the frosted glass. "Driver's pushing hard. Too hard, if you ask me."

Laura nodded politely, but offered no reply. She had learned long ago that silence was often the safest response. Instead, she tightened her grip on her satchel—the sum total of her worldly possessions—and watched as her breath formed small clouds in the increasingly frigid air of the coach.

The vehicle jolted again, throwing her sideways. She caught herself against the wooden panel, wincing as her shoulder struck the hard surface.

"You all right there, miss?" The elderly man's wife reached across, her gloved hand hovering uncertainly.

"Yes, thank you." Laura straightened, tucking a strand of dark hair back beneath her bonnet. "I'm fine."

But she wasn't fine. She hadn't been fine for longer than she could remember.

The stagecoach contained five passengers besides herself—the elderly couple, a portly businessman who had been dozing since they'd left Elk Ridge, and two rough-looking men who had barely spoken a word the entire journey. None of them knew her story, and she preferred it that way. In Lone Valley, she would be nobody's burden, nobody's responsibility, and most importantly, nobody's shame.

Another violent lurch sent the businessman jerking awake with a startled grunt.

"What in tarnation—" he began, just as the driver's voice carried through the howling wind, shouting something unintelligible to the horses.

The coach pitched forward suddenly, and Laura's stomach dropped as she felt the sickening sensation of the wheels sliding rather than rolling. Outside, the horses whinnied in panic.

"Hold on!" someone shouted, and then the world tilted.

Laura had no time to scream before she was thrown against the side of the coach. Glass shattered. Wood splintered. For a terrifying moment, she was weightless, and then—impact. Pain shot through her body as the stagecoach crashed onto its side, sending passengers tumbling against each other in a tangle of limbs and luggage.

Silence fell, broken only by the moan of the wind and the groans of the injured passengers.

Laura blinked, finding herself wedged awkwardly between the bench and what had been the ceiling but was now a wall. Her cheek stung, and when she touched it, her fingers came away with a smear of blood.

"Is everyone all right?" The elderly man's voice trembled as he extricated himself from where he'd fallen across his wife.

Murmurs and moans answered him. The businessman was holding his arm at an odd angle, his face contorted in pain. One of the silent men had a gash across his forehead that was bleeding profusely.

Laura pushed herself upright, ignoring the throbbing in her shoulder. "Mrs.—" she began, realizing she didn't know the elderly woman's name.

"Dobbins," the woman supplied weakly. "Margaret Dobbins. And this is my husband, Henry."

"Mrs. Dobbins, are you hurt?" Laura moved carefully toward her.

"Just shaken, I think." Margaret attempted a smile that looked more like a grimace. "What happened?"

"Driver probably lost control on the ice," Henry said, helping his wife to a more comfortable position. "This storm came on faster than anyone expected."

The businessman, still clutching his injured arm, managed to kick open what had been the door and was now above them. Freezing air and snow immediately swirled into the confined space.

"I'm going to check on the driver," he announced, awkwardly pulling himself up and out.

Laura hesitated only a moment before following, her practical nature overriding her fear. The injured needed attention, regardless of the storm.

Emerging from the overturned coach was like stepping into another world. The wind slapped her face with such force that she gasped, the air stolen from her lungs. Snow fell so thick she could barely see three feet ahead. The world had become a churning mass of white, disorienting and vast.

The businessman stood a few paces away, his figure barely discernible in the blizzard. He was staring at something on the ground. Laura struggled forward, her boots slipping in the deepening snow.

"The driver—" the businessman said, his voice hollow.

Laura followed his gaze and immediately wished she hadn't. The driver lay motionless, thrown from his seat during the crash. His neck bent at an impossible angle, eyes staring sightlessly at the darkening sky. There was no need to check if he was alive.

Laura quickly averted her eyes, a prayer forming silently on her lips. Lord, receive his soul.

"The horses are gone," the businessman observed numbly, gesturing to the broken harnesses dangling from the front of the coach.

Laura glanced around, trying to get her bearings. All she could see was white in every direction—no road, no landmarks, just the endless sweep of the blizzard.

"We need to get back inside," she said, raising her voice above the wind. "We can't stay out here."

The businessman nodded, his face already red from the cold. Together they returned to the relative shelter of the overturned coach, where the others waited anxiously.

"Driver's dead," the businessman announced bluntly as he dropped back inside. "Horses ran off."

A shocked silence fell over the group, broken only by Margaret Dobbins's soft sob.

"God rest his soul," Henry murmured, crossing himself.

"What do we do now?" asked one of the previously silent men, his voice surprisingly young.

Laura looked around at their faces—scared, uncertain, looking for leadership. It was a familiar feeling, being surrounded by people who needed something from her. For years, it had been Jasper looking at her this way when he was deep in the bottle, needing her to clean up his messes, to smooth things over, to keep them both alive.

"How far are we from Lone Valley?" she asked, pushing away thoughts of her brother.

Henry shook his head. "Can't say for certain. Maybe two miles? Could be more. We were still a good piece out when the storm hit."

"And Elk Ridge?"

"Farther back. At least fifteen, I'd reckon."

Laura bit her lip, calculating. Two miles in fair weather was nothing. Two miles in a blizzard might as well be fifty.

"We need to stay put," the businessman declared, cradling his injured arm. "Someone will come looking when we don't arrive."

"In this?" The younger of the two silent men gestured toward the open door above them, where snow continued to swirl in. "No one's coming in this weather, mister. Not today, maybe not tomorrow either."

"We could freeze to death by then," Laura said quietly, voicing what they all were thinking.

"Not if we're smart," Henry replied. "I spotted a rock outcropping just before we crashed. Can't be more than a hundred yards back. Better shelter than this coach, and we might find some wood to make a fire."

"A hundred yards in that?" The businessman gestured disbelievingly at the blizzard. "We'd get lost and freeze for certain."

"Not if we stay together," Henry insisted. "Form a line, hold on to each other."

The group fell into an anxious debate about their options. Laura listened silently, her mind working. She had come too far, endured too much to die in a blizzard on the edge of her new beginning.

Lone Valley. The name had called to her from the moment she'd heard it. A valley, nestled among mountains, protected and isolated. A place where a person could disappear, start fresh. Where Jasper couldn't find her.

Two miles. She had walked farther with less hope.

"I'm continuing to Lone Valley," she announced suddenly, cutting through the argument.

Five pairs of eyes turned to her in astonishment.

"Alone?" Margaret gasped. "Child, you'll die out there!"

"I might die here too," Laura replied calmly. "At least this way, I have a chance to reach shelter—real shelter, with warm fires and food."

"It's suicide," the businessman stated flatly.

"I've survived worse," Laura said, and she had. Nights sleeping rough when Jasper gambled away their rent money. Days without food when his drinking consumed what little they had. The constant moving, running, apologizing, mending, scraping by. "I know how to follow a road, even in snow."

"Miss..." Henry looked at her kindly. "I don't even know your name, but please reconsider. We're going to that outcropping, I saw. It's not far, and it's our best chance."

"It's Laura. Laura Rose Hartley." She smiled slightly, warming to the old man's genuine concern. "And I appreciate your worry, Mr. Dobbins, truly. But I've made my decision."

She began gathering her things—her satchel, thankfully still intact, and her woolen cloak, which she wrapped tightly around herself. From her bag, she pulled out a pair of mittens she had knitted herself during one of the many late nights, waiting for Jasper to stagger home.

"At least wait until morning," Margaret pleaded. "The storm might let up."

Laura shook her head. "It'll be dark soon. If I wait until morning, I'll have lost precious hours. And there's no guarantee the storm will ease." She hesitated, then added softly, "I have nothing and no one to go back to. Lone Valley is my only chance."

The younger man who had spoken earlier suddenly stood. "I'll go with you," he offered.

Laura assessed him quickly—barely older than herself, lean but strong-looking. "Why?"

He shrugged. "Same as you. Nothing waiting for me, and I don't fancy freezing in a rock cave for days."

She hesitated. Part of her wanted to reject his offer outright—she had learned the hard way not to trust men's sudden offers of help. But another part, the practical part, knew that having a companion in the blizzard increased her chances of survival.

"What's your name?" she asked.

"Thomas Wade," he replied. "Most call me Tom."

"Well, Tom, if you're coming, we need to leave now." She turned to the others. "I hope you all make it safely to that outcropping. God be with you."

"And with you, child," Margaret said, tears in her eyes. "You're in our prayers."

Laura nodded her thanks, then climbed out of the coach, Tom following close behind. The cold hit her with renewed force, making her gasp. The wind had, if anything, grown stronger, driving needles of ice against any exposed skin.

Looking back, she saw Henry helping the others out of the coach, organizing them for their trek to the rock outcropping. Then she turned her face toward what she hoped was the direction of Lone Valley and took her first step into the blizzard.

Chapter 2

She could no longer feel her feet. That was probably bad, Laura thought distantly, but she couldn't summon the energy to care. How long had they been walking? An hour? Two? Time had lost all meaning in the white wilderness that engulfed them.

Tom had fallen behind some time ago, his steps growing slower despite Laura's encouragement. She'd waited for him several times, but each stop allowed the cold to seep deeper into her bones. The last time she'd looked back, he was just a dark smudge in the whiteness, and now... now she couldn't see him at all.

"Tom?" she called, her voice pathetically weak against the roar of the wind. "Tom!"

No answer came. Had he turned back? Collapsed? Or was she simply too disoriented to see or hear him?

The thought that she might be responsible for leading him to his death made her stomach clench. But what could she do? She could barely see her own hands in front of her face. Going back would only mean two deaths instead of one.

"I'm sorry," she whispered, though the words were torn away by the wind before they even left her lips.

Laura forced herself to continue, one agonizing step after another. She had lost the road long ago—if she had ever been on it to begin with. Now she was simply moving forward, driven by the stubborn hope that she might stumble across Lone Valley, or at least some kind of shelter.

The memory of her brother's face rose unbidden in her mind. Jasper, red-faced with drink and rage when he had discovered her plans to leave.

"You can't just abandon me, Laura Rose!" he had shouted, using her full name the way he always did when he was angry. "After everything I've done for you!"

Everything he'd done to her, more like. The years of broken promises, of money gambled away, of being uprooted every time his debts or reputation caught up with them. The nights she'd lain awake, wondering if he was dead in a ditch somewhere, or if the men he owed would come for her when they couldn't find him.

Yet still, some small part of her felt guilty. He was her brother, her only blood left in the world. They had been orphaned young, forced to rely on each other. There had been good times too, especially when they were children and their parents had still been alive. Jasper teaching her to fish in a sun-dappled creek. Jasper defending her from bullies in school.

But those memories had grown distant, buried beneath the weight of his addiction. The brother she had loved was disappearing, drink by drink, replaced by a stranger who wore his face but none of his kindness.

The words of hope from Evelyn Whitaker had been a godsend. The kindly widow who owned the mercantile in Elk Ridge had taken a shine to Laura during her brief employment there. When Evelyn mentioned her cousin in Lone Valley needing help at her boarding house, Laura had seen it as the sign she'd been praying for.

"Lone Valley is perfect for a fresh start," Evelyn had told her, eyes twinkling with warmth. "Small enough to feel safe, big enough to offer opportunity. And far enough away that troublesome brothers might not find their way there so easily."

Laura had planned her escape carefully, saving what meager coins she could from mending clothes and helping at the mercantile. She'd waited until Jasper was deep in a drunken sleep before slipping away, leaving only a brief note explaining that she needed to make her own way now.

It had been cowardly, perhaps, but necessary. Face to face, she would have wavered. He would have promised to change, as he had a dozen times before, and she would have believed him, as she had a dozen times before.

Not this time. This time, she had chosen herself.

And now she might die for that choice.

The irony was not lost on her. After all her careful planning, after finally finding the courage to leave, she might perish just miles from her destination. She thought of Mrs. Dobbins' parting words... "You're in our prayers"—and wondered if God was listening to any of them in this howling wasteland.

"Lord," she whispered through cracked lips, "I know I've been distant. I know my faith has wavered. But if You can hear me now... I could use a miracle."

The wind seemed to mock her prayer, driving snow into her face with renewed force. Laura lowered her head and pressed on, each step heavier than the last. Her vision had begun to narrow, darkness creeping in at the edges. That was bad too, she knew. Very bad.

She stumbled, falling to her knees in the snow. The cold shock of it penetrated even her numbness, but she couldn't find the strength to stand again. Exhaustion washed over her in waves, along with a strange, treacherous warmth that tempted her to simply lie down and rest.

Just for a moment, a voice in her head whispered. Close your eyes just for a moment.

Laura knew, with the small part of her mind still functioning rationally, that closing her eyes would mean death. But the knowledge seemed distant and unimportant compared to the overwhelming need for rest.

As she wavered there on her knees, caught between the will to survive and the lure of surrender, a sound penetrated the roar of the wind. At first, she thought she had imagined it—a rhythmic thudding, growing louder.

Thud-thud-thud-thud.

Laura raised her head with effort, blinking snowflakes from her lashes as she peered into the white void. The sound grew clearer, unmistakable now.

Hoofbeats.

A dark shape materialized in the swirling snow, growing larger as it approached. A horse and rider, moving with purposeful speed despite the blizzard.

Her miracle.

Laura tried to call out, but her voice emerged as little more than a rasp. She tried to stand, to wave, to do anything that might catch the rider's attention, but her body refused to cooperate.

The horse and rider were going to pass her by, she realized with a surge of despair. They were angled slightly away from her position, and in the blinding snow, she was just another shadowy lump on the ground.

With the last reserves of her strength, Laura fumbled with the clasp of her cloak. The wool wasn't visible enough against the snow, but underneath—underneath she wore a dress of blue, the one spot of color in the white landscape.

Her fingers, stiff and clumsy in her mittens, finally managed to loosen the clasp. She shrugged the cloak from her shoulders and, mustering every ounce of remaining energy, waved it above her head like a flag.

"Help!" The word tore from her throat, carried away by the wind. "Please! Help me!"

For a moment, it seemed the rider hadn't seen or heard her. The figure continued on its path, about to disappear back into the curtain of snow.

Laura's arm dropped, the cloak falling limply beside her. So close. Her miracle had been so close.

Then, abruptly, the horse turned. The rider had seen her.

Relief washed over Laura so intensely that what little strength she had left deserted her. She slumped forward into the snow, consciousness slipping away even as the hoofbeats grew louder, approaching fast.

The last thing she was aware of was the sound of the horse coming to a halt nearby, the crunch of boots in snow, and then strong arms lifting her from the ground. A deep voice, concern evident even through her fading awareness, said something she couldn't quite make out.

And then darkness claimed her completely.

Chapter 3

Boone Callahan leaned into the wind, his body angled forward in the saddle as Rusher fought against the blinding snow. The gelding's muscles strained beneath him, each step a battle against nature's fury. They'd been riding for nearly an hour. The journey back to the ranch turned treacherous by the sudden ferocity of the storm.

"Come on, boy," Boone muttered, his voice lost in the howling wind. "Just a few more miles."

The supply run to Elk Ridge had been a fool's errand. He'd known the storm was coming—everyone had—but he'd gambled on having enough time to make it there and back before the worst hit. Now he was paying for that miscalculation, and Rusher along with him.

Beneath his heavy coat, Boone's shoulders ached from the constant tension of fighting the wind. His face burned from the relentless sting of ice crystals, the lower half protected only somewhat by the bandana pulled up over his nose and mouth. Even through his thick gloves, his fingers had gone numb, clutching the reins.

This was Montana in winter—unforgiving and merciless to those who underestimated her. Boone knew better. He'd been born and raised in this territory, had weathered storms that had claimed the lives of men who thought themselves its master. Nature had no masters, only survivors.

A sudden gust nearly unseated him, and Boone tightened his thighs around Rusher's barrel, steadying himself. The horse nickered in protest but pushed on, head down against the onslaught.

"That's it," Boone encouraged, leaning down to pat the gelding's frost-crusted neck. "We'll get you home, get you warm."

Home. The word conjured an image of the Callahan ranch house—solid timber walls, the stone fireplace his father had built with his own hands, lamplight glowing in windows that had watched over two generations of his family. It wasn't grand, but it was his, his responsibility since his mother's passing and his father's gradual yielding of the reins to his youngest son.

The other Callahan children had long since gone—Marcus to Colorado with his wife, Sara, married and moved west. Only Boone had remained, tied to the land by something deeper than duty, something that lived in his blood and bones.

His thoughts drifted briefly to Eliza, as they sometimes did in moments of solitude. Two years since she'd stood on the porch of that same ranch house, her trunk packed beside her, explaining that she couldn't waste her life as a rancher's wife when the promise of California gold beckoned.

"I need more than this, Boone," she'd said, gesturing vaguely at the endless Montana landscape. "More than cows and fence posts and the same four walls."

He'd offered nothing in response—no pleas, no promises, no anger. Just a nod, acceptance of what he should have seen coming. Eliza had always been restless, always looking toward distant horizons while he found everything he needed right where he stood.

The memory no longer cut as it once had. Time had cauterized that wound, leaving only a dull ache and a wariness he carried like his father's old pocket watch—constant, familiar, largely unnoticed until something made him reach for it.

A tightness in his chest made Boone cough, the cold air scraping his lungs. He needed to focus. Woolgathering in a blizzard was a good way to end up dead.

The visibility had worsened, if that was possible. He could barely see Rusher's ears in front of him, much less the trail. But the horse knew the way home, and Boone trusted the animal's instincts more than his own in these conditions.

"Just follow your nose, boy," he murmured, giving the gelding more rein.

Rusher snorted, then suddenly halted, ears pricking forward. Boone tensed, alert to the change. The horse had sensed something.

"What is it?" Boone leaned forward, straining to see through the swirling whiteness.

For a moment, there was nothing but the endless veil of snow. Then—a movement. Something that didn't belong in this wilderness of white. A splash of color, there and gone so quickly Boone thought he might have imagined it.

Rusher shifted beneath him, sidestepping nervously.

"Easy," Boone soothed, peering intently into the storm.

There it was again—a flash of blue against the snow, like a jay's wing in summer, absurdly out of place in this winter wasteland. Boone turned Rusher toward it, curiosity overriding his desire to reach home as quickly as possible.

As they drew closer, the blue resolved into a shape—fabric moving weakly in the wind. Boone's heart quickened. Someone was out here in the storm.

He urged Rusher forward, closing the distance rapidly. The figure was small, collapsed on their knees in the deep snow, barely moving. As he pulled up alongside, Boone saw it was a woman, her dark hair whipping around a pale face, eyes closed as if in sleep.

"Hey!" he called, but the wind stole his words.

The woman didn't respond—didn't move at all. Acting on instinct, Boone swung down from the saddle, his boots sinking deep into the snow. The cold immediately bit through his pants, a stark reminder of how deadly this exposure could be.

He crouched beside the woman, turning her face toward him. She was young, maybe early twenties, her features delicate but blue with cold. Her eyelashes were frosted, lips parted slightly as shallow breaths formed small clouds in the frigid air.

"Miss?" Boone tapped her cheek, trying to rouse her. "Miss, can you hear me?"

Nothing. She was alive, but barely—deep in the dangerous sleep that preceded freezing to death. Boone glanced around, looking for others, for any sign of where she had come from or how she had ended up alone in this blizzard. There was nothing visible but white in every direction.

No time to puzzle it out. The woman would be dead within minutes if he didn't get her warm.

Boone gathered her in his arms, surprised at how little she weighed. Her body was limp against his, head rolling against his shoulder. A small leather satchel was clutched in her frozen fingers, which he pried loose and slung over his shoulder. He spotted a cloak half-buried in the snow and grabbed that too, though it was wet and nearly frozen stiff.

Getting back on Rusher while holding the unconscious woman proved challenging, but Boone managed it with the practiced efficiency of a man accustomed to solving problems alone. He positioned her across his lap, cradling her against his chest, and wrapped his coat around her as best he could.

"Home, Rusher," he urged, turning the horse's head back in the direction they'd been traveling. "Fast as you can, boy."

The gelding needed no further encouragement, sensing the urgency in his master's voice. Despite the added weight, Rusher pushed forward with renewed purpose, as if understanding the precious nature of their burden.

Boone held the woman tightly, trying to shield her from the worst of the wind. She was so cold against him, her breathing shallow. He found himself murmuring to her the same encouraging words he'd been using with Rusher, though he knew she couldn't hear him.

"Stay with me," he said, the words caught and carried away by the wind. "Not much further now. Just stay with me."

For the first time in years, Boone found himself praying—not the formal, distant prayers he sometimes offered in church to maintain appearances, but something raw and urgent.

Lord, don't let her die. Not when help is so close.

The journey back to the ranch seemed interminable, each minute stretching as Boone divided his attention between the trail ahead and the still figure in his arms. Once or twice, he thought he felt her stir, but it might have been the motion of the horse.

Finally, the welcome shape of the ranch house appeared through the curtain of snow, lamplight glowing in the windows like a beacon. Relief surged through Boone, though he knew they weren't safe yet. The woman needed warming, and quickly.

As they approached, the front door flew open, spilling golden light onto the snow-covered ground. His father's silhouette appeared in the doorway.

"Boone?" Zeb called out, his voice barely carrying through the storm. "That you, son?"

"It's me, Pa!" Boone shouted back. "And I've got company. She needs help!"

Comprehension dawned on Zeb's face as Boone drew closer, and he rushed forward to meet them, snow immediately dusting his gray hair. Despite his age, Zeb moved with the vigor of a much younger man, reaching Rusher's side just as Boone began to dismount.

"Good Lord," Zeb exclaimed, helping to steady them as Boone carefully maneuvered off the horse with his burden. "Where'd you find her?"

"About three miles out," Boone replied, adjusting his grip to carry her more securely. "All alone in the snow. No idea where she came from."

"Bring her in quick," Zeb ordered, unnecessarily. "I'll tend to Rusher."

Boone nodded gratefully and strode toward the house, the unconscious woman cradled against his chest. The snow crunched beneath his boots, the last steps of a journey that had unexpectedly become a rescue mission.

Inside, the heat from the roaring fire in the hearth hit him like a physical wave after the bitter cold. The main room of the ranch house was large and open, combining living area and kitchen, with the substantial stone fireplace dominating one wall. The familiar smell of wood smoke and coffee wrapped around him like an embrace.

Boone carried the woman directly to the fire, kneeling to lay her gently on the thick rug before it. Her face, illuminated now by the dancing flames, seemed even more pale and drawn than it had appeared in the dim light of the blizzard.

"Who is she?"

Boone glanced up to see Matt Cutler, his ranch hand and friend, standing in the doorway to the kitchen, wiping his hands on a cloth. Matt's expression was one of surprise mixed with immediate concern.

"Don't know," Boone answered shortly, already working to remove the woman's snow-covered outer garments. "Found her half-dead in the snow. Help me get these wet things off her."

Matt moved forward without hesitation, helping to carefully remove the woman's boots and stockings, revealing alarmingly white feet. Her hands, when Boone carefully peeled away her mittens, were in a similar state—not blackened with frostbite yet, but dangerously cold.

"We need to warm her up," Matt said, stating the obvious.

"Blankets," Boone instructed, fighting to keep the worry from his voice. "The heavy wool ones from the chest. And heat some water—not boiling, but warm."

As Matt hurried to comply, Boone hesitated, looking down at the woman's dress, now damp from melting snow. She needed to be completely dry to warm properly, but the implications of undressing an unconscious, unknown woman were not lost on him.

The front door opened again, admitting a gust of cold air and his father, snow dusting his gray hair and beard.

"Rushers settled," Zeb announced, stomping his boots on the mat. "How is she?"

"Still unconscious," Boone replied, relief evident in his voice at his father's arrival. "Pa, she needs to get out of these wet clothes, but—"

Zeb understood immediately. "I'll handle it, son. You and Matt go fetch more firewood and heat up some broth. We'll need it when she wakes."

Boone nodded, grateful for his father's tactful intervention. Though he'd acted without hesitation to save the woman's life, there were matters of propriety to consider, especially with a stranger.

Rising to his feet, he cast one last glance at the still figure by the fire. Something about her face, vulnerable in unconsciousness, stirred a protective instinct he hadn't felt in a long time.

"She'll be all right," Matt said quietly, clapping a hand on Boone's shoulder. "Your pa knows what he's doing."

Boone nodded, tearing his gaze away. "Let's get that wood."

As they headed toward the back door, Boone found his mind returning to the woman he'd found in the snow. Who was she? What was her story? And why did he feel so inexplicably drawn to someone he'd literally just pulled from a snowdrift?

Questions without answers swirled in his mind as he stepped back out into the storm.

Lord, let her live. Whatever brought her out into that storm, whatever she's running to or from, let her have the chance to see it through.

It was the most sincere prayer he'd said in years.

Chapter 4

Laura woke slowly, awareness returning in gentle waves. First came the sensation—warmth surrounding her, the soft weight of blankets, the distant crackling of a fire. Then smell—wood smoke, coffee, and the faint scent of something savory cooking. Finally, she opened her eyes to an unfamiliar wooden ceiling. The beams darkened with age and smoke.

For a disorienting moment, she couldn't remember where she was or how she'd gotten there. Then memory flooded back—the stagecoach accident, the desperate walk through the blizzard, falling in the snow, and then... a rider. She had been rescued.

Laura turned her head slightly, taking in her surroundings. She lay on a bed in a small, simple room, covered with layers of quilts. A lamp burned low on a nearby dresser, casting a warm glow over plain wooden furniture. Through a window, she could see it was dark outside, snow still falling, though not as heavily as before.

A soft knock at the door drew her attention. Before she could respond, it opened slightly, and a man's head poked in, an older man with a kind face framed by a gray beard.

"Ah, you're awake," he said, his voice warm with relief. "How are you feeling, miss?"

Laura tried to speak, but her throat was painfully dry. She managed only a rasp before coughing.

"Here," the man said, entering fully and approaching with a cup of water. "Small sips now."

He helped her to sit up slightly, supporting her back with one arm while holding the cup to her lips with the other. The water was wonderfully cool and soothing.

"Thank you," Laura whispered when she'd drunk her fill.

"You're most welcome," the man replied, setting the cup aside and settling into a chair beside the bed. "I'm Zebuliah Callahan—Zeb to most folks. You're at the Callahan Ranch, about three miles outside of Lone Valley."

Lone Valley. The name sparked hope in Laura's chest. She had almost reached her destination after all.

"My son, Boone, found you in the blizzard," Zeb continued. "Lucky thing too—wouldn't have lasted much longer out there."

"Your son," Laura repeated, memory stirring of strong arms lifting her from the snow. "I remember... someone on horseback. I thought I was dreaming."

"No dream," Zeb assured her with a smile. "Though I imagine it seemed like one at the time. Boone was on his way back from a supply run cut short by the storm. Providence, I'd call it."

Laura nodded weakly. "I'm Laura," she offered. "Laura Rose Hartley."

"Miss Hartley," Zeb acknowledged with a small nod. "You're a fortunate young woman. Not many survive being caught in a Montana blizzard, especially alone."

The mention of "alone" triggered a sudden memory. "There was a man with me," Laura said urgently, trying to push herself up further. "Tom Wade. He fell behind. I couldn't—"

A wave of dizziness forced her back down, and Zeb reached out to steady her.

"Easy now," he cautioned. "You're still weak. As for your companion, I'm afraid there's nothing to be done tonight. The storm's still going, and it's pitch black out there. Come morning, if the weather's cleared, we can send out a search party."

Laura closed her eyes briefly, guilt washing over her. Poor Tom.

"The others," she said, opening her eyes again. "There was a stagecoach. It overturned about a mile or two back from where your son found me. Four other passengers—they were heading for a rock outcropping for shelter."

Zeb's expression grew grave. "I'll tell Boone. First thing tomorrow, we'll organize a search for all of them, if the weather permits." He studied her face for a moment. "May I ask what brings you to our area?"

Laura hesitated, uncertain how much to reveal. These people had saved her life, but old habits of caution were hard to break.

"I was on my way to Lone Valley," she said finally. "I have a position waiting for me there. When the stagecoach overturned and the driver was killed, I... I made the decision to continue on foot."

"A risky decision," Zeb observed, though there was no judgment in his tone.

"Yes," Laura agreed quietly. "I see that now."

A door opened somewhere outside the room, and Laura heard the heavy tread of boots on wooden floorboards, followed by a second, lighter set of footsteps.

"She awake, Pa?" a deep voice called.

"Just came around," Zeb replied, raising his voice slightly. "Come in and meet our guest properly."

The bedroom door opened wider, admitting two men. The first was tall and broad-shouldered, with dark hair and a face that seemed carved from the same rugged stone as the mountains surrounding them. His eyes, a startling blue, regarded her with an intensity that made Laura want to shrink back into the blankets.

The second man was shorter, leaner, with sandy hair and an open, friendly face that instantly put Laura more at ease.

"Miss Hartley, this is my son, Boone," Zeb introduced, "and our ranch hand, Matt Cutler."

"Ma'am," Matt greeted with a cheerful smile. "Good to see you with some color back in your cheeks. You were about as blue as a jay when Boone brought you in."

"Matt," Boone said warningly, then turned his attention to Laura. His expression remained guarded, but something in his eyes softened slightly. "How are you feeling?"

"Better," Laura replied honestly. "Thanks to you."

Boone shifted his weight, clearly uncomfortable with her gratitude. "Anyone would have done the same," he said dismissively.

"Not everyone would have been out in that storm to begin with," Laura countered softly. "Nor would they have spotted me."

Boone didn't respond directly, but his gaze lingered on her face a moment longer than necessary before he turned to his father.

"Storm's letting up some," he reported.

"Good," Zeb nodded. "Miss Hartley was telling me about the stagecoach accident she was in. Sounds like we might have several people in need of help out there."

"We should go look for them," Laura said, trying once again to sit up. This time she managed it, though the effort left her dizzy. "I can show you where—"

"You're not going anywhere," Boone interrupted, his tone brook no argument. "You nearly died out there once. I won't risk having to rescue you again."

His bluntness took Laura aback. She wasn't accustomed to being spoken to so directly, especially by a stranger. But before she could respond, Matt stepped in smoothly.

"What Boone means, in his charming way," he said with a pointed look at his boss, "is that you need to rest and recover. Frostbite's nothing to mess with, and you've had a close call."

"That's exactly what I mean," Boone said, not softening his tone in the slightest. "It would be foolish for you to go back out there in your condition."

Laura might have bristled at being called foolish under normal circumstances, but she was too exhausted to summon much indignation. Besides, he wasn't wrong. Her limbs felt like lead, and even sitting upright was taxing her limited strength.

"I understand," she conceded quietly. "But please find the others if you can. They could still be alive. Three men and a woman near the accident. One other man, I'm not sure where I lost him. We had been walking together and then, at some point, I lost sight of him wandering through the storm."

Something in her plea seemed to reach Boone because his expression softened fractionally. "We'll do our best," he promised.

An awkward silence fell, broken by Matt clearing his throat. "I've got some beef stew on the stove," he announced. "Miss Hartley might be feeling up to something more substantial than broth now."

"That sounds wonderful," Laura said gratefully, suddenly aware of the hollow feeling in her stomach. "If it's not too much trouble."

"No trouble at all," Matt assured her with a grin. "Cooking's about the only thing I do around here that doesn't get complaints." He shot a teasing glance at Boone.

"That's because it's the only thing you do right," Boone retorted, but there was no real heat in his words, and Laura detected the faint curl of his lip that might have been a suppressed smile.

This glimpse of camaraderie between the two men revealed something about Boone that his stern exterior concealed—he was capable of warmth, just selective about showing it.

"I'll help you up to the table if you feel strong enough," Zeb offered. "Or we can bring a tray in here if you prefer."

Laura considered how weak she still felt, but was reluctant to be more of a burden than she already was. "I think I can make it to the table," she decided, pushing back the covers.

It was only then that she realized she was wearing an oversized man's shirt that hung past her knees. Heat flooded her cheeks as she looked up questioningly.

Zeb, reading her thoughts, quickly explained. "We had to get you out of those wet clothes, or you'd never have warmed up. I handled it myself, miss," he assured her. "Proper as could be under the circumstances. The shirt's one of Boone's old ones—cleanest thing we had that would work as a nightshirt."

"I understand," Laura murmured, embarrassment mingling with gratitude. "Thank you for your... discretion."

Boone, she noticed, had turned away slightly, a faint redness visible on the back of his neck. The sight was oddly endearing—this rugged man, embarrassed by the mere mention of feminine undergarments.

"Your clothes are dry now," Matt piped up, helpfully changing the subject. "I'll fetch them for you."

"Thank you," Laura said, gathering the quilt around herself.

The men left the room to allow her privacy, Zeb promising to return in a few minutes to help her to the table. When the door closed behind them, Laura sat for a moment, collecting herself.

The events of the past day felt surreal—the stagecoach accident, the desperate trek through the blizzard, her near-death in the snow, and now finding herself in the home of strangers who had saved her life. It was almost too much to process.

Yet beneath the disorientation was a profound sense of gratitude. She had survived, thanks to Boone Callahan's timely appearance in the storm. Whatever she thought of his gruff manner, she owed him her life.

Matt returned with her clothes, knocking respectfully before passing them through a barely opened door. Laura dressed quickly, grateful to be back in her own garments despite their simplicity—a plain blue woolen dress with a high collar and long sleeves, practical and modest.

The motion of dressing left her light-headed, and she had to pause several times to steady herself. Her fingers felt stiff and clumsy, her feet still partially numb. These were worrying signs, but at least she had all her fingers and toes, which was more than many frostbite victims could say.

When she was decent, Laura called softly that she was ready. Zeb returned immediately, offering his arm for support. She took it gratefully, finding her legs wobbly and unreliable as she stood.

"Easy now," Zeb cautioned as they moved slowly toward the door. "No rush."

The main room of the Callahan ranch house was spacious and open, dominated by a large stone fireplace. A wooden table with benches stood nearby, already set with bowls and spoons. The fire cast a warm glow over everything, creating pools of light and shadow that made the simple space feel cozy despite its utilitarian furnishings.

Boone and Matt looked up as she entered, Matt with an encouraging smile, Boone with an assessing gaze that seemed to catalog her every weakness and strength in a single glance.

"You should be in bed," he stated flatly.

"Boone," Zeb said warningly.

"It's all right," Laura assured Zeb, refusing to be cowed by Boone's bluntness. "I need to sit up for a while. And I'm hungry."

Matt jumped in before Boone could respond. "Then you're in luck, Miss Hartley. My stew is famous in these parts—well, famous to the three of us, anyway." He ladled a generous portion into a bowl and set it before her as Zeb helped her onto the bench.

Laura inhaled the rich aroma of beef, onions, and carrots, her stomach rumbling in response. She hadn't realized how hungry she was until that moment.

"It smells wonderful," she said, picking up her spoon with fingers that still felt strangely disconnected from her hands.

The first mouthful was heaven—savory and hearty, warming her from the inside in a way that the fire and blankets couldn't quite manage. Laura closed her eyes briefly in appreciation.

"This is delicious," she told Matt after swallowing. "You're a fine cook."

Matt beamed at the compliment. "Told you," he said to Boone, who merely grunted in response as he took his own seat across from Laura.

Zeb joined them, and for a few minutes, they ate in companionable silence. Laura was grateful for the reprieve from the conversation, using the time to gather her thoughts and her strength. She was still weak, she realized, the simple act of eating taxing her more than it should.

"So, Miss Hartley," Zeb said eventually, breaking the silence. "You mentioned you were headed to Lone Valley for a position?"

Laura nodded, setting down her spoon to take a sip of water. "Yes. Mrs. Whitaker in Elk Ridge—she owns the mercantile there—recommended me to her cousin, Ms. Patterson. She needs help at her boarding house and café."

"Louella Patterson," Zeb nodded in recognition. "Good woman. Makes the best apple pie in the territory."

"That's what Mrs. Whitaker said," Laura smiled faintly.

"How long were you in Elk Ridge?" Boone asked suddenly, his gaze direct and penetrating.

Laura hesitated, unsure how much of her story to share. "Not long," she answered carefully. "Just over two months."

"And before that?" he pressed.

The directness of his questioning made Laura uncomfortable, but she saw no reason to lie. "Various places. My brother and I moved around quite a bit."

"Your brother?" Zeb inquired. "He's not with you?"

"No," Laura replied, her voice cooling slightly. "Jasper and I... we've gone our separate ways."

Something in her tone must have signaled her reluctance to elaborate, because Zeb smoothly changed the subject. "Well, you're welcome to stay here until you're recovered enough to travel to town. The storm might keep us all housebound for a day or two, anyway."

"That's very kind," Laura said gratefully. "But I would rather not impose. You've already done so much for me."

"Nonsense," Zeb dismissed her concern with a wave of his hand. "We can't very well turn you out into the snow, and it's no imposition to have another face at the table."

Boone said nothing, but Laura noticed the slight tightening of his jaw. She wondered if he disapproved of his father's hospitality or simply preferred his solitude undisturbed.

"At least let me earn my keep," she offered. "I can cook and mend, and I'm not afraid of hard work."

Matt laughed. "I'm not sure Boone's ready to surrender his kitchen to a stranger."

Zeb chuckled. "Don't worry about earning your keep, Miss Hartley. Regaining your strength is contribution enough for now."

Laura wanted to protest further, but found herself suddenly overwhelmed by exhaustion. The brief activity of eating and conversing had drained what little energy she had managed to recover. She swayed slightly on the bench, steadying herself with a hand on the table.

Boone was on his feet immediately, his movement so swift Laura barely registered it until he was beside her.

"You need to rest," he said, his voice softer than before. It wasn't quite concern in his tone, but something close to it.

"I think you're right," Laura admitted, too weary to argue.

Without warning, Boone slipped one arm around her back and the other beneath her knees, lifting her as easily as if she weighed nothing. Laura gasped at the sudden contact, one hand instinctively grabbing the front of his shirt for balance.

"I can walk," she protested weakly.

"You're about to fall over," Boone countered, already carrying her back toward the bedroom.

Laura wanted to object on principle—she wasn't accustomed to being handled so directly, especially by a man—but she couldn't deny his reasoning. Her body felt impossibly heavy, her limbs leaden with fatigue.

The strange intimacy of being carried against Boone's chest left her flustered. She could feel the solid strength of him, smell the faint scent of pine and leather that clung to his clothes. Despite his brusque manner, his hold was gentle, careful not to jostle her.

In the bedroom, he set her down on the edge of the bed with surprising delicacy for such a large man. Laura caught a glimpse of his face as he straightened—stern as ever, but with something unreadable in his eyes.

"Thank you," she said softly, arranging her skirts around her legs.

Boone nodded once, already turning to leave. "Rest," he said, pausing at the door. "Tomorrow will be soon enough to figure out what comes next."

With that, he was gone, leaving Laura alone with her thoughts. She changed back into the borrowed shirt, her movements slow with exhaustion, and slipped beneath the quilts. The bed was warm and comfortable, the pillow soft beneath her head.

As she drifted toward sleep, Laura thought about Boone Callahan—his gruff manner belied by the gentleness of his actions, the intensity in his blue eyes when he looked at her, as if trying to solve a puzzle whose pieces didn't quite fit together.

There was something complex about him, she thought drowsily. A reason for the walls he had built around himself. But that was none of her business. In a day or two, when the storm passed, and she was stronger, she would continue to Lone Valley and leave the Callahan ranch behind.

The thought brought an unexpected pang of something like regret, which Laura dismissed as simple gratitude. Of course, she felt a connection to the man who had saved her life. It was natural, and it would pass.

With that reassurance, she surrendered to sleep, unaware that in the main room of the ranch house, Boone Callahan stood by the window, staring out at the slowly abating storm. He was similarly preoccupied with the unexpected guest fate had delivered to his door.

Chapter 5

Morning dawned clear and blindingly bright, the storm having spent its fury overnight. Boone was up before sunrise, as was his habit, moving quietly through the house to avoid waking their guest. He built up the fire, put coffee on to boil, and stepped outside to check on the animals and assess the damage.

The blizzard had transformed the world. Snow lay deep across the yard, drifted against the barn and corrals in smooth, sculptural waves. The sky above was a clear, hard blue, the sun just beginning to crest the eastern mountains, turning the snow-covered landscape into a sea of glittering diamond light.

Boone inhaled deeply, the frigid air filling his lungs with crystalline sharpness. Days like this made the harshness of Montana winters worthwhile—the pristine beauty of freshly fallen snow, the absolute silence broken only by the occasional creak of pine boughs releasing their white burden.

But beauty wouldn't save the lives of those still stranded out in that wilderness. Boone's thoughts turned to the task ahead—searching for the survivors of the stagecoach accident and the man who had been walking with Miss Hartley. If they had found adequate shelter and fuel for a fire, they might have survived the night. If not...

He pushed the grim thought aside and headed for the barn. The horses would need extra feed after the cold night, and Rusher deserved special attention after yesterday's ordeal.

Inside the barn, the familiar smells of hay, horses, and leather greeted him, along with the relative warmth generated by the animals' bodies. Rusher nickered a greeting from his stall, ears pricked forward in anticipation of breakfast.

"Morning, boy," Boone said, running a hand down the gelding's sturdy neck. "You did good yesterday."

Rusher nudged him impatiently, more interested in feed than praise. Boone chuckled and set about his chores, finding comfort in the routine. These were the rhythms of ranch life, unchanging and reliable in a way people rarely were.

As he worked, Boone found his thoughts returning to Laura Rose Hartley. There was something about her that nagged at him, something beyond her unexpected appearance in the blizzard. A wariness in her eyes, perhaps, or the careful way she had sidestepped questions about her past.

Not that it was any of his business. She would be gone soon enough, off to her position in town, and life at the ranch would return to normal. Which was exactly as it should be.

Yet, he couldn't quite shake the memory of how light she had felt in his arms, how vulnerable despite the quiet strength she'd shown. There was a story there, one Boone wasn't sure he wanted to know, yet found himself curious about, nonetheless.

"Morning."

The voice startled him from his thoughts. Boone turned to find Matt standing in the barn doorway, bundled against the cold.

"Coffee's ready inside. Your pa sent me to fetch you—says we should get moving on that search soon as we've eaten."

Boone nodded, giving Rusher a final pat before following Matt back toward the house. "How's our guest?" he asked, trying to sound merely conversational.

"Still sleeping. Last I checked," Matt replied. "Your pa says to let her rest—she needs it after what she's been through."

They trudged through the deep snow, their boots crunching with each step. The sun was fully up now, casting long blue shadows across the pristine white.

"Going to be slow going," Boone observed, surveying the landscape. "Snow's deep."

"Reckon we can take the sleigh," Matt suggested. "More supplies that way too, in case we find survivors."

Boone nodded his agreement. The ranch's sleigh wasn't used often, but it would serve them well today, allowing them to bring extra blankets, food, and medical supplies.

Inside, they found Zeb at the stove, frying bacon and eggs. The smell filled the warm kitchen, making Boone's stomach growl.

"Thought you boys could use a hearty breakfast before heading out," Zeb said, sliding the food onto plates.

They ate quickly, discussing the best route to take for their search. Boone explained where he had found Laura, and based on her description, they mapped out the likely location of the overturned stagecoach and the rock outcropping where the other passengers might have sought shelter.

"I'll stay here with Miss Hartley," Zeb said as they finished their meal. "Don't want her waking up alone in a strange house. Besides, someone should be here in case anyone makes their way to the ranch on their own."

Boone nodded, grateful for his father's thoughtfulness. Though he'd never admit it aloud, he'd been concerned about leaving Laura alone while she was still recovering.

They were gathering their gear when a soft sound made them all turn. Laura stood in the bedroom doorway, dressed in her blue dress from the day before, her dark hair neatly braided though falling loose in places. She looked pale but steady on her feet.

"Good morning," she said, her voice stronger than it had been the night before.

"Miss Hartley," Zeb greeted warmly. "You should be resting."

"I've rested enough," she replied with a small smile. "And please, call me Laura."

Boone studied her, noting the shadows beneath her eyes that belied her claim of adequate rest, but also the determined set of her jaw. She was stronger than she looked, this woman.

"We were just discussing the search," he said, gesturing to the rough map they'd drawn on a piece of paper. "If you're feeling up to it, any details you can provide would help."

Laura nodded and approached the table, moving carefully, but with purpose. "The stagecoach overturned about here, I think," she said, pointing to a spot on their map. "The rock outcropping Mr. Dobbins mentioned was visible from there, maybe a quarter mile back in the direction we'd come from."

"Dobbins?" Zeb inquired.

"Henry and Margaret Dobbins," Laura explained. "An elderly couple who were on the coach with me. There was also a businessman with an injured arm and two other men. One of them, Tom Wade, decided to come with me when I chose to continue toward Lone Valley."

Boone frowned. "That was a foolish risk in such weather."

Laura's eyes flashed, a spark of fire that surprised him. "I'm well aware of that now, Mr. Callahan. But at the time, it seemed the better option than waiting to freeze or starve."

Her direct response caught Boone off guard. Most women of his acquaintance would have demurred or apologized when faced with his blunt criticism. Laura Rose Hartley did neither.

"Fair enough," he conceded with a slight nod. "We'll head out shortly. My father will stay here with you."

"I'd like to come," Laura said, straightening her shoulders.

"Absolutely not," Boone replied immediately.

"I know where to look," she insisted. "I could help."

"You could collapse," Boone countered. "You're barely recovered from nearly freezing to death."

"Boone's right, Laura," Zeb interjected gently. "You need more time to regain your strength. Besides, the snow's deep—it would be hard going, even for someone at full health."

Laura looked ready to argue further, but something in Zeb's kind but firm tone seemed to reach her. She sighed, her shoulders dropping slightly.

"You're right," she admitted reluctantly. "I just feel responsible. Maybe I should have stayed with the group. I could have helped them all stay warm... offered assistance..."

"That's not on you," Matt said, his usually jovial face serious. "Everyone made their choice. You and Wade chose to press on. No one forced anyone."

Laura nodded, though she didn't look entirely convinced. Boone found himself wanting to reassure her, an unfamiliar urge he quickly suppressed.

"We'll find them if they're out there," he said instead, his tone matter-of-fact rather than comforting. "And we'll bring back whoever we can."

With that, he turned away, focusing on gathering the supplies they would need. Behind him, he could hear Zeb offering Laura breakfast, his father's natural hospitality smoothing over any awkwardness.

Within half an hour, Boone and Matt had the sleigh loaded and the horses harnessed. They'd chosen the strongest pair from the stable, both experienced with pulling through deep snow.

As they prepared to depart, Laura came out onto the porch, wrapped in a borrowed coat against the cold. The morning sunlight caught in her dark hair, highlighting strands of auburn Boone hadn't noticed before.

"Be careful," she called, her breath forming small clouds in the frigid air. "And thank you."

Boone nodded once in acknowledgment, strangely moved by her genuine concern. Then he clicked to the horses, and the sleigh began to move, runners sliding smoothly over the pristine snow as they set out on their search for survivors.

Behind them, Laura remained on the porch, watching until they disappeared from view, a solitary figure against the white landscape of the Callahan ranch.

Chapter 6

Laura watched the sleigh until it disappeared into the vast whiteness, Boone and Matt becoming nothing more than dark specks
against the pristine snow before vanishing completely. The cold bit
at her cheeks, but she remained on the porch, her thoughts with
the missing passengers. Had they survived the night? The rock outcropping would have provided some shelter, but without adequate
warmth...

"You'll catch your death standing out here," Zeb said gently from
behind her. "Come back inside where it's warm."

She turned, offering him a small smile. "I was just thinking about
the others."

"Boone will find them if they're to be found," Zeb assured her,
holding the door open. "My son's stubborn that way—doesn't give
up easily."

Laura stepped back into the welcoming warmth of the ranch house.
"I've noticed that about him," she said, unwrapping the borrowed coat
from her shoulders. "He seems... determined."

"That's one word for it," Zeb chuckled, taking the coat and hanging it on a peg by the door. "Some might say bullheaded. But it's served him well running this ranch."

Laura lowered herself carefully into a chair at the kitchen table, still mindful of her weakened state. Though she'd insisted on getting up, her body protested with each movement, muscles aching from the ordeal in the blizzard.

"How long has he been running things?" she asked, genuinely curious about the man who had saved her life.

Zeb poured coffee into a mug and set it before her. "Going on five years now, more or less. I'm still around, of course, but these old bones don't take to the hard work like they used to. Boone's got a good head for ranching, always has."

Laura wrapped her hands around the warm mug, grateful for its heat against her still-tender fingers. "It seems like a lot of responsibility for someone so young."

"He's always been older than his years," Zeb said, a hint of pride in his voice as he settled into the chair opposite her. "Even as a boy, took everything serious-like. His brother Marcus was the troublemaker, his sister Sara was the dreamer, but Boone—he was always the steady one."

Laura sipped her coffee, contemplating this glimpse into Boone's character. It fit with the stern, responsible man she'd encountered.

"What about you, Laura?" Zeb asked. "You mentioned a brother—Jasper, was it? Is he your only family?"

Laura tensed slightly, the familiar wariness creeping over her at questions about her past. But Zeb's kind face held only genuine interest, not prying curiosity.

"Yes," she admitted after a moment. "Our parents died when I was young. Jasper raised me, after a fashion." She tried to keep the bitterness from her voice, but wasn't entirely successful.

"After a fashion?" Zeb repeated gently.

Laura stared into her coffee, debating how much to share. These people had saved her life; they deserved some honesty. Yet, old habits were hard to break.

"Jasper has... struggles," she said finally. "He turns to drink when things get difficult. Which is often." She looked up, meeting Zeb's understanding gaze. "We moved around a lot. Never stayed in one place long enough to put down roots."

"And now you're looking to put down some roots of your own in Lone Valley," Zeb observed.

"Yes." Laura straightened slightly, a small smile touching her lips. "Mrs. Whitaker in Elk Ridge was kind enough to recommend me to her cousin. I've worked in kitchens before, and I can clean and manage rooms."

"Louella runs a fine establishment," Zeb nodded. "She's been alone since her husband passed five years back. Could use a steady hand to help, I imagine."

"That's my hope," Laura agreed.

"And your brother?" Zeb asked carefully. "He's not joining you?"

Laura shook her head, her eyes dropping back to her coffee. "No. We... parted ways. It was time."

Something in her tone must have signaled the end of that line of questioning because Zeb smoothly changed the subject. "Well, you're welcome here until you're strong enough to head into town. Might be a few days yet, given what you've been through."

"I don't want to impose," Laura began, but Zeb waved away her concern.

"Nonsense. We've got the room, and frankly, it's nice having a fresh face at the table." He smiled warmly. "Gets tiresome looking at the same three ugly mugs day in and day out."

Laura laughed despite herself, the sound unexpected even to her own ears. It felt good—natural in a way she hadn't experienced in a long time.

"There now," Zeb said, his eyes twinkling. "That's better. A pretty girl like you should laugh more often."

A comfortable silence fell between them as they drank their coffee. Laura relaxed in Zeb's company. There was something steady and reassuring about the older man, like a tree whose roots ran deep into the earth.

"I do have one request, though," Laura said after a moment. "I'd like to be useful while I'm here. I'm not accustomed to idleness, and I owe you all so much for taking me in."

Zeb considered her for a moment, seeming to weigh her strength against her determination. "I suppose there might be some light mending that needs doing," he conceded. "And I wouldn't say no to some help with dinner later, if you're feeling up to it."

Laura brightened at the prospect of purposeful activity. "I'd like that."

"But first," Zeb said firmly, "you need to rest a bit more. Doctor's orders."

"You're a doctor?" Laura asked, surprised.

Zeb laughed, the sound warm and rich. "No, but I've patched up enough cowboys and calves in my day to know when someone needs recovery time. The body heals at its own pace, Laura. Can't rush it, no matter how determined the spirit might be."

Laura nodded reluctantly, acknowledging the wisdom in his words. She was tired, the simple act of getting dressed and having breakfast having drained more of her limited energy than she cared to admit.

"I'll rest," she agreed, "but only for a little while."

"That's all I ask," Zeb said, standing and collecting their empty mugs. "Why don't you settle in the rocking chair by the fire? I've got some reading material if you're interested—not much, mind you, but we keep a Bible and a few books around."

"That would be nice, thank you."

Laura moved to the chair, arranging a quilt over her legs. The fire crackled pleasantly, casting a warm light over the rustic main room. There was something deeply comforting about this space—no pretense, no excessive ornaments, just solid, well-used furniture and the marks of a life well-lived.

Zeb brought her a small stack of books: the promised Bible, a collection of Charles Dickens stories, a well-thumbed almanac, and a surprisingly pristine copy of "Pride and Prejudice."

Laura raised an eyebrow at the last one, and Zeb chuckled. "That was my late wife, Mary's. She loved her stories about proper English folk and their romances. Said it was as far from Montana ranching as a body could get without actually leaving."

"She sounds as if she had a good sense of humor," Laura observed, running her fingers over the book's cover.

"That she did," Zeb agreed, a wistful smile crossing his weathered face. "Never met a woman who could laugh at life's hardships quite like my Mary could. Raised three children out here when this was barely more than wilderness, and never lost her joy in the process."

The love and respect in his voice as he spoke of his late wife touched Laura deeply. She couldn't remember ever hearing a man speak of anyone with such genuine affection.

"I'm sorry for your loss," she said softly.

"Been ten years now," Zeb replied, his eyes distant for a moment before refocusing on her. "But thank you. I miss her every day, though I reckon she's in a better place."

He cleared his throat, clearly wanting to move away from melancholy thoughts. "I'll be outside tending to a few chores. You rest and give a holler if you need anything."

"I will," Laura promised, already settling deeper into the rocking chair's embrace as fatigue washed over her.

Once Zeb had donned his coat and headed outside, Laura enjoyed the peace and quiet house. The only sounds were the crackling of the fire, the occasional settling of the wooden structure, and the distant howl of the wind around the eaves.

She picked up "Pride and Prejudice," finding something comforting in holding a book that had once brought joy to another woman in this same house. Opening to the first page, she began to read, but found her attention wandering.

Her thoughts turned to Boone and Matt, out searching in the deep snow. Had they found the stagecoach yet? Were the Dobbinses and the others still alive? And what of Tom Wade, who had set out with her and vanished in the storm?

She said a silent prayer for all of them, including her rescuers. The faint memory of being carried through the snow in Boone's strong arms surfaced unbidden—the solid warmth of him against the freezing air, the steady beat of his heart under her cheek, the surprising gentleness in hands that looked made for hard labor.

Laura pushed the thought away, unsettled by the warmth it created in her chest. Boone Callahan had saved her life, nothing more. His gruff manner made it clear he wasn't looking for gratitude or attachment, and she certainly wasn't looking for... anything. Her plan was set: recover, continue to Lone Valley, start her position with Ms. Patterson, and finally build a stable life for herself. A life without Jasper's chaos and unpredictability.

The thought of her brother sent a pang of guilt through her. Was he worried about her, or merely angry over her absence? Laura closed her eyes, pushing away the familiar knot of emotions that thoughts of Jasper always brought—love tangled with resentment, loyalty with frustration, hope with bitter disappointment.

"Not now," she whispered to herself. "Not today."

Despite her best intentions to stay awake, the warmth of the fire, her lingering exhaustion, and the quiet of the house soon lulled Laura to sleep. The book sliding forgotten onto her lap as her head tipped to the side.

Chapter 7

The next thing she knew, Laura was being gently shaken awake. She opened her eyes to find Zeb standing over her, his expression tense.

"They're back," he said simply.

Laura sat up quickly, blinking away sleep and disorientation. "Did they find anyone?"

"Yes," Zeb confirmed, helping her to her feet. "Three survivors from the stagecoach. Matt's taking them straight to town—the doctor there can look after them better than we can. Boone's just arrived with the news."

Heart pounding, Laura followed Zeb to the front door, where Boone was stomping snow from his boots on the porch. He looked exhausted, his face reddened from cold and wind, snow dusting his dark hair and shoulders.

"Mr. Callahan," Laura said as he entered, her eyes searching his face. "Who did you find?"

Boone's blue eyes met hers, something unreadable in their depths. "The elderly couple—the Dobbinses—and the businessman with the injured arm. They'd made it to the outcropping and managed to keep a small fire going through the night."

"And the others?" Laura asked, though she feared she knew the answer from the grim set of his mouth.

Boone shook his head, removing his hat and coat. "We found one man frozen about fifty yards from the stagecoach. Looks like he never made it to the shelter. As for Tom Wade…"

He hesitated, and Laura felt her heart sink. "Tell me," she said quietly.

"We found him about a half-mile back from where I found you," Boone said, his voice gentler than she'd heard it before. "He didn't make it, Miss Hartley. I'm sorry."

The news hit Laura like a physical blow. She sank into a nearby chair, hands trembling slightly. "He shouldn't have come with me," she whispered. "If he'd stayed with the others…"

"You can't know that," Boone said firmly. "There's no way to predict who lives and who dies in a blizzard like that."

Laura nodded, accepting the logic of his words, even as grief and guilt warred within her. She hadn't known Tom Wade well—they'd only met on the stagecoach—but he had been kind, offering to accompany her when she'd decided to press on to Lone Valley.

Laura closed her eyes briefly, a prayer forming silently in her heart for the souls of the departed. When she opened them again, she found both Callahan men watching her with concern.

"I'm all right," she assured them, straightening her shoulders. "Or I will be. What will happen to the… the bodies?"

"Matt's taking care of notifying the authorities in town," Boone said. "They'll be properly buried once the ground thaws enough for digging."

A heavy silence fell over the room, broken only by the crackling of the fire. Zeb moved first, heading toward the kitchen. "I'll put on some coffee. You look like you could use something hot, son."

Boone nodded gratefully, sinking into a chair at the table. Laura noticed how he winced slightly as he sat, his movements stiffer than usual.

"Are you hurt?" she asked.

He shook his head dismissively. "Just cold and tired. It was slow-going with the snow so deep."

Laura wasn't entirely convinced, but didn't press the issue. Instead, she asked, "The survivors—they're being taken to Lone Valley?"

"Yes," Boone confirmed. "Doc Jenkins there will look after them. They're shaken up and suffering mild frostbite, but they should recover."

"That's something to be thankful for, at least," Laura murmured.

Zeb returned with three mugs of steaming coffee, setting them on the table. "The Lord provides, even in the darkest times," he said, his voice gentle but firm with conviction.

Laura wrapped her hands around her mug, grateful for its warmth. "Yes," she agreed quietly. "Though sometimes it's difficult to see His plan."

"That's where faith comes in," Zeb said, taking his seat. "Trusting, even when the path isn't clear."

Boone remained silent, staring into his coffee with an unreadable expression. Laura wondered if he shared his father's easy faith or if he, like her, sometimes struggled to understand God's design in the face of tragedy.

"Will you still head to town tomorrow?" Boone asked abruptly, looking up at her.

The question caught Laura off guard. "I... I'm not sure," she admitted. "I should, but..."

"You're not strong enough yet," Zeb interjected firmly. "Another day or two of rest wouldn't hurt."

"Pa's right," Boone said, surprising Laura with his agreement. "The trail to town will still be difficult, even if the weather holds. Better to wait until you've got your full strength back."

Laura hesitated, torn between her desire to begin her new position and the undeniable wisdom of their advice. "I don't want to impose on your hospitality any longer than necessary."

"It's no imposition," Zeb assured her.

Boone's expression remained neutral, but he nodded once in agreement with his father's words. "Besides," he added pragmatically, "I need to go back into town in a couple of days, anyway. I can take you then."

"Thank you," Laura said, relief washing over her. The thought of traveling again so soon, even the relatively short distance to Lone Valley, had been daunting. "I promise I won't be idle while I'm here. I meant what I said about earning my keep."

"I'll hold you to that," Boone said, the barest hint of a smile touching his lips. "Matt's hopeless with mending, and Pa's cooking would try the patience of a saint."

"Watch yourself, boy," Zeb warned, but his eyes twinkled with good humor. "I kept you fed for more than twenty years."

"And it's a miracle I survived," Boone retorted, the easy banter between father and son warming the atmosphere despite the somber news they'd just discussed.

Laura found herself smiling despite the weight of grief. There was something healing about witnessing their affectionate teasing—a glimpse of normal family life she had rarely experienced with Jasper.

"I can certainly handle mending and cooking," she offered. "Though I can't promise anything fancy."

"Anything's better than salt pork and beans three nights in a row," Boone said, raising an eyebrow at his father.

"It's protein," Zeb defended mildly. "Keeps a man going."

Laura couldn't help the small laugh that escaped her. "I think I can manage something a bit more varied, Mr. Callahan."

"If I'm going to eat your cooking, you might as well call me Boone," he said, meeting her eyes directly for the first time since he'd returned. "No need to stand on ceremony here."

Laura felt an unexpected flutter in her chest at the small concession toward friendliness. "Boone, then," she agreed.

A moment of silence stretched between them, neither looking away until Zeb cleared his throat meaningfully. Boone immediately dropped his gaze back to his coffee, and Laura felt heat rising to her cheeks without quite understanding why.

"Well," Zeb said, his tone deliberately casual, "since you're staying a bit longer, Laura, perhaps you'd like to help me inventory our pantry. It'll give you an idea of what we've got to work with for meals."

"I'd be happy to," Laura said, grateful for the chance to be useful and the distraction from whatever had just passed between her and Boone.

"I'll check on the stock," Boone said, rising from his chair with that same slight wince Laura had noticed earlier.

As he headed for the door, Laura couldn't help but notice again how stiffly he moved. Perhaps it was just the cold, as he'd claimed, but something told her there was more to it than that.

"Boone," she called before she could think better of it. He paused, looking back at her questioningly. "Thank you. For finding them and bringing them back. It can't have been easy."

Something shifted in his expression—a softening around the eyes, a slight relaxation of his stern mouth. "It needed doing," he said simply. Then he was gone, the door closing firmly behind him.

Zeb watched his son leave, then turned to Laura with a thoughtful expression. "Boone doesn't say much, but he feels things deeply. Always has."

"I'm beginning to see that," Laura admitted.

Zeb smiled, a knowing glint in his eye that Laura couldn't quite interpret. "Come on, then. Let's see what we've got to work with for dinner. And you can tell me more about yourself, if you're of a mind to."

As they moved toward the pantry, Laura wondered about the man who had saved her life—the contradiction of his gruff exterior and the unmistakable kindness of his actions. There was more to Boone Callahan than met the eye, and despite her best intentions, she was increasingly curious to discover what lay beneath that stoic surface.

Chapter 8

By late afternoon, Laura had familiarized herself with the Callahan kitchen and pantry, relieved to find it reasonably well-stocked despite the obvious bachelor management. There were plenty of dried beans, flour, salt pork, other meats, and preserves, along with root vegetables stored in the cool cellar beneath the house.

True to her word, she set about preparing a proper supper, despite Zeb's insistence that she shouldn't overtax herself. The activity felt good after so much rest, and there was something soothing about the familiar tasks of cooking—measuring, mixing, and watching over bubbling pots.

She had decided on a hearty stew of salt pork, beans, and vegetables, with fresh biscuits to accompany it. Nothing fancy, as she'd warned, but wholesome and filling after a day spent working in the cold.

Zeb kept her company, sitting at the kitchen table, whittling a small piece of wood while they talked. He was easy to talk to, asking questions without prying, sharing stories of his life on the ranch and his late wife without dwelling too much on sadness.

"Mary would have liked you," he told Laura as she worked biscuit dough with flour-covered hands. "She had a soft spot for those with grit."

Laura smiled at the unexpected compliment. "I wish I could have met her."

"She was something special," Zeb said, his knife pausing in its steady work. "Came out here as a city girl from back East, not knowing a steer from a heifer. But she adapted, learned everything she needed to run a household out here in the wilderness. Never complained, not even during that first terrible winter when we nearly lost everything."

"It takes a special kind of strength to build a life out here," Laura observed, thinking of the vast, beautiful, but unforgiving landscape surrounding them.

"That it does," Zeb agreed. "Different from a man's strength, but every bit as important. Mary used to say a man might build the walls, but a woman makes them a home."

Laura considered this as she cut the dough into rounds. "I've not had a home since my parents passed," she admitted. "Not a permanent one, anyway."

"Everyone needs roots, Laura," Zeb said gently. "A place to belong."

"That's what I'm hoping to find in Lone Valley," she said, arranging the biscuits on a baking sheet. "A fresh start. A chance to build something of my own, without—" She stopped herself, not wanting to speak ill of Jasper despite everything.

"Without your brother's troubles weighing you down," Zeb finished for her, his perception uncomfortably accurate. "There's no shame in seeking your own path, you know. Sometimes the kindest thing we can do for those we love is to stop enabling their worst behaviors."

Laura looked up sharply, surprised by his insight.

"I've known my share of men who found too much comfort in a bottle," Zeb said with a sad smile. "Seen what it does to those who love them, too. It's a hard road, especially for family."

Laura nodded, unable to find words for a moment. "It is," she finally said. "And I tried—for years, I tried to help him. But nothing changed. It only got worse, and I was drowning along with him."

The admission felt both painful and freeing. She had never spoken so openly about Jasper's problems to anyone before.

"There comes a point where you have to save yourself," Zeb said quietly. "It doesn't mean you love them any less."

Laura blinked back sudden tears, turning to slide the biscuits into the oven to hide her emotion. "Thank you," she said when she trusted her voice again. "For understanding."

"Life has a way of teaching us all sorts of lessons we never asked to learn," Zeb replied, returning to his whittling. "The trick is what we do with that knowledge afterward."

The kitchen door opened then, admitting a gust of cold air and Boone, his cheeks red from the cold, his dark hair windblown. He paused just inside the doorway, seeming surprised by the domestic scene before him—Laura at the stove, his father at the table, the kitchen filled with the aromas of cooking food.

"Something smells good," he said after a moment, removing his coat and hanging it on a peg by the door.

"Laura's making stew and biscuits," Zeb informed him.

"You didn't have to do that," Boone said to Laura, though she detected no disapproval in his tone—only surprise.

"I wanted to," she replied, stirring the stew to avoid meeting his intense gaze. "It's the least I can do to thank you both for your hospitality."

Boone made a noncommittal sound and moved to wash his hands at the basin. Laura couldn't help noticing again how he favored his left side, moving with a careful stiffness that went beyond mere cold or fatigue.

"Stock all accounted for?" Zeb asked his son.

"All present and hungry," Boone confirmed. "No losses from the storm, thankfully."

"That's good news," Laura said, genuinely relieved. She knew enough about ranching to understand that losing cattle to bad weather could be financially devastating.

Boone glanced at her, seeming surprised by her comment. "Yes," he agreed. "We were lucky this time."

"Not just luck," Zeb said, looking meaningfully at his son. "Good management. Moving them to the sheltered pasture before the storm hit made the difference."

Boone shrugged off the praise, clearly uncomfortable. "Just common sense."

"And plenty of hard work," Zeb added, giving Laura a conspiratorial wink. "Though my son would sooner bite his tongue than admit it."

Laura smiled at the accurate observation, earning a slightly defensive look from Boone.

"Any word from Matt?" he asked, clearly wanting to change the subject.

"Not yet," Zeb replied. "But I expect he'll stay in town tonight. No sense making the journey back in the dark after such a long day."

Boone nodded, then winced as he lowered himself into a chair at the table. The movement didn't escape Laura's notice.

"You are hurt," she said, her tone leaving no room for denial. "What happened?"

Boone shot her a look that might have intimidated a less determined woman. "It's nothing. Slipped on some ice while loading the sleigh."

"Favorin' your ribs," Zeb observed, setting aside his whittling. "Probably bruised them in the fall."

"I'm fine," Boone insisted, throwing his father an irritated glance.

"Well, if you're fine, then you won't mind if I take a look," Laura said firmly, wiping her hands on her apron. "I've had plenty of experience with injuries like that, living with Jasper."

She immediately wished she hadn't mentioned her brother, but it was too late to take back the words. Both men looked at her with sudden interest, though Zeb's was tempered with understanding, while Boone's held a sharp curiosity.

"Your brother was prone to injuries?" Boone asked, his tone carefully neutral.

Laura busied herself checking the biscuits to avoid his perceptive gaze. "He was prone to fights," she said, trying to keep her voice matter-of-fact. "Especially after he'd been drinking. I learned to patch him up."

A heavy silence followed her admission. Laura could feel Boone's eyes on her back, no doubt piecing together parts of her story she hadn't intended to reveal.

"Well," Zeb said finally, breaking the awkward moment, "those skills might come in handy now, if my son will swallow his pride long enough to accept help."

Boone looked like he wanted to refuse, but a particularly sharp movement caused him to wince visibly. "Fine," he conceded grudgingly. "After supper."

Laura nodded, relieved that he wasn't going to be stubborn about it. Injured ribs needed proper wrapping to heal correctly, and left untreated, they could cause significant pain for weeks.

The meal came together shortly thereafter, and they sat down to eat, the stew and fresh biscuits a welcome change from the simple fare the Callahan men were accustomed to. Laura couldn't help feeling a small sense of pride as both men helped themselves to second helpings without prompting.

"This is really good, Laura," Zeb said appreciatively. "Been a while since we've had anything this tasty that didn't come from Louella's café in town."

"It's just simple cooking," Laura demurred, though pleased by the compliment.

"Simple or not, it beats what we've been eating," Boone said, breaking open a steaming biscuit. It wasn't effusive praise, but coming from him, Laura suspected it was significant.

"Thank you," she said, meeting his eyes briefly. "I enjoy cooking when I have the chance. It's... soothing, somehow."

Boone nodded as if he understood, though he didn't comment further. The rest of the meal passed pleasantly, with Zeb sharing stories about the ranch's early days and Laura occasionally asking questions about Lone Valley and its residents.

After they'd finished eating and the dishes were cleared away—Zeb insisting on handling that task himself since Laura had cooked—she turned her attention to Boone's injury.

"Where do you keep your medical supplies?" she asked him directly.

He sighed, seemingly resigned to her ministrations. "Cabinet in the washroom. I'll get them."

"I can—" Laura began, but he was already heading toward the small adjoining room, moving stiffly but determinedly.

"He hates being fussed over," Zeb said quietly once Boone was out of earshot. "Always has, even as a boy. Broke his arm when he was ten, climbing in the hayloft, and tried to convince us it was just a sprain, so his ma wouldn't worry."

Laura smiled at the image of a young, stoic Boone trying to downplay his injury. "The more things change..."

"Exactly," Zeb chuckled. "Some things are simply bone-deep."

Boone returned with a small wooden box of medical supplies—bandages, witch hazel, a small bottle of whiskey for disinfecting, and various other necessities for ranch life, where minor injuries were common.

"Where should we do this?" Laura asked, taking the box from him.

"Here's fine," Boone said, gesturing to the main room. "Better light by the fire."

Laura nodded, setting the box on the table near the hearth. "You'll need to remove your shirt so I can see the extent of the bruising."

A flicker of something—perhaps discomfort—crossed Boone's face, but he complied without comment, unbuttoning his flannel shirt with deliberate movements to minimize the pain in his side.

Zeb, sensing his son's discomfort at being examined in front of an audience, made a show of yawning. "Think I'll turn in early," he announced. "Been a long day. Good night to you both."

With a meaningful glance at Boone that Laura couldn't quite interpret, Zeb retreated to his bedroom off the main room, leaving them alone by the fire.

Boone finished removing his shirt, revealing a lean, muscular torso marked by a life of physical labor. Laura kept her expression neutral despite the flush she felt rising to her cheeks. She had tended to Jasper's injuries often enough, but this felt distinctly different.

"Let me see," she said, gesturing for him to turn slightly to catch the firelight.

The bruising along his left ribs was impressive—a spreading pattern of purple and blue that wrapped around his side. Laura winced in sympathy.

"That's more than a simple fall on ice," she observed, eyes narrowing. "What really happened?"

Boone hesitated, then sighed. "One of the bodies was frozen under a drift. Matt and I had to dig him out to load him onto the sleigh. I lost my footing and fell against the edge of the sleigh runner."

Laura's expression softened. Even in death, he had treated the strangers with dignity, risking injury to ensure they were properly recovered.

"You should have said something sooner," she chided gently, reaching for the bandages. "Ribs need proper binding, or they'll take twice as long to heal."

"Wasn't the most pressing concern at the time," Boone replied, watching as she unrolled a length of clean cloth.

"Well, it is now," Laura said firmly. "Take a deep breath and hold it while I wrap these. It's going to hurt, but it will help in the long run."

Boone did as instructed, his jaw tightening as she began the careful process of binding his ribs. Laura worked efficiently, trying to be gentle while still wrapping the bandage tightly enough to provide proper support. Standing so close to him, she was acutely aware of his breathing, the warmth of his skin under her fingers, the clean scent of soap mixed with the outdoor smells of pine and horses that seemed to cling to him.

"Jasper taught you how to do this," Boone said suddenly, breaking the silence. It wasn't quite a question.

Laura's hands paused briefly before continuing their work. "Not intentionally," she replied, focusing on the bandage. "But yes, I learned from tending to him after... incidents."

"Must have been difficult," Boone observed, his voice carefully neutral.

Laura secured the end of the bandage before stepping back to assess her work. "It was what it was," she said with a small shrug. "Jasper wasn't always... like that. After our parents died, he tried his best. But somewhere along the way, he lost himself."

She hadn't meant to say so much, but something about the quiet room, the crackling fire, and Boone's steady presence made the words flow more easily than usual.

"And you?" Boone asked, reaching for his shirt. "Did you lose yourself too?"

The question caught Laura off guard with its perception. She looked up, meeting his intense blue gaze directly. "Sometimes I think I never had the chance to find myself in the first place," she admitted. "I was always either Jasper's responsibility or his caretaker. Never just... Laura."

The vulnerability of the admission hung in the air between them. Boone's expression softened almost imperceptibly, and for a moment, Laura thought he might reach out to her. Instead, he nodded once, as if confirming something to himself.

"Well, Laura," he said, her name sounding different somehow in his deep voice, "thank you for the doctoring. And the meal."

"You're welcome," she replied softly, beginning to pack away the medical supplies. "The binding will need to be changed in a day or two."

"I'll manage," Boone said, buttoning his shirt. "It's not my first run-in with bruised ribs."

Laura arched an eyebrow at him, a tiny smile playing at the corner of her mouth. "Somehow, I'm not surprised to hear that."

Their eyes met again, and something shifted in the space between them—a moment of understanding, perhaps, or recognition of something shared despite their different paths.

"You should rest," Boone said, breaking the silence as he carefully rose to his feet. "It's been a long day."

Laura nodded, suddenly aware of her own fatigue creeping back. "Yes, I suppose it has." She gathered the medical supplies, placing them back in the wooden box. "Will you check on the survivors when you go into town?"

"I will," he promised. "And let you know how they're faring."

"Thank you." She hesitated, then added, "For everything, Boone. Not just the rescue, but... for bringing them back. All of them. It means a great deal to know they weren't left out there alone."

Boone looked uncomfortable with her gratitude, but nodded once in acknowledgment. "Get some sleep, Laura."

As he walked away toward his own room, Laura remained by the fire for a moment, reflecting on the strange path that had led her to this ranch, to these people. For the first time in longer than she could remember, she felt something like peace settling around her—fragile and tentative, but present nonetheless.

She hadn't come to Montana looking for anything more than stability and independence. Yet somehow, in the midst of tragedy and danger, she had found something unexpected: a place where, for the moment at least, she felt safe.

With that comforting thought, Laura retired to her borrowed room, the events of the day catching up with her as her head touched the pillow. Her last conscious thought was of Boone's steady blue eyes and the surprising gentleness hidden beneath his gruff exterior.

Chapter 9

Laura woke to the sound of a tin pail clattering against the side of the well outside her window. Blinking in the soft gray light of early morning, she listened to the rhythmic creak of the pump handle, followed by the splash of water. The ranch was already awake and moving.

Despite having slept soundly, Laura felt a lingering weariness in her bones, a reminder of her ordeal in the blizzard. Still, she was determined not to spend the day idle. She rose quickly, washed her face in the basin, and dressed in her simple navy-blue work dress—the most practical of the few garments she'd brought with her.

As she pinned her hair into a practical coil at the nape of her neck, Laura caught sight of her reflection in the small mirror above the washstand. Color had returned to her cheeks, and the haunted look in her eyes had diminished. Three days at the Callahan ranch had already begun to restore her in ways she hadn't expected.

Voices drifted from the kitchen—male voices engaged in quiet conversation. Laura paused at her door, not wanting to interrupt.

Through the crack, she could see Boone and Zeb seated at the table, mugs of coffee between them.

"—not saying she has to leave right away," Boone was saying, his deep voice carrying a note of frustration. "But we need to be practical about this."

"Seems to me offering her work is practical," Zeb replied evenly. "You said yourself we're shorthanded with Davis laid up in town."

Laura's heart skipped a beat. Were they discussing her?

"I know what I said." Boone's voice had that same controlled patience she'd noticed before when he was trying not to show irritation. "But she's meant for town life. She's got that position waiting at the boarding house."

"A position that'll still be there in a week or two," Zeb pointed out. "Louella's not going to hire someone else that quick, especially not in winter."

There was a moment of silence, and Laura heard the scrape of a chair.

"You've seen how capable she is," Zeb continued. "Good cook, knows her way around mending and such. She's stronger than she looks, too. Not afraid of work."

"That's not the point, Pa."

"Then what is the point, son?"

Another pause, longer this time. Laura held her breath, knowing she shouldn't be eavesdropping but unable to move away.

"I just think..." Boone began, then sighed heavily. "I don't want her to feel obligated to stay because we helped her."

"Have you asked what she wants?" Zeb's question hung in the air.

Laura decided this was her cue. She smoothed her dress, took a breath, and opened the door fully, stepping into the kitchen with what she hoped was a natural smile.

"Good morning," she said.

Both men looked up, Zeb with an easy smile, Boone with a flash of something that might have been guilt before his expression settled back into its usual reserve.

"Morning, Laura," Zeb greeted her cheerfully. "Coffee's hot if you'd like some."

"Thank you," she said, moving to pour herself a cup. "I hope I'm not interrupting anything important."

"Not at all," Zeb assured her, though Boone remained silent, his eyes on his coffee mug. "We were just discussing ranch business. How did you sleep?"

"Well, thank you," Laura replied, taking a seat at the table with them. She glanced at Boone, noticing how he held himself carefully to avoid stressing his injured ribs. "And you? How are your ribs feeling this morning?"

Boone looked up, seeming surprised by her direct question. "Better," he said simply. "Your binding helped."

Laura nodded, pleased. "Good. They'll need time to heal properly, though. You should avoid heavy lifting for at least a week."

A small frown creased Boone's forehead. "Not much choice about that on a ranch."

"Which brings us back to what we were discussing," Zeb interjected, giving his son a pointed look. "Boone, why don't you tell Laura what we were talking about?"

Boone shot his father a look that might have withered a less determined man, but Zeb merely raised his eyebrows expectantly.

With a slight sigh of resignation, Boone turned to Laura. "We're shorthanded," he stated bluntly. "One of our ranch hands, Davis, broke his leg a week before you arrived. He's laid up in town for at least another month."

Laura nodded, waiting for him to continue.

"Pa thinks—" Boone began, but Zeb cleared his throat meaning-fully. Boone's jaw tightened before he amended. "I was wondering if you might consider staying on at the ranch for a while. Working here instead of heading to town right away."

"Working here?" she repeated. "Doing what, exactly?"

"Whatever needs doing," Boone said with a small shrug that he im-mediately seemed to regret as he winced. "Cooking, mending, helping with the lighter ranch chores. Nothing too strenuous while you're still recovering."

Laura considered this, turning the mug slowly between her palms. "And my position in town?"

"We'd let Mrs. Jenkins know," Boone assured her. "She'd under-stand, especially given the circumstances."

"It would just be temporary," Zeb added. "Until Boone is healed up... Davis is back on his feet. Or until spring makes travel easier, whichever comes first."

Laura's mind raced with the implications. Working at the ranch would mean postponing her plans for independence in town. Yet, it would also give her more time to regain her strength in a place where she already felt safe. And there was something undeniably appealing about the prospect of staying at the ranch a little longer, learning its rhythms, being useful.

She glanced at Boone, trying to gauge his true feelings about the arrangement. His expression was carefully neutral, but she could sense a certain tension in the set of his shoulders.

"If you'd rather go to town as planned, that's fine too," he said, apparently misinterpreting her hesitation. "You're not obligated to help us just because—"

"I'd like to stay," Laura interrupted, her decision crystallizing as she spoke the words. "I want to repay your kindness, and I'm not afraid of hard work."

Boone studied her face for a moment, as if searching for signs of reluctance. "The pay wouldn't be much," he warned.

"I don't need much," Laura countered. "Room and board, and perhaps a small wage I can save toward my fresh start in town."

A ghost of a smile flickered across Boone's face. "Practical," he observed.

"I've had to be," she replied simply.

"Then it's settled," Zeb declared, looking pleased. "Laura stays on as our temporary ranch hand."

"And cook," Laura added with a small smile. "If last night's reaction to my stew was any indication."

Zeb laughed, a warm, genuine sound that filled the kitchen. "Oh, definitely cook. My cooking's kept us alive, but not much more than that."

Even Boone's stern expression softened slightly at this. "True enough," he conceded.

"So," Laura said, straightening with new purpose, "what needs doing first?"

"Breakfast," both men said simultaneously, then exchanged looks that made Laura laugh despite herself.

"I think I can manage that," she said, rising from her chair. "Though I'll need someone to show me around the rest of the ranch later, so I know what I'm getting into."

"I can do that," Boone offered, surprising her with his readiness. "Got some mending to do on a harness in the barn this morning, anyway. You can come along, and I'll give you the tour."

"Thank you," Laura said, meeting his eyes.

Zeb cleared his throat, bringing them back to the present. "Well, I'd best go check on those new calves. Don't want them getting chilled." He stood, reaching for his coat. "Don't worry about me for breakfast, Laura. I'll grab something when I come back in."

After Zeb left, Laura set about preparing breakfast, aware of Boone's presence at the table behind her. He sat in silence, but it wasn't uncomfortable—more contemplative, as if he was adjusting to the idea of her staying.

"I hope you didn't feel pressured," he said as she cracked eggs into a bowl. "About staying, I mean."

Laura glanced over her shoulder at him. "I didn't," she assured him. "I make my own decisions, Boone."

He nodded, seeming satisfied with her answer. "Good."

Laura turned back to her task, whisking the eggs with a fork. "Though I am curious," she ventured after a moment, "about why you offered. Your father seemed more enthusiastic about the idea than you did."

There was a pause, and Laura wondered if she'd overstepped. But when Boone spoke, his voice was thoughtful rather than offended.

"Pa sees things... differently than I do sometimes," he said carefully. "He's always been quick to welcome people, to see the best in them."

"And you haven't?" Laura asked, keeping her tone light as she sliced bread for toasting.

"I've learned to be more cautious," Boone replied, a subtle edge to his words. "But that doesn't mean I don't recognize capable hands when I see them."

Laura smiled slightly at the grudging compliment. "Well, I'll try not to make you regret your decision," she said, placing slices of bread in the cast-iron skillet to toast.

"I don't think you will," Boone said quietly, almost to himself.

The rest of the breakfast preparation passed quietly. Laura found that she enjoyed cooking in the Callahan kitchen, which was well-organized despite its obvious masculine management. By the time she placed a plate of scrambled eggs and toast in front of Boone, along with a small jar of preserved apple butter, she had discovered in the pantry. She was feeling more at home than she had in quite some time.

"This looks good," Boone said, eyeing the food appreciatively. "Better than Pa's infamous breakfast hash."

"Infamous?" Laura questioned, taking her own seat across from him.

A rare smile tugged at the corner of Boone's mouth. "Let's just say there's a reason Matt always claims to have eaten before he arrives in the morning."

Laura laughed, and for a moment, Boone's eyes lingered on her face with an expression she couldn't quite decipher. It disappeared as quickly as it had come, replaced by his usual reserve, as he turned his attention to his food.

"What made you decide to come to Lone Valley?" he asked suddenly. "Of all places."

Laura considered her answer, absently spreading apple butter on her toast. "I needed somewhere... new," she said finally. "Somewhere Jasper wouldn't think to look for me. Mrs. Whitaker—she owned the mercantile where I worked back in Elk Ridge—she mentioned Lone Valley. Said it was small but growing, and that Ms. Patterson was looking for help at her boarding house."

"And that was enough?" Boone asked, genuine curiosity in his voice. "Just the promise of work?"

"Sometimes that's all you need," Laura replied, meeting his gaze steadily. "A chance to start fresh, to be someone other than who you've always been."

Something flickered in Boone's eyes—recognition, perhaps. "I suppose that's true," he acknowledged.

Chapter 10

Boone and Laura finished breakfast, and Laura insisted on clearing up while Boone took his medicine for the pain in his ribs. Once the kitchen was tidy, she found him waiting by the door, a heavy wool coat in his hands.

"You'll need this," he said, holding it out to her. "It's quite cold out there, despite the sunshine."

Laura assumed it was one of his coats—far too large for her, but undoubtedly warmer than her wool wrap. "Thank you," she said, slipping it on. The sleeves hung well past her hands, and the hem nearly reached her ankles.

Boone's lips twitched at the sight of her swallowed by his coat. "Bit big," he observed dryly.

"It will do," Laura countered, rolling up the sleeves. "Warm is all that matters."

Outside, the ranch was transformed by sunlight. The snow lay crisp and white across the yard, sparkling in the morning sun. The air was cold but refreshingly clean. Laura breathed deeply, feeling her spirits lift at the beauty of the place.

The main ranch house sat at the center of a small complex of buildings. A large barn stood nearby, its weathered boards bright against the snow. Beyond it, Laura could see corrals, a smokehouse, and what appeared to be a bunkhouse—currently empty with Matt in town and Davis laid up.

"It's beautiful," she said honestly, taking in the vista of mountains rising beyond the ranch buildings.

Boone followed her gaze, nodding slightly. "It is," he agreed, a note of pride in his voice. "Been in the family since my grandfather's time. Started with just the house and twenty acres. Now we run cattle on over six hundred."

"That's impressive," Laura said, genuinely amazed at what the Callahan family had built.

"It's taken work," Boone said simply, but she could hear the satisfaction beneath his modest words. "Come on, I'll show you around."

He led her first to the barn, walking slightly ahead to break a path through the snow. Laura noticed how, despite his injured ribs, he moved with the easy confidence of a man completely at home in his surroundings.

The barn door creaked as Boone pulled it open, revealing a warm, hay-scented interior. Several horses turned their heads from their stalls, nickering softly in greeting. Saddles and tack hung neatly along one wall, while farm implements were arranged along another. A ladder led up to a hayloft overhead.

"Most of the heavy work happens out with the herd," Boone explained, moving into the center of the barn. "But there's plenty that needs doing here—feeding the horses, maintaining equipment, making sure everything's in working order."

"It's well-organized," Laura observed, noting how every tool seemed to have its place.

"Has to be," Boone replied. "Can't afford to waste time looking for something when you need it." He moved toward a workbench where a leather harness lay spread out. "This is what I need to mend today. Stitching's coming loose."

Laura approached, examining the worn leather. "The thread's rotted," she noted. "You'll need to replace the whole section, not just patch it."

Boone looked at her with mild surprise. "You know leather work?"

"Some," Laura admitted. "Jasper worked for a livery stable for a while. I helped with repairs when they were shorthanded."

Boone nodded thoughtfully. "Skill like that could be useful here." He hesitated, then added, "Though I didn't bring you out to put you to work right away. Just meant to show you around."

"I don't mind helping," Laura said, already rolling up the oversized sleeves more securely. "Four hands make quicker work than two, especially when one of you has injured ribs."

Boone looked like he might protest, but then seemed to think better of it. "All right," he conceded. "Tools are in that drawer there. I'll get the waxed thread."

They settled into a comfortable rhythm, working side by side at the bench. Laura carefully unpicked the rotted stitching while Boone prepared new sections of leather to reinforce the weak points. It was peaceful work, requiring concentration, but not so much that conversation was impossible.

"How long have you been running the ranch?" Laura asked as she worked.

"Took over most of the management when I was eighteen," Boone replied, measuring a strip of leather against the harness. "Pa had a bad fall, broke his leg in two places. By the time he healed up, I'd gotten a taste for it, so he stepped back. Let me take the lead."

"That's a lot of responsibility for someone so young," Laura observed.

Boone shrugged his good shoulder. "I'd been working the ranch my whole life. Knew what needed doing."

"Still," Laura persisted, glancing at him, "managing everything, making all the decisions—that's different from just doing the work."

Boone was quiet for a moment, focused on cutting the leather. "It was," he finally acknowledged. "Made some mistakes at first. Lost a few heads to winter storms that first year because I didn't move them to the sheltered pastures soon enough. Miscalculated our hay stores another time." He paused. "You learn."

The simple statement contained volumes—about responsibility, growth, and the unforgiving nature of their surroundings. Laura understood immediately why Boone carried himself with such quiet confidence. He'd earned it through hard lessons.

"What about you?" Boone asked, breaking into her thoughts. "You mentioned working at a mercantile before coming here?"

Laura nodded, threading a needle with the waxed thread he'd provided. "For the past couple of months. Before that, we moved around a lot. Jasper would find work, lose it, and we'd move on to the next town."

"Must have been difficult, never staying in one place."

"It was," Laura admitted, beginning to stitch the reinforced section of the harness. "Just when I'd start to make friends or feel settled, we'd have to leave again." She concentrated on making neat, even stitches as she continued. "After a while, I stopped trying to put down roots. It was easier that way."

Boone was silent for a long moment, watching her work. "You're good at that," he observed, nodding toward her stitching.

Laura recognized the change in subject for what it was—not indifference to her story, but an acknowledgment that some memories were better left undisturbed. "Thank you," she said simply.

They worked in silence for a while, the only sounds the soft nickering of horses in their stalls and the creak of leather as they handled the harness. Outside, the sun climbed higher, sending shafts of light through the barn's high windows to illuminate dancing dust motes in the air.

"Pa thinks highly of you," Boone said suddenly, his voice casual as he examined a buckle on the harness.

Laura glanced up, surprised by the comment. "That's kind of him. I've only known him a few days."

"He's a good judge of character," Boone continued, not meeting her eyes. "Says you've got grit."

"High praise from a Montana rancher," Laura remarked with a small smile.

"It is," Boone agreed, looking up at her then. "Not everyone can survive what you did—the blizzard, I mean."

Laura's hands stilled on the harness. "I didn't do anything special," she said quietly. "Just kept moving as long as I could."

"That's exactly what I mean," Boone said, his blue eyes intent on her face. "Most people would have given up, waited for help that might never come. You didn't."

There was something in his voice—respect, certainly, but something else that Laura couldn't quite name. It warmed her unexpectedly, this acknowledgment of her strength from a man who clearly valued self-reliance above most things.

"Thank you," she said simply, returning to her stitching to hide the flush she felt rising to her cheeks.

They completed the harness repair working together, Laura's neat stitching complementing Boone's practiced handling of the heavy leather. When they finished, Boone tested the repair, tugging firmly on the mended section.

"Good work," he said with approval. "Better than I could have done."

Laura couldn't help feeling pleased at the genuine compliment. "What's next on your list?" she asked, eager to continue making herself useful.

Boone seemed to consider this, looking at her thoughtfully. "You up for meeting the horses properly? If you're going to be working here, you should know who you're feeding."

Laura nodded eagerly. "I'd like that."

Boone led her down the row of stalls, introducing each horse in turn—Rusher, his own chestnut gelding; Daisy, Zeb's gentle bay mare; Thunder, Matt's spirited black stallion; and several others used for ranch work. The final stall held a beautiful dappled gray mare who regarded them with intelligent dark eyes.

"This is Willow," Boone said, a new softness entering his voice as the mare stretched her neck toward him. "She's the gentlest one we have. Good for someone who's not used to riding much."

The implication was clear, and Laura felt a flutter of anticipation. "Are you suggesting I might need to ride while I'm here?"

"Eventually," Boone said, stroking Willow's nose. "Can't get around the ranch proper without a horse. But only when you're stronger," he added quickly.

"I'd like that," Laura said honestly. "It's been years since I've ridden regularly."

Boone glanced at her. "But you can ride?"

"Yes," Laura confirmed. "My father taught me. Though I'm surely out of practice."

"It comes back," Boone assured her. He hesitated, then asked, "Would you like to say hello to her properly?"

At Laura's nod, he opened the stall door and gestured her inside. Willow regarded Laura with gentle curiosity as she approached slowly, hand extended.

"Talk to her," Boone suggested from behind her. "Let her get to know your voice."

"Hello, Willow," Laura said softly, feeling a bit foolish but following his advice. "Aren't you beautiful? Such a lovely girl."

The mare's ears pricked forward at the sound of her voice, and she stretched her neck to sniff Laura's outstretched hand. After a moment's consideration, Willow nudged Laura's palm gently with her velvet muzzle.

"She likes you," Boone observed, and Laura could hear the smile in his voice without turning to see it.

"She's wonderful," Laura said, stroking the mare's neck. Something about the simple contact with the gentle animal soothed a part of her soul that had been restless for so long. She turned to look at Boone over her shoulder, unable to keep the delight from her face. "Thank you for introducing us."

Boone was leaning against the stall door, watching her with an expression that made Laura's heart skip strangely. His usual reserve had softened, and there was a warmth in his eyes she hadn't seen before.

"You're welcome," he said simply.

The moment stretched between them, quiet and unexpectedly intimate in the hushed barn with only the horses as witnesses. Laura was suddenly very aware of how small the stall was, how close Boone stood, how his eyes hadn't left her face.

The sound of the barn door opening broke the spell. "Boone? You in here?" Zeb's voice called.

Boone straightened, his expression shifting. "Here, Pa," he called back. "By Willow's stall."

Zeb appeared a moment later, smiling when he saw Laura with the mare. "Making friends already, I see," he observed.

"Boone was introducing me to everyone," Laura explained, giving Willow a final pat before stepping out of the stall.

"Good," Zeb nodded approvingly. "A ranch hand should know the stock." He turned to Boone. "Matt's back from town. Thought you'd want to know."

"About time," Boone said, though there was no real irritation in his tone. "He bring news of the survivors?"

"That he did," Zeb confirmed. "All three are doing well, according to Doc Jenkins. The Dobbins are staying with relatives in town. The businessman—Holloway, I think his name was—is already talking about heading back east as soon as the weather permits."

Laura felt relief wash over her at the news. "I'm so glad they're recovering," she said sincerely.

"Doc says they were lucky," Zeb added. "Another hour or two in that storm, and they might not have made it."

The sobering thought hung in the air for a moment before Zeb continued in a more cheerful tone. "Matt's got other news, too. Seems there's to be a social at the church next Sunday after church—weather permitting, of course. Reverend Tanner's idea, to lift spirits after the blizzard."

"A social?" Laura echoed, intrigued despite herself.

"Nothing fancy," Zeb assured her. "Just folks gathering for food and fellowship. Might be a good chance for you to meet some of the townsfolk, seeing as you'll be staying in Lone Valley eventually."

Laura hadn't considered this aspect of staying at the ranch longer—that it would delay her integration into the community she'd chosen for her fresh start. A social would be the perfect opportunity to begin making connections.

"That sounds wonderful," she said. "Though I don't have anything suitable to wear for a social gathering."

"Louella Patterson is about your size," Zeb suggested. "I'm sure she'd lend you something if needed. Matt can ask when he heads back to town."

"Or we could go ourselves," Boone said unexpectedly. Both Laura and Zeb turned to look at him in surprise. He shrugged slightly, wincing at the movement. "Need to go into town anyway to tell Ms. Patterson about the change in Laura's plans. Might as well let her choose something herself."

"That's thoughtful of you, son," Zeb said, a hint of something like satisfaction in his voice that made Boone's ears redden slightly.

"It's practical," Boone muttered.

Laura hid a smile. "I would appreciate the chance to speak with Ms. Patterson personally," she said. "It seems the polite thing to do, given the circumstances."

"Then it's settled," Zeb declared. "You'll ride into town tomorrow or the next day, weather permitting."

Boone nodded once, then gestured toward the barn door. "We should go see what other news Matt's brought. Coming, Laura?"

The simple inclusion—his assumption that she would naturally join them for ranch business—warmed Laura unexpectedly. It was a small thing, perhaps, but it made her feel like she truly belonged, if only temporarily.

"Of course," she said, falling into step beside him as they left the barn.

Outside, the sun had climbed higher, turning the snow-covered ranch into a dazzling landscape of white and blue. Laura squinted against the brightness, grateful for Boone's steadying hand at her elbow as they navigated a slippery patch near the barn door.

Matt was waiting for them by the corral. "Well, look who's up and about!" he called cheerfully. "Miss Hartley, good to see you on your feet."

"Please, call me Laura," she replied, smiling at his infectious good humor. "And thank you for all you did during the rescue. I'm in your debt."

Matt waved away her thanks with a gloved hand. "Just doing what needed doing."

As Matt launched into a detailed report about conditions in Lone Valley, Laura found her attention drawn to Boone. There was something compelling about him standing there in the snow-bright light, listening intently to his ranch hand, occasionally asking a clarifying question or giving a brief instruction. This was Boone in his element—competent, decisive, completely at ease with the responsibility of managing the ranch and the people who depended on him.

It struck Laura suddenly how different he was from Jasper, whose attempts at responsibility had always crumbled under pressure. Where Jasper was volatile and unpredictable, Boone was steady and reliable. Where her brother sought escape from his troubles, Boone faced challenges directly, with quiet determination.

The realization left her feeling oddly unsettled. She had come to Montana to escape Jasper's influence, yet here she was, still defining her experiences in relation to him. If she truly wanted a fresh start, she would need to learn to see people—to see Boone—on their own terms, not as comparisons to her past.

"Laura?" Boone's voice broke into her thoughts. "Everything all right?"

She realized the men had finished their conversation and were looking at her with varying degrees of concern. "Yes, sorry," she said quickly. "Just got lost in thought for a moment."

"I was saying Matt's brought mail from town," Boone explained. "There's a letter for you."

Laura's heart skipped a beat. "For me? Who would be writing to me?"

Matt reached into his coat pocket and extracted a slightly crumpled envelope. "From a Mrs. Whitaker in Elk Ridge," he said, handing it to her. "Town was asking after you, so I mentioned you were staying here for now. Postmaster said this came for you."

Laura accepted the envelope with trembling fingers, recognizing Evelyn Whitaker's neat handwriting immediately. "Thank you," she said, tucking it into her pocket. She would read it later, in private.

"No telegrams or urgent news about sales or business?" Boone asked Matt, returning to ranch matters.

"Nothing like that," Matt confirmed. "Town's still digging out from the storm, but things are getting back to normal. Oh, and Doc Jenkins sends his regards. Says he'd like to see Laura when she's up to the journey, just to check she's recovering properly."

"We'll stop by his office when we go to town," Boone decided, glancing at Laura for confirmation. She nodded her agreement.

The men continued discussing ranch business—feed supplies, cattle in the north pasture, repairs needed on the line cabin—while Laura listened, trying to absorb as much as she could about the operation she would be helping with. It was complex work, she realized, requiring constant attention to countless details, from the health of individual animals to the management of vast grazing lands.

Eventually, they moved toward the house, where Laura insisted on preparing lunch for everyone. Matt's enthusiastic appreciation for her cooking was both flattering and amusing, especially compared to Boone's more reserved compliments.

"This stew is something else, Miss Laura," Matt declared, helping himself to a second bowl. "If you cook like this every day, I might gain some weight."

"Careful," Zeb warned with a twinkle in his eye. "She'll start thinking we only hired her for her cooking."

"Didn't we?" Matt asked innocently, earning a stern look from Boone that didn't quite hide his own amusement.

The easy camaraderie around the table was healing in a way for Laura. For so long, meals with Jasper had been tense affairs, fraught with the potential for his mood to sour with each drink. Here, surrounded by these straightforward, hardworking men, she felt a knot of tension she'd carried for years begin to loosen.

After lunch, Boone suggested she rest for a while before taking on any more chores. "You're still recovering," he reminded her when she protested. "No point pushing too hard and setting yourself back."

Reluctantly, Laura agreed, retreating to her room with Evelyn's letter. She settled onto the bed, broke the seal, and unfolded the single sheet of paper inside.

My dear Laura,

I pray this letter finds you well and safely arrived in Lone Valley. The journey is not an easy one in the best of times, and winter travel adds its own challenges.

I write with news that may be unwelcome, but which you should know. Your brother came to the store a day after your departure, asking after you. He was not in a state to be reasoned with, I'm afraid. When I told him only that you had moved on to seek better opportunities, he became quite agitated, insisting that you would not have left without telling him.

I did not reveal your destination, but I fear he may be determined to find you. He mentioned heading west to follow the stagecoach routes. I tell you this not to alarm you, but to prepare you. Should he somehow discover your whereabouts?

Please know that you remain in my prayers. You made the right choice in seeking a fresh start, Laura. Do not let fear of your brother's reaction dim your resolve or cloud the new life you are building.

With the fondest regards,

Evelyn Whitaker

Laura lowered the letter slowly, a cold weight settling in her stomach. The thought of Jasper searching for her, angry and determined, brought back memories she'd been trying to leave behind. She could picture him all too clearly—red-faced, voice raised, demanding to know why she had abandoned him.

A soft knock at her door startled her from her troubled thoughts. "Laura?" Boone's voice called. "Everything all right?"

She quickly folded the letter. "Yes," she called back, composing herself. "Come in."

The door opened, and Boone stood framed in the doorway, his tall figure nearly filling the space. His observant eyes took in her expression immediately. "Bad news?" he asked, nodding toward the letter.

Laura hesitated, then sighed. "News I expected, but hoped wouldn't come," she admitted. "Jasper asked after my whereabouts. He's looking for me."

Boone's expression darkened. "Does he know you're here? In Lone Valley?"

"Mrs. Whitaker didn't tell him," Laura assured him. "But he's heading west, following the stagecoach routes."

Boone was quiet for a moment, considering. "Montana Territory's a big place," he said finally. "Lots of small towns between here and Elk Ridge. Even if he makes it this far, there's no reason he'd connect you to this ranch."

His practical assessment was reassuring, and Laura felt some of her tension ease. "You're right," she acknowledged. "And I can't spend my life looking over my shoulder."

Boone nodded approvingly. "For what it's worth, if he did somehow find you here, you wouldn't be facing him alone."

Chapter 11

Sleep had proven elusive after reading Evelyn's letter. Every time Laura closed her eyes, images of Jasper—angry, desperate, searching for her—had flooded her mind. The thought of him following the stagecoach routes, questioning people about her whereabouts, left her feeling hunted. She needed distraction, and physical labor was the best remedy she knew.

She made her way to the kitchen quietly, not wanting to wake the Callahan men. The embers in the stove still glowed faintly, and she carefully added kindling, coaxing the fire back to life. There was something soothing about simple morning tasks—stoking the fire, measuring coffee grounds, pumping water into the kettle.

By the time the coffee was brewing, filling the kitchen with its rich aroma, Laura had already mixed biscuit dough and sliced salt pork for frying. She worked efficiently, finding comfort in the rhythm of the tasks. If she kept busy enough, perhaps she could outrun the worries that had chased her through the night.

She heard floorboards creaking, and Laura turned to see Boone, watching her with a mixture of surprise and approval.

"You're up early," he observed, his voice rough with sleep.

"Couldn't sleep," Laura admitted, turning back to flip the slices of salt pork in the skillet. "Thought I might as well make myself useful."

Boone moved to the stove, pouring himself a cup of coffee. "Thinking about your brother?"

Laura's hands stilled momentarily.

"Yes," she acknowledged, resuming her work. "Among other things."

Boone studied her over the rim of his mug. "Whatever Mrs. Whitaker wrote has you spooked."

It wasn't a question, but Laura answered anyway. "Not spooked. Just... cautious. A bit on edge, perhaps. Jasper can be unpredictable when he's drinking, and according to Mrs. Whitaker, he was quite agitated about my leaving."

"Unpredictable how?" Boone asked, his tone casual but his eyes sharp.

Laura hesitated, not wanting to speak ill of Jasper despite everything. "He has a temper," she said finally, sliding the biscuits into the oven. "He's never hurt me," she added quickly, seeing Boone's expression darken. "But he can be... intimidating. Things get broken. Words get said."

Boone's jaw tightened, but he only nodded, taking another sip of coffee. "Seems to me you had good reason to leave, then."

"I did," Laura agreed quietly. "But that doesn't mean I don't worry about him."

"That's your good heart talking," Boone said, surprising her with the unexpected observation. "But you deserve better than living in fear of someone's moods."

Laura busied herself with breakfast preparations to hide the sudden moisture in her eyes.

"Thank you," she said when she trusted her voice. "For understanding."

Boone made a noncommittal sound, but Laura sensed his support nonetheless. Laura finished making breakfast while Boone set the table.

"What needs doing around the ranch today?" she asked.

"Plenty. Always is. Fence in the south pasture needs mending. Matt's going to work on that. Pa's heading to check on the herd in the north section. I've got to repair the roof on the smokehouse where the snow damaged it."

"And me?" Laura prompted when he didn't continue.

Boone looked at her appraisingly. "Figured you might want to help around the house today. It's cold out, and you're still recovering."

Laura straightened her shoulders. "I'm perfectly recovered, and I'd rather be working outside. I need—" She stopped herself, not wanting to admit how desperately she needed distraction. "I'd like to be useful. Really useful, not just cooking and cleaning."

Something in her tone must have convinced him because after a moment Boone nodded. "All right. There's always wood that needs chopping for the stove and fireplace. Not the big logs—Matt handles those—but splitting the smaller pieces. Think you can manage that?"

"Yes," Laura said confidently, though she'd never actually chopped wood before. How difficult could it be? "What else?"

The faintest hint of amusement flickered in Boone's eyes, as if he suspected her inexperience but was willing to let her learn the hard way. "There's chicken feed to distribute, eggs to collect. The hen house could use a good cleaning out, too."

"I can handle all of that," Laura assured him, turning to remove the biscuits from the oven before they burned.

"Don't overdo it," Boone cautioned, his voice softening. "No shame in pacing yourself."

Laura was saved from having to respond by Zeb's arrival in the kitchen, his face lighting up at the sight of breakfast nearly ready.

"Now this is a fine way to start the day," he declared, inhaling deeply. "Laura, you're spoiling us."

Laura smiled, pleased by his appreciation. "Just earning my keep, Mr. Callahan."

"Zeb," he corrected gently. "If my son gets to be called by his given name, I think I'm entitled to the same courtesy."

"Zeb," Laura amended, setting a platter of fried salt pork on the table.

Matt arrived moments later, drawn in by the smell of food, and they all sat down to breakfast. As the men discussed the day's work, Laura found her gaze repeatedly drawn to Boone. There was something compelling about him, the strong line of his jaw, the way his dark hair fell across his forehead, the quiet authority in his voice as he gave Matt instructions about the fence repair.

She caught herself staring and quickly looked away, focusing intently on her plate. These kinds of thoughts were dangerous. Boone Callahan might be kind, honorable, and unexpectedly perceptive, but he was also her temporary employer and landlord. Moreover, she had no intention of staying at the ranch any longer than necessary. She needed her independence, her fresh start in town. Developing any sort of attachment to Boone or the ranch would only make that eventual transition more difficult.

As soon as breakfast was finished, Laura insisted on tackling the outdoor chores, despite Zeb's protests about the cold.

"Bundle up, at least," he said, concern evident in his voice.

Laura promised she would and hurried to her room to add an extra layer beneath the oversized coat Boone had lent her. By the time she stepped outside, the men had already dispersed to their various tasks. The ranch yard was empty save for a few chickens pecking hopefully at the frozen ground.

Laura headed first to the woodpile near the side of the house. A small axe leaned against the chopping block, its handle smooth from years of use. She picked it up, testing its weight in her hands. It was heavier than she'd expected.

She positioned a piece of wood on the block, raised the axe, and brought it down with as much force as she could muster. The axe blade glanced off the side of the wood, barely making a dent. Laura frowned, repositioning the log. Her second attempt was more successful, the blade biting into the wood but stopping halfway through.

After fifteen minutes of struggle, she had managed to split exactly three pieces of wood, and her arms ached from the unfamiliar exertion. This was clearly going to be more difficult than she'd anticipated.

"Might help if you widen your stance a bit."

Laura turned to find Boone watching her from a few yards away, a coil of rope slung over one shoulder. She hadn't heard him approach.

"I'm figuring it out," she said, trying not to sound defensive.

Boone set down the rope and moved toward her. "Mind if I show you?"

Laura relinquished the axe, stepping back as Boone positioned himself in front of the chopping block. His movements were fluid and practiced as he set a log upright, raised the axe, and brought it down in one smooth motion. The wood split cleanly in two.

"It's about technique more than strength," he explained, setting up another log. "Stand with your feet shoulder-width apart. Keep your back straight. When you swing, let the weight of the axe do most of the work."

He demonstrated again, making the task look effortless. Then he held out the axe to her. "Your turn."

Laura took the axe, determined to master this skill. She positioned herself as Boone had shown, feet planted firmly, back straight. She lifted the axe and swung, focusing on letting its weight carry the motion. The blade connected solidly with the wood, splitting it nearly in half.

"Better," Boone said with approval. "Try again."

Under his watchful eye, Laura split two more logs, each attempt more successful than the last. Her arms still ached, but there was satisfaction in seeing the growing pile of firewood at her feet.

"You're a quick learner," Boone observed.

"I've had to be," Laura replied, setting up another log. "Moving around so much with Jasper, I was always having to pick up new skills quickly."

"I'll leave you to it, then. Don't push yourself too hard. The chickens still need tending, and that's no small job."

As he walked away, Laura called after him, "Thank you for the lesson."

Boone half-turned, giving her a brief nod before continuing toward the smokehouse with his rope.

Laura worked steadily for the next hour, splitting enough wood to fill the box by the kitchen stove. Her arms trembled with fatigue by the time she finished, but there was a deep satisfaction in the physical accomplishment. She'd proven—to herself, as much as to Boone—that she could handle this task.

The chicken coop proved to be its own challenge. The hens scattered in alarm when she entered, making the task of collecting eggs a game of patience and persistence. By the time she'd gathered all the eggs in her basket and distributed fresh feed, the front of her skirt was covered in dust and feathers.

Cleaning the coop was even messier work. Laura shoveled out old straw and droppings, trying to breathe through her mouth to avoid the pungent smell. She spread fresh straw, filled the water trough, and made sure the coop was secure against predators before finally stepping back outside into the fresh air.

The rest of the morning passed in a blur of activity. Laura found tasks to occupy herself—helping Matt carry tools to the fence line, sorting through a bin of root vegetables in the cellar to remove any that had begun to spoil, scrubbing the kitchen floor until it gleamed. The physical labor was precisely what she needed, keeping her mind too occupied for worries about Jasper or unwelcome thoughts about Boone Callahan's kind eyes.

By midday, every muscle in Laura's body ached pleasantly, and her mind felt clearer than it had since receiving Mrs. Whitaker's letter. She prepared a simple lunch of bean soup and bread, leaving it warming on the stove for the men to help themselves whenever their work allowed.

Zeb was the first to return, stomping snow from his boots on the porch before entering. His eyebrows rose at the gleaming kitchen floor.

"Been busy, I see," he remarked.

Laura smiled, wiping her hands on her apron. "Just trying to be useful."

"Useful, she says," Zeb chuckled, shaking his head as he removed his coat. "You've split wood and cleaned out the chicken coop. Now the floor's clean enough to eat off of. That's more than useful, Laura."

"I like to keep busy," she said simply, ladling soup into a bowl for him.

Zeb accepted the soup with a nod of thanks, settling at the table. "Nothing wrong with hard work," he agreed. "But there's no need to prove yourself here. You've already more than earned your keep."

Laura joined him at the table with her own bowl of soup. "It's not about proving myself," she said, though she wasn't entirely sure that was true. "I just... need the distraction."

Zeb's kind eyes studied her face. "Worried about your brother still?"

"Yes," Laura admitted. "And thinking too much in general. Work helps."

"I understand that," Zeb said, breaking a piece of bread. "Boone's the same way. After his mother passed, that boy worked from sunup to sundown, barely stopping to eat. Said he was just doing what needed doing, but I knew better. Work was his way of keeping the grief at bay."

Laura looked up, surprised by this glimpse into Boone's past. "How old was he when your wife died?"

"Fourteen," Zeb said, his voice softening with memory. "Old enough to understand what was happening, young enough to still need his mother desperately. It hit him hard, though he tried not to show it."

"You must have been devastated," Laura said gently.

Zeb's eyes grew distant. "I was. Mary was everything to me. But I had two boys and a daughter who needed me to keep going, so that's what I did." He paused, a small smile touching his lips. "Boone stepped up in ways I never expected. Took on responsibilities way beyond his years. He's always been like that—solid as a rock when things get hard."

The portrait Zeb painted of young Boone resonated deeply with Laura. She, too, had learned to be responsible beyond her years after her parents' deaths. She could easily imagine a teenage Boone stoically shouldering adult burdens while grieving over his mother.

"He doesn't talk much about her," Zeb continued, "but I catch him sometimes, looking at her portrait when he thinks no one's watching."

Laura thought of the small portrait she'd noticed hanging on the wall—a pretty woman with Boone's eyes and a gentle smile. She'd wondered about her, but hadn't wanted to pry.

"Loss shapes us," she said quietly. "Sometimes in ways we don't even realize until years later."

Zeb looked at her thoughtfully. "Sounds like you know something about that yourself."

"My parents died when I was sixteen," Laura explained. "Influenza outbreak. It was quick—less than a week from first symptoms to... the end. Jasper was eighteen. Suddenly, we were alone in the world, trying to figure out how to survive."

"That's a heavy burden for young shoulders," Zeb said sympathetically.

Laura nodded, stirring her soup absently. "Jasper tried, at first. He really did. He got work at the sawmill, made sure I stayed in school. But then he started drinking, just a little at first. Said it helped him sleep." She sighed. "You can guess the rest."

"The bottle's a poor substitute for facing grief," Zeb observed. "But an easy one to reach for."

"By the time I was seventeen, I was the one keeping us afloat," Laura continued. "Jasper would work just long enough to earn drinking money, then disappear for days at a time. When he lost his job at the sawmill, we had to leave town. That became the pattern—move somewhere new, Jasper would find work, lose it when the drinking got bad, and we'd move on."

"And you never thought of striking out on your own until recently?" Zeb asked.

Laura hesitated. "He's my brother," she said simply. "The only family I had left. And sometimes, between the bad spells, he'd be himself again—the Jasper I remembered from before. He'd promise to do better, and I'd believe him."

"Hope's a powerful thing," Zeb said, nodding. "Hard to give up on someone you love."

"But eventually, I had to," Laura admitted. "For my own sake. The last few months in Elk Ridge, I started saving every penny I could. When Jasper disappeared on another drinking binge, I saw my chance and took it. I waited until he stumbled home and was deep in sleep." She looked down at her hands, a mixture of guilt and resolution in her heart. "I left him a note. Told him I loved him, but couldn't live that way anymore."

"That took courage," Zeb said.

Laura shook her head. "Sometimes it feels like cowardice. Running away instead of trying harder to help him."

"You can't help someone who won't help themselves," Zeb said, echoing what Laura had told herself countless times. "And from what you've said, you tried for years."

"I did," Laura agreed. "But I still worry about him. Even knowing how angry he might be with me, I can't help wondering if he's safe, if he's eaten today, if he's found shelter in this cold weather."

Zeb reached across the table and patted her hand, a fatherly gesture that brought unexpected tears to Laura's eyes. "That's because you've got a good heart, Laura Hartley. But don't mistake caring for responsibility. Your brother's choices are his own."

Laura blinked away the moisture in her eyes, nodding. "You're right. I know you're right."

"Knowing and feeling are different things," Zeb said wisely. "Give yourself time."

The back door opened then, and Boone entered, bringing with him a gust of cold air. He paused, looking between Laura and his father, as if sensing the serious nature of their conversation.

"Everything all right?" he asked, his gaze lingering on Laura's face.

"Just fine," she assured him, rising to fetch him a bowl of soup.

Boone looked to his father for confirmation, and Zeb nodded slightly.

"The roof's patched," he reported, accepting the bowl Laura offered him. "Should hold until spring when we can replace the damaged section properly."

"Good," Zeb said, returning to his own soup. "Laura here's been working harder than both of us put together."

Boone glanced around the spotless kitchen, then back at Laura with a raised eyebrow. "So I see."

"It wasn't all housework," Laura said, a touch defensively. "I finished splitting a pile of wood, tended the chickens, helped Matt with his tools."

The corner of Boone's mouth twitched in what might have been the beginning of a smile. "I know. Saw the woodpile. You did good."

The simple praise warmed Laura more than it should have. She busied herself with getting Boone bread for his soup to hide her pleased expression.

After lunch, Zeb announced he was heading back out to check the cattle in the western pasture, leaving Laura and Boone alone in the kitchen. An unexpected awkwardness settled between them as Laura cleared the dishes.

"More chores for this afternoon?" Boone asked finally, breaking the silence.

Laura nodded, grateful for the practical topic. "I thought I might start on some mending. I noticed a stack of shirts and socks in the corner of the main room."

"That pile's been growing for months," Boone admitted. "None of us has much skill with a needle."

"Well, I do," Laura said, pleased to have a useful indoor task for the afternoon. Her muscles were already protesting the morning's unaccustomed labor.

"I need to ride out and meet Matt at the fence line," Boone said, rising from the table. "Probably won't be back until suppertime."

"I'll have something ready," Laura promised. "Any requests?"

Boone considered for a moment. "There's a ham in the cellar that needs using. Beyond that, I trust your judgment."

As he put on his coat and hat, Laura was struck by the domestic normalcy of their exchange. It was the sort of conversation a husband and wife might have—him heading out to work; her managing the household, discussing the evening meal. The thought was both comforting and alarming. She had no business thinking of Boone Callahan in those terms.

"Be careful out there," she said instead, keeping her tone light. "Your ribs still need time to heal."

Boone nodded, that almost-smile appearing again. "Yes, ma'am," he said, a hint of teasing in his deep voice.

After he left, Laura stood in the kitchen for a long moment, unsettled by her own thoughts. This was exactly what she'd been trying to avoid—getting comfortable, developing attachments, forgetting that her stay at the Callahan ranch was temporary.

She reminded herself of her goals. Independence. Stability. A life free from the chaos and uncertainty that had defined her for years with Jasper. Those things wouldn't come from lingering at the ranch or developing feelings for a man who had his own life here, a life that didn't include her beyond her temporary usefulness.

Laura fetched the pile of mending and settled in the chair by the window, where the afternoon light was strongest. As she sorted through the items—socks with holes at the heels, shirts missing buttons, a tear in what looked like Boone's Sunday jacket—she forced her mind to focus on practical matters.

She would stay at the ranch for a week or two longer, she decided, earning enough money to supplement what she'd brought with her. Soon she would move to Lone Valley as originally planned. She would thank the Callahans for their hospitality, take the position with Ms. Patterson, and begin building the independent life she'd dreamed of for so long.

And if her heart gave a painful twinge at the thought of leaving the ranch and its inhabitants behind, well, that was a feeling she would simply have to overcome.

Chapter 12

The afternoon passed in a rhythm of needle and thread, with Laura's thoughts circling between memories of the past and plans for the future. She was so absorbed in her work that she barely noticed the light fading until the chill in the room began to seep into her bones. With a start, she realized the fire had burned low, and the early winter evening was setting in.

She rose, stretching muscles stiff from sitting, and added wood to the fireplace. The warmth began to return to the room as she lit the oil lamps, their gentle glow creating pools of light against the gathering darkness outside.

It was time to start supper. Laura retrieved the ham from the cellar, along with potatoes, carrots, and onions. She worked steadily, peeling and chopping vegetables, preparing the ham with a glaze of honey and mustard she found in the pantry. Soon, the kitchen was filled with savory aromas that made her own stomach growl in anticipation.

As she worked, Laura tried to maintain the firm resolve she'd felt earlier. This was just a temporary arrangement. The comfort she felt in the Callahan kitchen, the ease with which she'd fallen into ranch routines—these were dangerous illusions. She couldn't afford to get attached to this place or its people.

Yet it was becoming increasingly difficult to maintain that emotional distance, especially with Zeb's fatherly kindness and Boone's allure. Even Matt's cheerful presence had quickly become something she looked forward to. After years of guarding herself against Jasper's volatile moods, the steadiness of these men was both unfamiliar and deeply appealing.

The sound of horses approaching pulled Laura from her thoughts. She wiped her hands on her apron and moved to the window, watching as Boone and Matt rode into the yard. They looked cold but satisfied, the way men often did after a day of productive labor.

Laura turned back to her cooking, adding the finishing touches to the meal. She heard the men on the porch, stomping snow from their boots, then the door opening. Cold air rushed in, quickly replaced by the warmth of male voices as Boone and Matt entered, bringing with them the scents of horses, hay, and the crisp winter air.

"Something smells mighty fine in here," Matt declared, removing his hat.

"Ham with honey glaze," Laura replied, smiling at his enthusiasm. "And potato and carrot hash. Should be ready in about twenty minutes."

"You're an angel, Miss Laura," Matt said fervently. "A genuine, heaven-sent angel."

Boone rolled his eyes at his ranch hand's dramatics, but there was no real irritation in the gesture. "Go get cleaned up, Matt. You smell like a horse."

"Yes, boss," Matt said, heading toward the washroom.

Once Matt was gone, Boone moved closer to the stove, drawn by the appetizing smells. "Need any help?" he asked, surprising Laura. It was the first time he'd offered to assist with meal preparation.

"You could set the table," she suggested. "Everything else is nearly done."

Boone nodded, moving to the cupboard to retrieve plates and utensils. They worked in companionable silence for a few minutes, moving around each other with growing ease in the small kitchen space.

"How's the fence coming along?" Laura asked as she stirred the hash.

"Good," Boone replied, setting out cups for coffee. "Should finish it tomorrow if the weather holds."

The simplicity of the exchange struck Laura. It was this very normalcy that both comforted and troubled her.

"I got through most of the mending," she said, deliberately keeping the conversation on practical matters. "Though there's a tear in a Sunday jacket that assume is yours and needs more attention than I could give it today."

Boone glanced at the pile of neatly folded clothes on the chair by the window. "You didn't have to do all that in one day," he said. "There was no rush."

"I like keeping busy," Laura said simply.

Boone studied her for a moment. "So I've noticed. Running from something, or toward something?"

The unexpected perception of the question caught Laura's attention. "I'm not running," she said automatically, then sighed at his skeptical look. "Perhaps a bit of both," she admitted more honestly.

Boone nodded. "Nothing wrong with that," he said, turning to finish setting the table. "We've all got things we're trying to outrun or catch up to."

The front door opened again, and Zeb entered, bringing another rush of cold air.

"Land's alive. It's getting bitter out there," he declared, rubbing his hands together. "Wind's picked up something fierce. Might be another storm brewing."

"Possibly," Boone countered, frowning.

Zeb shrugged, hanging up his coat. "Just saying, there's a feeling in the air I don't much like."

"Well, supper's ready regardless of the weather," Laura interjected, setting the platter of glazed ham on the table. "And there's hot coffee to warm you up."

Matt rejoined them, freshly washed and combed, and they all sat down to eat. The meal was a success, with the men helping themselves to second and even third helpings. Laura relaxed into the easy conversation around the table, mostly centered on ranch matters, but occasionally venturing into stories from the past.

"—and then the horse throws Boone clear over the fence," Zeb was saying, eyes twinkling with mirth. "Lands him right in the mud puddle on the other side."

"I was ten," Boone protested, though Laura detected no real annoyance in his tone. "And that horse had it in for me from the start."

"Best part was," Matt added, clearly having heard the story before, "he gets up, covered in mud from head to toe, and says with perfect dignity, 'I meant to do that.'"

Laura couldn't help laughing at the image of a mud-covered young Boone trying to maintain his pride. Boone glanced at her, a spark of shared amusement passing between them.

"I seem to recall," Boone said dryly, turning back to Matt, "that you once got yourself chased up a tree by the Anderson's prize bull."

Matt clutched his chest in mock offense. "A strategic retreat. Very different situation."

"He was up there for three hours," Boone told Laura, the corner of his mouth curving upward. "Singing hymns to try to calm the bull down."

"Did it work?" Laura asked, enjoying this glimpse of Boone's subtle humor.

"Not even slightly," Matt admitted cheerfully. "Old man Anderson finally came along and led that monster away. Told me I had a worse singing voice than his deaf aunt."

Laughter filled the kitchen. This was what a family meal should be—stories, gentle teasing, shared history. It made her realize how much she'd missed this kind of simple connection during the years with Jasper, when meals were often tense, silent affairs punctuated by his sudden outbursts or morose withdrawal.

After supper, the men insisted on cleaning up while Laura rested. She protested at first, but the weariness in her body from the day's exertions convinced her to accept their offer. She settled in the rocking chair by the fireplace in the main room, content to listen to the quiet clatter of dishes and the murmur of male voices from the kitchen.

Zeb joined her first, taking the chair opposite hers. "Weather's definitely changing," he remarked, glancing toward the window where darkness had fully fallen. "Can hear the wind picking up. Might be in for a rough night."

"I hope not another blizzard," Laura said, remembering all too clearly her terrifying experience in the last storm.

"Doubt it'll be that bad," Zeb reassured her. "Just some wind and snow. Nothing unusual for this time of year."

Boone and Matt emerged from the kitchen, Matt announcing that he was turning in early to rest up for finishing the fence tomorrow. After he'd gone, Boone took the third chair by the fire, stretching his long legs toward the warmth.

For a time, they sat in silence, watching the flames dance in the fireplace. Laura found her gaze drawn to Boone's profile, softened in the firelight. The stern lines of his face were relaxed, making him look younger, less burdened. She wondered what he was thinking, this quiet man who revealed so little of himself.

"Miss Laura," Zeb said suddenly, breaking the silence. "Would you mind fetching that book from the shelf there? The red one with the gold lettering."

Laura rose, moving to the small bookshelf in the corner of the room. She found the book Zeb had described—a well-worn volume of poetry. As she handed it to him, curiosity got the better of her.

"You enjoy poetry?" she asked, surprised.

"Mary loved it," Zeb explained, handling the book with gentle reverence. "Used to read it aloud in the evenings. I've kept up the habit, though I'm not half the reader she was."

He opened the book to a marked page, the paper thin and yellowed with age. "This was one of her favorites," he said, clearing his throat before beginning to read in a gravelly but steady voice:

Hope is the thing with feathers
That perches in the soul,
And sings the tune without the words,
And never stops at all...

As Zeb continued reading Emily Dickinson's poem, Laura found herself stealing glances at Boone. His expression had softened further, a distant look in his eyes that suggested he too was remembering his mother's voice reciting these same words.

There was something deeply moving about this glimpse into their family tradition—the way Zeb honored his late wife's memory, the reverent quiet with which Boone listened. It spoke of a love that endured beyond loss, of bonds that remained unbroken despite the passage of time.

When Zeb finished reading, a gentle silence filled the room, broken only by the crackling of the fire.

"That was beautiful," Laura said. "Thank you for sharing it."

Zeb smiled, closing the book carefully. "Poetry helps us make sense of things sometimes, doesn't it? Puts words to feelings we can't quite express ourselves."

Laura nodded, thinking of her own tumultuous emotions of late—her fears about Jasper, her growing attachment to the ranch and its people, her determination to maintain her independence. No poem could fully capture that complex tangle of feelings, but there was comfort in knowing others had also struggled to make sense of their hearts.

The wind outside had grown stronger, rattling the windows and sending occasional gusts down the chimney that made the fire flicker.

"Storm's definitely coming," Boone observed, rising to add another log to the fire. "Good thing we got the fence mostly fixed today."

"And the smoke house roof," Zeb added. "Nothing worse than trying to patch a roof in the middle of a snowstorm."

Laura shivered slightly at the thought of being caught outside in such weather again. The memory of the blizzard was still too fresh, too frightening.

Boone noticed her reaction. "No need to worry," he said quietly. "You're safe here."

The simple assurance touched Laura deeply. Safety had been a rare commodity in her life with Jasper, where his volatile moods could shatter calm in an instant. Here, in this warm room with these steady men, she felt truly protected.

But that sense of security was itself a danger. Laura couldn't afford to become dependent on others for her safety or happiness. She had embarked on this journey to build a life of self-reliance, not to trade one form of dependence for another.

"I should turn in," she said, rising from her chair. "It's been a long day."

"Of course," Zeb said, offering her a kind smile. "Sleep well, Laura."

"Good night," Boone added, his deep voice rumbling in the quiet room.

In her bedroom, Laura changed into her nightgown and slipped beneath the heavy quilt. Outside, the wind continued to grow, whistling around the corners of the house like a living thing seeking entry. Despite the ominous sounds, Laura felt no fear.

Chapter 13

Boone lay in the loft bed, the rough-hewn timbers above him groaning under the assault of the wind. He'd moved up here when Laura had arrived. His normal downstairs bedroom being given to her had only made sense, a space that had been his since he was a boy. It felt strange to be up here, further from the heart of the house. He shifted, the straw mattress rustling beneath him, the ache in his ribs a dull throb that had become a constant companion. The storm was brewing, just as his pa had predicted. He could hear the increasing fury of the wind, a high-pitched whine that threatened to tear at the very foundations of the house.

But it wasn't the storm that truly held his attention. It was the quiet stillness emanating from the downstairs bedroom, the room he now thought of as Laura's room. He imagined her there, tucked beneath the quilts, hopefully sleeping soundly despite the growing tempest outside. He pictured her face as she'd been earlier, firelight dancing in her eyes as she'd laughed, a genuine, unguarded laugh that had resonated deep within him.

He scrubbed a hand over his face, the weariness of the day settling heavily upon him. What was happening to him? He, Boone Callahan, the man who'd sworn off any romantic entanglements, the rancher who'd buried his heart beneath layers of hard work and stoic resolve, was now...what? Distracted. Intrigued. Downright...concerned for a woman he'd known less than a week.

It was foolish. Utterly foolish. He'd built walls around his heart for a reason. Two years ago, Eliza had ripped it open and left him bleeding, exposed to the harsh elements of betrayal and heartbreak. He'd vowed then, never again. The ranch, his family, his faith—those were the anchors in his life, the things he could depend on. Love, romance...those were fickle illusions, shimmering promises that turned to dust.

And yet... Laura. She was different. He tried to deny it, to categorize her as just another soul in need of help, a temporary presence on the ranch. But he couldn't. There was a strength and grit about her, a resilience forged in the fires of hardship, that mirrored something deep within himself. He saw it in her eyes, a flicker of pain, yes, but also an unwavering spark of determination, a refusal to be broken.

He thought of her at the woodpile earlier, her initial awkwardness giving way to focused determination as she mastered the axe, her small frame working with surprising strength. He recalled her gentle hands tending to his injured ribs, the quiet competence with which she managed the kitchen, the unexpected vulnerability in her voice when she'd spoken of her brother.

He was drawn to her, undeniably so. It was more than just gratitude for her help, more than simple compassion for her difficult circumstances. It was something deeper, something...dangerous. He felt a stirring within him, a thawing of the ice that had encased his heart for so long. And it terrified him.

He couldn't afford to let those walls crumble. Not again. He had a ranch to run, a family to legacy to hold together. Emotional entanglements, especially with a woman who was clearly searching for her own path, were a distraction he couldn't afford. She was heading to town, to the boarding house. Her stay at the ranch was temporary. He needed to remember that. He had to remember that.

He forced himself to focus on the storm, on the practicalities of ranch life. Had Matt secured the gate to the north pasture? Were the calves sheltered adequately? He needed to think about practicalities, about cattle and fences, and the endless demands of ranch work. Anything but Laura.

He rolled out of bed, the cold air biting at his skin. He needed to move, to do something. He pulled on his boots, grabbed his coat, and headed down the ladder, the familiar creak of the wood a grounding sound in the storm's escalating symphony.

He found Zeb still in the main room, sitting in his usual chair by the dying embers of the fire, the poetry book lying open on his lap. Zeb looked up as Boone entered, his keen eyes assessing his son's restless energy.

"Can't sleep?" Zeb asked, his voice low, barely audible above the wind's howl.

Boone shook his head, moving to the fireplace and adding another log, the dry wood catching quickly and sending a fresh burst of warmth into the room. "Storm's picking up."

Zeb nodded, his gaze thoughtful. "Aye, it is. Feel it in my bones. Reminds me of that blizzard back in '78. Lost a good portion of the herd that year."

Boone remembered stories of that storm, tales of hardship and resilience passed down through the family. "We did all we could at that time."

"We did," Zeb agreed, his voice laced with a quiet faith that had weathered countless storms, both literal and metaphorical. He closed the poetry book, placing it carefully on the small table beside his chair. "Sometimes, son, all we can do is our best, and trust the rest to the Lord."

Boone nodded, appreciating the quiet wisdom in his father's words. Faith. It was the bedrock of their lives here, in this harsh and beautiful land. He'd wrestled with his faith after Eliza's betrayal, questioning, doubting. But beneath the layers of hurt and anger, the foundation remained. It had to.

He turned, leaning against the mantelpiece, his gaze fixed on the flickering flames. "Pa," he began, hesitating slightly, "what do you think of Laura staying on for a while?"

Zeb's eyebrows rose slightly, a subtle hint of knowing amusement in his eyes. "Think it's a good thing. She's capable and hardworking. You said yourself we need the help with Davis laid up."

"That's not what I meant," Boone said, a flicker of impatience in his voice.

Zeb's gaze softened, the amusement fading, replaced by a gentle understanding that only a father could possess. "No?" he asked, his tone deliberately neutral. "Then what did you mean, son?"

Boone hesitated again, struggling to articulate the tangled emotions swirling within him. "Just...wondering what you thought. About her. As a person." He hated how awkward it sounded, how evasive. He wasn't used to talking about feelings, especially not these kinds of feelings.

Zeb leaned back in his chair, studying Boone with unhurried patience. "Think she's a fine young woman. Strong spirit. Kind heart. Been through more than her share of hardship, I reckon. But it hasn't broken her. Not inside."

Boone nodded, feeling a strange sense of relief at his father's assessment, a validation of the unspoken feelings he was grappling with. "She has grit," he said, echoing Zeb's earlier words about Laura.

"Grit and grace," Zeb corrected gently. "Don't underestimate the grace, Boone. It's a powerful thing. Grace is." He paused, then added, his voice even softer, "Reminds me a little of your ma, in some ways."

Boone's breath hitched slightly at the unexpected comparison. His mother. Kind, gentle, but with a quiet strength that had been the anchor of their family. To compare Laura to her...it was a profound compliment, a deeply significant observation coming from his father.

He swallowed, his throat suddenly tight. "She's...heading to town eventually," he said, the words sounding too abrupt, too dismissive, even to his own ears.

Zeb simply nodded, his expression unreadable. "Folks have their own paths to walk, Boone. We can't always know where they'll lead."

Silence settled between them again, the wind howling outside, a reminder of the wild unpredictability of life. Boone stood there, staring into the fire, his thoughts a whirlwind of conflicting emotions. He wanted to deny the feelings stirring within him, to retreat back into the safety of his guarded heart. But Zeb's comparison to his ma had shifted something within him. The walls he'd built felt a little less solid, a little less impenetrable. And that, he realized with a jolt, was both terrifying and...hopeful.

Chapter 14

A crash from the barn jolted Laura awake with the dawn. She sat bolt upright in bed, heart hammering against her ribs. The wind had died down overnight, leaving an eerie stillness in its wake, broken only by the muffled commotion from outside.

She dressed quickly, pulling on her dress and wrapping a shawl around her shoulders against the morning chill. As she made her way to the kitchen, she found Zeb already there, stirring a pot of oatmeal on the stove.

"Morning," he greeted, his weathered face creasing into a smile. "Sounds like Boone's having a time of it in the barn."

"What happened?" Laura asked, moving to the stove to help.

"One of the stall doors came loose in the night. Wind probably," Zeb explained, passing her the wooden spoon. "He's been out there since before first light."

Laura nodded, taking over the stirring. Her gaze drifted toward the window. Another crash echoed across the yard.

"Coffee's ready," Zeb noted, nodding toward the pot. "He could probably use some."

Laura understood the unspoken suggestion. She poured a steaming mug of the dark brew, wrapped a thick biscuit from yesterday's batch in a cloth, and added a generous slice of ham. Balancing the impromptu breakfast carefully, she headed for the door.

"Might want to announce yourself," Zeb called after her. "He gets mighty focused when he's working on something."

The cold morning air bit at Laura's cheeks as she crossed the yard. Fresh snow had fallen during the night, not a blizzard as they'd feared, but enough to blanket everything in pristine white. Her boots crunched through the top layer, leaving a trail of footprints behind her.

The barn door stood partially open, a wedge of golden lamplight spilling onto the snow. Laura paused at the threshold, shifting the mug and food to one hand so she could knock on the rough wooden planks.

"Boone?" she called. "I've brought you some coffee."

No answer came, but she could hear movement inside—the scrape of tools, the soft nickering of horses. She pushed the door wider with her shoulder and stepped into the warm, hay-scented interior.

Boone stood with his back to her, muscles tensed beneath his flannel shirt as he wrestled with a broken stall door. He'd removed his coat despite the cold, and Laura could see the strain in his shoulders as he worked, his breath forming in small clouds in the chilly air.

"Boone," she tried again, louder this time.

He turned sharply, surprise evident in his features. For a moment, he simply stared at her, as though struggling to shift his focus from the task at hand. A shadow lingered in his eyes, something troubled that hadn't been there the night before.

"Thought you might need this," Laura said softly, offering the steaming mug.

He hesitated, then set down his hammer and crossed to her, taking the mug with a nod of thanks. His calloused fingers brushed against hers briefly, sending an unexpected warmth through her hand that had nothing to do with the hot coffee.

"And this," she added, holding out the cloth-wrapped biscuit and ham.

"Thanks," he murmured, his voice gruff but not unkind. He took a large sip of the coffee, then accepted the food, taking a hearty bite.

Laura studied him as he ate, noticing details she'd somehow missed before. The fine lines at the corners of his eyes. The way his dark hair curled slightly at his neck, in need of a trim. The careful way he held the mug, strong hands gentle around the fragile ceramic.

He ate with quiet intensity, focused on the task as he was with everything else. When he finished, he brushed the crumbs from his hands and met her gaze directly for the first time that morning.

"Was there anything else?" he asked, the words not dismissive but genuinely questioning.

Laura suddenly felt foolish. What had she expected? A lengthy conversation? Words of gratitude? This was Boone Callahan, a man of few words and fewer sentiments.

"No," she answered, taking a step back. "I just thought you might be hungry."

Boone nodded, taking another long drink of coffee. Then, wiping his mouth with the back of his hand, he finally spoke again, his gaze still not quite meeting hers directly.

"Town run today," he stated, more than asked. "Supplies. Figured you might want to come. See about... things."

He trailed off, and Laura understood immediately. He meant for her to finalize plans for leaving, to perhaps even find a place in Lone Valley. A pang, sharper than she expected, resonated within her.

"Thought you'd be keen on speaking with Ms. Patterson about your job," he continued, a hint of something unreadable in his tone. "See about borrowing that dress for the social on Sunday from Ms. Patterson?"

The assumption, though logical, felt like a subtle push away from the ranch, away from him. She tried to dismiss the irrational hurt that bloomed in her chest. After all, wasn't that exactly her plan? To establish herself in Lone Valley, to build an independent life away from the ranch?

"Yes," she said, the word sounding strange to her own ears. "Yes, that would be helpful. Thank you."

Boone nodded once, turning back to the broken stall door. "Leaving in an hour," he said over his shoulder. "Need to finish this first."

Laura retreated from the barn, confusion swirling in her mind. Why did his suggestion about town feel so... disappointing? Wasn't it what she wanted? She'd only known the man for days, yet already the thought of leaving the ranch, of leaving him, left a hollow feeling in her chest.

No, she reminded herself firmly. This was exactly as it should be. Her stay at the Callahan Ranch was temporary, a brief respite on her journey to independence. Getting attached to Boone, to Zeb, to the ranch itself—that was a dangerous path she couldn't afford to walk.

Back in the house, she found Zeb, and Matt seated at the table. They both looked up when she entered.

"How's our resident carpenter?" Matt asked, grinning.

"Still working," Laura replied, moving to the stove to dish herself a bowl of oatmeal. "He said we're going to town today."

"Ah, well," Zeb nodded, reaching for his coffee. "Been needing supplies."

Laura took her seat at the table, stirring sugar into her oatmeal. "He mentioned the social on Sunday."

"Church social," Matt clarified, his eyes lighting up. "Best dancing and food this side of Helena. You coming?"

Laura hesitated. "I... I'm not sure. I don't really have anything suitable to wear."

"Nonsense." Zeb waved a hand dismissively. "Folks around here aren't fancy."

Laura nodded.

"I'll see," she said. "I'm not much for dancing, though."

Matt laughed. "Neither is Boone, but that doesn't stop Ms. Patterson from trying to drag him onto the floor every time. Says a man that tall should 'put his God-given height to good use.'"

The image of Boone being pulled onto a dance floor by a determined woman made Laura smile despite herself.

"He's actually not half bad," Zeb admitted. "When Mary was alive, she made sure all our children could dance proper. Said it was a civilized skill."

Laura glanced at Zeb, surprised by this unexpected glimpse into Boone's upbringing. She tried to picture him dancing, those large hands gentle on a partner's waist, his usual stern expression softened by music and movement. The thought sent a curious flutter through her stomach.

"Well," she said, rising to clear her bowl, "I suppose I'll find out on Sunday."

Chapter 15

An hour later, Laura was seated beside Boone on the wagon bench, a thick blanket draped across her lap. The snow from the night before sparkled in the winter sun, transforming the landscape into a glittering expanse that hurt the eyes to look at directly.

Boone handled the reins with confidence, his communication with the horses almost entirely unspoken—a gentle click of his tongue, a subtle adjustment of the reins, an occasional soft word. Laura watched his hands, fascinated by the contrast between their obvious strength and the delicate precision with which they guided the team.

"Beautiful," she commented, gesturing to the snow-covered hills.

Boone nodded, his eyes scanning the horizon. "Good snowpack this year. Means plenty of water come spring."

Always practical, Laura thought. Always thinking of the ranch.

Laura wrapped her borrowed coat more tightly around herself, grateful for its warmth.

"Cold?" Boone asked, glancing at her.

"I'm fine," she assured him. "This coat is warmer than anything I've owned in years."

Something flickered across his face—perhaps concern, perhaps something else entirely—but he said nothing, merely nodded and returned his attention to the road.

As they crested a hill, Lone Valley came into view below them, a small cluster of buildings nestled in the valley floor. From this distance, it looked like a toy town, smoke rising from chimneys in thin, straight lines against the clear blue sky.

"There it is," Boone said unnecessarily. "Lone Valley."

Laura studied the town that was to be her new home. It was smaller than she'd imagined, barely more than a wide spot in the road with a handful of buildings lining what appeared to be a single main street. Yet even from this distance, there was a feeling of solidity to it, of permanence.

The wagon began its descent, the horses picking their way carefully down the snowy slope. As they drew closer, Laura could make out individual buildings—a church with a modest steeple, storefronts with painted signs, houses clustered around the town center.

"Not much," Boone said, as though reading her thoughts. "But it's home to good people."

"It looks lovely," Laura replied honestly. There was something appealing about the town's modest size, its unassuming presence in the vast landscape. A place where everyone would know everyone else, where you couldn't simply disappear into anonymity.

They reached the outskirts of town, and Boone guided the wagon onto the main street. Despite the cold, people moved about their business—a woman sweeping the boardwalk in front of what appeared to be a millinery shop, men loading crates outside a saloon, children bundled against the cold running with shouts of laughter between buildings.

Boone pulled the wagon to a stop in front of a building with a sign proclaiming it "Miller's General Store."

"Need to get supplies," he said, setting the brake. "Then we can stop by Ms. Patterson's place. It's just down the street."

He climbed down from the wagon, then turned to help Laura. His hands gripped her waist firmly as he lifted her down, the strength in his arms making the task seem effortless. For a moment, after her feet touched the ground, his hands lingered at her waist, steadying her on the slippery snow. Laura felt a jolt of awareness, a spark that traveled from his hands through her entire body.

Their eyes met briefly before Boone dropped his hands, stepping back. "Watch your step," he said, his voice gruffer than usual. "It's icy."

Laura nodded, unable to speak past the sudden tightness in her throat. What was wrong with her? It was a simple, practical assistance, nothing more. Yet, her heart raced as though she'd run up a hill.

The bell above the door jingled as they entered the general store, a wave of warmth and the mingled scents of coffee, leather, and spices greeting them. The interior was crowded but neat, shelves stacked with goods from floor to ceiling along every wall.

A balding man with spectacles looked up from where he was measuring fabric for a woman and smiled broadly. "Boone Callahan! Thought that storm might've kept you away a bit longer."

"Takes more than a bit of wind to keep me home, Jude," Boone replied, stamping snow from his boots.

Jude's curious gaze shifted to Laura, eyebrows rising slightly. Boone cleared his throat.

"Miss Laura Hartley," he introduced. "She's staying at the ranch for a spell, helping out. Laura, this is Jude Miller, owns the place."

"A pleasure, Miss Hartley," Jude said, his eyes twinkling with barely concealed curiosity. "Any friend of the Callahans is welcome here."

Laura smiled, recognizing the thinly veiled interest in his tone. She wondered what assumptions were already forming in his mind. A single woman staying at the Callahan Ranch would surely set tongues wagging in a small town like this.

"Thank you, Mr. Miller," she replied politely. "It's lovely to meet you."

"Miss Hartley's on her way to a position at Ms. Patterson's boarding house," Boone added, his tone matter-of-fact. "Got caught in the blizzard on her way to town."

Understanding dawned on Jude's face. "Ah, you're the gal from the stagecoach! Word got around about that accident. Terrible business. We're all mighty grateful to Boone here for finding you in that storm."

Laura nodded, feeling a flush creep up her neck. She didn't particularly want to be the subject of town gossip, but she supposed it was inevitable.

"I have a list," Boone said, clearly redirecting the conversation as he pulled a folded paper from his pocket and handed it to Jude. "And whatever Miss Hartley might need."

Jude took the list with a nod. "Let me finish up with Mrs. Hayes here, and I'll get right to it. You folks look around, help yourselves to coffee by the stove."

Laura was grateful for the opportunity to escape Jude's curious gaze. She moved deeper into the store, amazed at the variety of goods packed into the relatively small space. Everything from farm implements to delicate ribbons lined the shelves, a testament to the isolation of the community and their need for self-sufficiency.

She lingered by a display of fabrics, her fingers drifting over a bolt of soft blue calico. It had been so long since she'd had a new dress, something chosen for beauty rather than mere practicality.

"That's a pretty color," came a voice from behind her.

Laura turned to find a young woman about her own age, with warm brown eyes and a friendly smile. She was dressed simply but neatly, her brown hair tucked under a modest bonnet.

"I was just thinking the same," Laura admitted.

"You must be Miss Hartley," the woman said. "I'm Hannah Edwards. I help Ms. Patterson at the boarding house sometimes."

"It's lovely to meet you."

Hannah's smile brightened. "So you've been staying at the Callahan place? How exciting! And a bit scandalous," she added, with a mischievous twinkle in her eye.

Laura felt her cheeks heat. "It wasn't planned. The blizzard—"

"Oh, don't mind me," Hannah interrupted with a wave of her hand. "Everyone who matters knows Boone Callahan is the most honorable man in the county. Besides," she lowered her voice conspiratorially, "his father being there makes it all proper, anyway."

Laura relaxed slightly, grateful for Hannah's easy acceptance. "You're very kind."

"Nonsense. Just practical. We'll be seeing more of each other once you're settled at Ms. Patterson's, I expect. Are you coming to the social on Sunday after church?"

"I... I'm not sure. I don't really have anything suitable to wear."

Hannah's eyes lit up. "Oh, you simply must come! And don't worry about clothes. I have several dresses that would fit you beautifully. In fact," she glanced at the blue calico, "you must let me loan you a dress."

Laura was taken aback by the immediate offer of friendship and assistance. "That's very generous of you, but—"

"I won't hear any objections," Hannah said firmly. "It's settled. Will you be visiting Ms. Patterson next?"

"Most likely."

"Perfect. I will rush home now and gather the perfect dress I have in mind for you and bring it to the boarding house."

Hannah glanced over Laura's shoulder, her eyes widening slightly. "Oh my, I believe Mr. Callahan is looking for you."

Laura turned to see Boone standing at the end of the aisle, his tall frame imposing even at a distance.

"Of course. Thank you again, Hannah."

Hannah squeezed her arm before hurrying away, casting one last curious glance at Boone as she passed him.

"Ready?" Boone asked as Laura approached. "Jude's putting together our order. Thought we might head over to Ms. Patterson's while we wait."

Laura nodded, falling into step beside him as they left the store. Outside, the day had warmed slightly, the sun strong enough to begin melting the snow on the boardwalks. They walked side by side down the street, their breath forming small clouds in the air before them.

Chapter 16

Louella Patterson's establishment sat at the far end of the main street, a two-story building with a painted sign announcing "Lone Valley Café & Boarding House." The smell of fresh bread and coffee wafted from the open door, making Laura's stomach growl despite the breakfast she'd eaten earlier.

A half-dozen patrons sat at tables around the room. Conversation paused briefly as heads turned to observe the newcomers, then resumed with increased urgency, no doubt discussing the unexpected arrival of Boone with an unknown woman.

A small, bustling woman with steel-gray hair pulled into a tight bun emerged from what Laura assumed was the kitchen, wiping her hands on her apron. Her sharp eyes took in the pair of them, widening slightly before her face split into a broad smile.

"Boone Callahan, as I live and breathe," she declared, approaching them with quick steps. "Haven't seen you in town for an age."

"Ms. Patterson," Boone nodded in greeting. "This is Miss Laura Hartley. She was supposed to be arriving for a position with you before the blizzard hit."

Ms. Patterson's expression shifted from curiosity to concern in an instant. "Oh my dear girl, you're the one from the stagecoach accident! When you didn't arrive, I feared the worst. It's a terrible tragedy for those poor souls who were lost."

She took Laura's hands in her own, her grip surprisingly strong. "Are you quite recovered? You look a bit pale still."

"I'm much better, thank you," Laura assured her. "Mr. Callahan and his father have been very kind, taking me in and caring for me."

Ms. Patterson's gaze darted between Laura and Boone, a knowing look in her eye that made Laura's cheeks warm.

"Well," Ms. Patterson said, "I'm just relieved you're safe. And I still have the position open for you, of course. The room's ready whenever you'd like to move in."

Laura nodded, attempting to summon the enthusiasm she knew she should feel. This was what she wanted, after all. Independence. A fresh start. Yet, the prospect of leaving the ranch, of leaving Boone and Zeb, left her feeling strangely hollow.

"Thank you," she said, forcing a smile. "That's very kind."

"Nonsense." Ms. Patterson waved a hand dismissively. "I need the help, and my cousin Evelyn spoke very highly of you in her letter. Now, sit down, both of you. I'll bring coffee, and you can tell me all about your harrowing ordeal."

She ushered them to a table by the window, bustling off to the kitchen before either could object. Boone pulled out a chair for Laura. The busy hum of the café filling the space between them. Laura glanced around, taking in what would soon be her workplace. The café was clean and welcoming, with checkered tablecloths and simple curtains at the windows. The patrons seemed content, several casting curious glances in their direction.

"This is a fine establishment," Boone commented, following her gaze around the room.

"It is," Laura agreed. "Ms. Patterson seems... enthusiastic."

A corner of Boone's mouth quirked upward, the closest thing to a smile she'd seen from him yet. "That's one way of putting it. Woman's got more energy than half the men in town put together."

Ms. Patterson returned with two steaming mugs of coffee and a plate of fresh biscuits. "Eat," she instructed, setting the plate between them. "You both look like you could use some feeding up."

"Thank you, ma'am," Boone said, taking a biscuit.

"Now," Ms. Patterson said, pulling up a chair to join them, "tell me everything. The whole town's been buzzing about the stagecoach and the blizzard. Poor Tom Wade, God rest his soul. Such a tragedy."

Laura shifted uncomfortably, the memory of Tom's kind face as he'd agreed to accompany her through the storm still fresh in her mind. The guilt of his death weighed heavily on her, despite Boone's assurances that it wasn't her fault.

"It was... difficult," she said. "If Mr. Callahan hadn't found me when he did, I fear I would have shared Mr. Wade's fate."

Ms. Patterson turned to Boone, genuine gratitude in her eyes. "You're a good man, Boone Callahan. Your mother would be proud."

Something flashed across Boone's face—pain, perhaps, or simply discomfort at the praise. He nodded once in acknowledgment, but said nothing.

"And how have you been recovering, dear?" Ms. Patterson asked, turning back to Laura.

"I'm fully recovered now, thank you. Mr. Callahan and his father have been very hospitable."

"I'm sure they have. They're good people," Ms. Patterson replied. "And when do you think you'll be ready to start your position here? Not that I'm rushing you, of course, but it would be good to know."

Before Laura could answer, Boone spoke. "She's been helping at the ranch. The ranch is shorthanded, with Davis laid up in Helena."

Ms. Patterson raised an eyebrow, looking between them again. "I see. Well, the position will be here whenever you're ready, Miss Hartley. No rush at all."

Laura felt a rush of gratitude toward Boone for providing her with an excuse to delay her move to town. She wasn't ready to leave the ranch; she realized with a start. Not yet.

"Thank you for understanding," she said to Ms. Patterson. "I'd like to repay the Callahans' kindness by helping a bit longer, if that's acceptable."

"Of course, dear." Ms. Patterson patted her hand. "Now, will we see you both at the social on Sunday? Reverend Tanner was just saying this morning how we need some new faces to liven things up."

"We'll be there," Boone confirmed, surprising Laura. She hadn't realized he'd already decided they would attend.

A commotion near the counter drew Ms. Patterson's attention. "Excuse me, dears. Duty calls." She bustled away to deal with a customer dispute over the last slice of apple pie.

Left alone with Boone, Laura sipped her coffee, gathering her courage to address his assumption. "So we're attending the social?"

Boone looked momentarily flustered, the first time she'd seen his composure slip. "Figured you'd want to meet folks in town," he said, the words coming out more gruffly than usual. "We always attend the socials. Tradition."

"I see," Laura nodded, trying to ignore the flutter of disappointment at his practical explanation. What had she expected? That he specifically wanted her company? "Hannah Edwards invited me as well."

"Edwards. Good family," Boone nodded approvingly. "Father's the town blacksmith."

"She seems very nice," Laura agreed. "She's offered to lend me a dress and should be here soon with them."

Boone shifted slightly, looking almost uncomfortable at the mention of women's clothing. "Good," he said simply, taking another biscuit.

They fell into silence again, but it wasn't the comfortable quiet of their wagon ride. Something had shifted between them, a tension that hadn't been there before. Laura couldn't quite put her finger on it, but it felt important, significant.

"About Ms. Patterson's offer," she began hesitantly.

"It's your decision," Boone interrupted, his tone carefully neutral. "When you're ready to move to town, just say the word. No obligation to the ranch."

The words stung more than they should have. No obligation. As though her presence at the ranch was merely tolerated, not valued or wanted. She forced a nod, focusing on her coffee cup to hide the hurt in her eyes.

"Of course," she said quietly. "Thank you."

A shout from the street drew their attention. Through the window, Laura could see a cluster of men gathered outside the saloon across the way, their voices raised in argument. One man shoved another, sending him stumbling backward into the street.

Boone frowned, setting down his coffee cup. "Stay here," he murmured.

Before Laura could protest, he strode out of the café. She moved to the window, watching as Boone approached the group, his tall frame instantly commanding attention. The arguing men fell silent as he spoke, his words inaudible through the glass but his calm authority evident in his stance.

The tension in the group visibly deflated, men nodding and stepping back. One of them seemed to be thanking Boone, shaking his hand vigorously.

"Man has a way about him, doesn't he?" Ms. Patterson observed, appearing beside Laura at the window. "Always has. Even as a boy, he could settle an argument without raising his voice."

Laura nodded, watching as Boone said something that made the entire group laugh, the conflict completely diffused. "He's... different," she admitted.

Ms. Patterson chuckled knowingly. "Boone Callahan is like a Montana winter—cold and hard on the surface, but that snow's what makes everything bloom come spring." She patted Laura's arm. "You remember that, dear."

Before Laura could respond to the cryptic advice, the café door opened and Boone returned, bringing a gust of cold air with him.

"Everything all right?" Laura asked.

Boone nodded, resuming his seat. "Just a misunderstanding about a card game." He glanced at his pocket watch, then drained his coffee cup. "Should head back to the store. Jude's probably got our order ready by now."

They bid farewell to Ms. Patterson, who extracted a promise from Laura to return soon to discuss the details of her position. Outside, the day had warmed further, the snow on the boardwalks turning to slush that squelched underfoot. As they made their way down the street, Laura noticed Hannah hurrying their way, dress in hand.

Chapter 17

As they walked back toward the general store, a tall man with a clerical collar emerged from a building with a small cross mounted above the door. He spotted them immediately, his face lighting up with recognition.

"Boone Callahan," he called, striding toward them with an outstretched hand. "Good to see you in town."

"Reverend Tanner," Boone greeted, shaking the man's hand. "This is Miss Laura Hartley. She's staying at the ranch for a while, helping out."

The reverend turned his warm smile to Laura, taking her offered hand in both of his. "Miss Hartley, a pleasure. I've heard about your ordeal in the blizzard. God's mercy was surely with you that day."

"It was," Laura agreed, feeling the genuine faith behind the minister's words. "I'm very fortunate Mr. Callahan found me when he did."

"Not fortune, my dear," Reverend Tanner corrected gently. "Providence. The Lord's hand guiding Boone to you in your time of need."

Laura nodded, the words resonating with her own thoughts during those desperate moments in the snow. "Yes, I believe you're right."

The reverend's smile widened, his eyes crinkling at the corners. "Will you be joining us for Sunday service? And the social afterward?"

"We're planning on it," Boone answered for both of them.

"Excellent, excellent," Reverend Tanner clasped his hands together. "It will be a pleasure to have you both there. Now, I won't keep you any longer. I'm sure you have errands to complete before the journey back to the ranch. God bless you both."

With a final nod, he continued on his way, leaving Laura with a warm impression of genuine kindness and faith.

"He seems very nice," she commented as they resumed walking.

"Good man," Boone agreed. "Fair and honest. Doesn't preach at you, but makes you want to listen all the same."

It was perhaps the longest personal opinion Boone had shared, and Laura was intrigued by his respect for the reverend. "You attend services regularly?"

Boone nodded. "Most Sundays, weather permitting. My ma always insisted, and I honor that still," he added, the words coming reluctantly, as though pulled from some deep, private place. "Faith was... important to her."

"My parents were the same," she offered. "Though I admit, life with Jasper these past few years made regular attendance difficult. He wasn't... comfortable in church."

Boone glanced at her, something unreadable in his eyes. "Faith finds a way, even outside church walls."

The simple statement struck Laura with its quiet wisdom. It wasn't what she expected from the taciturn rancher, yet it aligned perfectly with the complexity she was beginning to glimpse beneath his stoic exterior.

They reached the general store to find their order prepared, packages neatly stacked and ready for loading. Jude helped Boone carry everything to the wagon after he had settled his account.

With their errands complete and a borrowed dress in hand, they prepared to head home. Boone helped Laura up onto the bench first, then climbed up beside her, the wagon shifting slightly under his weight. As he reached for the reins, his arm brushed against hers, sending that same jolt of awareness through her body.

She stole a glance at his profile as he guided the wagon out of town, strong and steady, against the backdrop of the mountains. There was a quiet confidence about him, a certainty in his movements, that spoke of a man completely at ease with himself and his place in the world.

They were well out of town, the buildings of Lone Valley receding behind them when Boone broke the silence.

"What did you think? Of the town," he clarified when she looked at him questioningly.

Laura considered the question, gazing back at the diminishing buildings. "It's smaller than I expected," she admitted. "But it has a certain... charm to it. The people seem kind."

Boone nodded, his eyes on the road ahead. "Good folks, mostly. Like anywhere, got a few bad apples, but they generally keep to themselves."

"Ms. Patterson seems nice, if a bit... enthusiastic," Laura observed, smiling slightly at the memory of the woman's bustling energy.

A hint of amusement crept into Boone's expression. "Known her since I was a boy. Heart of gold, mouth that never stops running."

The unexpected touch of humor made Laura laugh, the sound bright in the crisp air. Boone glanced at her, something softening in his eyes at her laughter.

The wagon rocked gently over the uneven road, the rhythm almost hypnotic. Laura found her thoughts drifting, her gaze alternating between the spectacular scenery and the man beside her.

"Mind if I ask you something?" she ventured after a while.

Boone nodded, an invitation to continue.

"Why ranching? What draws you to this life?"

He was quiet for so long that Laura thought he might not answer. When he finally spoke, his voice was thoughtful, as though he was working out his response as he went.

"It's... honest work," he began slowly. "Land asks a lot of you, but it never lies. Put in the effort, respect what it needs, and it gives back. Not always in the ways you expect, but it gives back." He paused, his gaze sweeping across the vast landscape. "And there's freedom to it. Not easy freedom—working for yourself is harder than working for someone else in many ways. But there's a rightness to it."

He fell silent again, and Laura sensed he was struggling to articulate something deeply personal.

"My father's father settled this land," he continued, his voice deepening with pride. "Built something from nothing. Every fence post, every barn beam, every acre cleared—it's all family history written on the land." He glanced at her briefly, then back to the road. "Hard to explain to someone who hasn't felt it."

"I think I understand," Laura said softly. "It's about belonging somewhere. Having roots."

Boone nodded, looking almost relieved that she'd grasped his meaning. "That's part of it, yes."

"I've never had that," Laura admitted, surprising herself with her candor. "Not since my parents died. With Jasper, we were always moving on, always running from something or chasing some new opportunity that never materialized."

Boone's hands tightened slightly on the reins, the only indication that her words had affected him. "Must've been hard," he said simply.

"It was," Laura agreed, gazing at the mountains on the horizon. "I used to dream about having a place of my own. Something permanent. Something no one could take away."

"That why you came to Montana?"

"Yes," she nodded. "I needed... a fresh start. I persuaded Jasper to come this way, hoping I could part ways with him in this vast land. I wanted someplace where Jasper wouldn't think to look for me. Somewhere I could build something for myself."

Boone was silent for a long moment. "You think he'll come looking?"

The question sent a chill through Laura that had nothing to do with the winter air. "I don't know for certain," she admitted. "Part of me hopes he's too far gone in the bottle to bother. Part of me..." she trailed off, unable to voice the conflicted feelings she still harbored for her brother.

"You still care about him," Boone observed, not a question but a statement.

Laura nodded, her throat tight with emotion. "He's my brother. The only family I have left. But I couldn't keep living that way, watching him destroy himself and trying to pull me down with him."

"Takes courage," Boone said quietly. "Leaving. Starting over."

The simple validation in his words warmed something deep inside Laura. Few people in her life had ever acknowledged the strength it took to endure what she had, to make the hard choices she'd been forced to make.

"That it does, Boone," she said.

They fell back into silence, but it was different now—companionable, almost intimate. Laura felt as though something significant had shifted between them, some barrier lowered.

The rest of the journey passed mostly in this comfortable quiet, broken only by occasional observations about the landscape or the ranch work ahead. As they crested the final hill before the Callahan Ranch came into view, Laura found herself feeling a curious sense of homecoming that she hadn't expected.

The buildings of the ranch, nestled against the backdrop of the mountains, looked solid and welcoming. Smoke rose from the chimney of the main house, and even from this distance, Laura could see Zeb on the porch, raising a hand in greeting as he spotted the wagon.

"Home," Boone said simply, and for a fleeting moment, Laura allowed herself to imagine it was true—that this place could be her home too, not just a temporary haven.

The thought was as terrifying as it was tempting.

As the wagon rolled into the yard, Laura noticed Matt emerging from the barn, a broad grin spreading across his face as he hurried to help with the supplies. This, she realized with a pang, was what she'd always longed for—not just a place, but people who noticed when you returned, who welcomed you back.

Boone brought the wagon to a stop, setting the brake before climbing down. He came around to Laura's side, reaching up to help her down. His hands were strong and sure at her waist, and for a moment, as her feet touched the ground, she found herself standing very close to him. Close enough to see the flecks of amber in his brown eyes, to feel the warmth radiating from him despite the chill in the air.

Something flickered in his expression, a momentary softening that made her heart skip. Then he stepped back, the moment broken, and turned to Matt, who had reached the wagon.

"Anything happen while we were gone?" Boone asked, his voice steady, as if the moment of connection hadn't occurred.

"All quiet," Matt replied, already reaching for the packages in the wagon. "Fixed the loose boards on the chicken coop. Old Bessie's calf is looking stronger."

Laura moved toward the house, her mind still caught in that brief moment with Boone. What had she seen in his eyes? What had he seen in hers?

As she reached the porch, Zeb greeted her with a smile. "How was town, Laura?"

"It was lovely," she replied, returning his smile. "Everyone was very welcoming."

"And Ms. Patterson? You spoke with her about the position?"

Laura nodded, her smile faltering slightly. "Yes, she's holding it for me whenever I'm ready."

Zeb studied her face, his wise eyes seeming to see more than she intended to reveal. "No rush on that," he said gently. "You're welcome here as long as you like."

"I should help unload the supplies," Laura murmured, touched by his kindness.

Zeb waved a hand dismissively. "Let the men handle it. You've had a long day already."

Laura watched as Boone and Matt efficiently unloaded the wagon, carrying supplies to their proper places. She couldn't help noticing the easy strength with which Boone lifted even the heaviest items, the fluid grace of his movements despite his size.

She turned away, disconcerted by the direction of her thoughts. This growing awareness of Boone Callahan was dangerous, a complication she couldn't afford. Her plans didn't include developing feelings for a man who was clearly content with his solitary life, a man who had offered her shelter out of duty and kindness, nothing more.

Yet as she entered the house, Laura couldn't quite silence the whisper of her heart, the treacherous hope that perhaps, just perhaps, there might be room in her carefully constructed plans for something—someone—she hadn't anticipated.

Chapter 18

The church bell of Lone Valley rang out across the crisp morning air, its clear tones calling the faithful to worship. Laura smoothed her borrowed dress—a pretty blue affair Hannah had insisted suited her perfectly—and took a deep breath to steady her nerves. The Callahan wagon rolled to a stop in front of the white clapboard building, where townsfolk streamed inside, greeting each other with warm smiles and hearty handshakes.

"Looks like a good turnout," Zeb remarked, climbing down from the back of the wagon with surprising agility for his years.

Boone set the brake and came around to Laura's side. Her pulse quickened as his strong hands encircled her waist. For a moment, she looked directly into his eyes as he set her on the ground, her hands resting lightly on his shoulders. Something flickered in his gaze before he released her and stepped back.

"Thank you," she murmured, adjusting her shawl against the morning chill.

Boone merely nodded, his attention seemingly caught by the approaching townspeople.

"Zeb! Boone!" A portly man with ruddy cheeks approached, hand outstretched. "Fine morning for worship, isn't it?"

"Morning, Titus," Zeb greeted, shaking the man's hand. "It is indeed."

The man's curious gaze fell on Laura, eyebrows rising slightly.

"Titus, this is Miss Laura Hartley," Zeb introduced. "She's staying with us for a spell, helping out at the ranch."

"The young lady from the stagecoach accident," Titus nodded, taking Laura's hand respectfully. "Word travels fast in a small town. Bless you, my dear. The Lord certainly had His hand on you that day."

"He did," Laura agreed softly.

More introductions followed as townspeople gathered around, each curious about the newcomer accompanying the Callahans. Laura did her best to remember names and faces, though they blurred together in a whirl of friendly greetings. Through it all, she was acutely aware of Boone's steady presence beside her, not hovering exactly, but a solid, reassuring anchor in the sea of unfamiliar faces.

Hannah Edwards appeared, weaving through the crowd to reach Laura. "You look lovely!" she exclaimed, admiring how the dress fit. "I knew that blue would bring out your eyes."

"Thanks to you," Laura replied warmly. "It's perfect."

"Come, let me introduce you to a few people before the service starts," Hannah offered, taking Laura's arm. She glanced at Boone. "I'm stealing her for a moment, Mr. Callahan. I promise to return her safely."

Something that might have been amusement crossed Boone's face as he nodded his assent. Laura allowed herself to be led away, casting one glance back to see Boone watching them go, his expression un-readable.

Hannah guided her toward a group of young women standing near the church steps. "Everyone, this is Laura Hartley. She's staying at the Callahan Ranch," she announced.

Laura endured another round of introductions, fielding questions about her background with careful edits to her story. She mentioned coming west for a new start, her position with Ms. Patterson, and her temporary arrangement at the Callahan Ranch. She deliberately omitted Jasper, the drinking, and her desperate escape. These people didn't need to know the uglier parts of her past.

"The Callahan Ranch," one woman named Mary repeated with a meaningful glance at the others. "How... interesting. Boone Callahan doesn't typically take in strays."

"I'm hardly a stray," Laura corrected politely but firmly. "Mr. Callahan rescued me during the blizzard when the stagecoach couldn't continue. It was Christian charity, nothing more."

"Of course," Mary backpedaled, though her smile suggested she believed otherwise. "It's just that Boone has kept to himself since—"

"The bell's ringing," Hannah interrupted, shooting Mary a warning look. "We should head inside."

Laura followed the group into the church, wondering what Mary had been about to say. Since what? The question lingered as she entered the simple but lovingly maintained sanctuary. Wooden pews lined either side of a central aisle facing a modest pulpit. Light streamed through plain glass windows, illuminating the space with natural brightness.

She spotted Boone and Zeb already seated in the middle of the church. Boone glanced up as she approached, shifting slightly to make room beside him. Laura slid into the pew, acutely aware of his proximity, the clean scent of soap, and the faint aroma of leather and pine that seemed to cling to him.

"Everything all right?" he asked quietly.

"Yes, just meeting the townspeople," she replied.

He studied her face for a moment, as though sensing there was more she wasn't saying, but the arrival of Reverend Tanner at the pulpit drew their attention forward.

"Good morning, brothers, and sisters in Christ," the reverend began, his warm voice filling the sanctuary without seeming to raise it. "What a blessing to see so many faces here today, both familiar and new."

His gaze briefly met Laura's, and he offered a welcoming smile before continuing.

"Today I want to speak about trust. Trust in the Lord, trust in His plan, and the courage it takes to open our hearts when life has given us reason to close them."

Laura felt Boone stiffen slightly beside her. She risked a glance at his profile, finding his jaw tight, his gaze fixed unwaveringly on the reverend.

"In Proverbs 3:5-6, we are told, 'Trust in the Lord with all your heart and lean not on your own understanding; in all your ways submit to him, and he will make your paths straight.' But how many of us truly follow this wisdom? How often do we instead close ourselves off, convinced that we know best, that we can protect ourselves from pain if we just keep our hearts guarded enough?"

Reverend Tanner paused, his gaze sweeping across the congregation. "The truth is, my friends, that no wall is high enough to keep out God's purpose for our lives. No heart is so carefully guarded that His love cannot penetrate it. And perhaps the blessings we most desperately need are the very ones we're most afraid to accept."

The sermon continued, weaving scripture with practical wisdom about faith, vulnerability, and God's unfailing plan, even in the face of hardship. Laura found herself deeply moved by the reverend's words, which seemed to speak directly to her own struggle between independence and connection, between fear and trust.

She was so absorbed in the message that she barely noticed when Boone's hand brushed against hers on the pew between them. It was the briefest of touches, perhaps entirely accidental, yet it sent a jolt of awareness through her entire body. She didn't move her hand away, and neither did he, their little fingers remaining close enough that she could feel the warmth radiating from his skin.

When the service concluded with a hymn, Laura rose with the congregation, her voice joining others in "Amazing Grace." She couldn't help noticing that Boone sang too, his deep baritone quiet but true, the words seemingly coming from memory. It was another glimpse of the man beneath the stoic exterior, one that tugged at something deep within her.

As the congregation filed out into the churchyard, Laura was swept up in more introductions and conversations. Women complimented her dress, men tipped their hats respectfully, and children darted between groups, already released from the constraints of proper church behavior. Through it all, she was aware of Boone's location, even when they were separated by several groups of people. He stood with some of the ranch owners, talking cattle and weather, his tall frame easy to spot in the crowd.

"He keeps looking at you, you know," Hannah commented, appearing at Laura's side with a cup of coffee from the table that had been set up for refreshments.

"Who does?" Laura asked, though she knew perfectly well.

Hannah gave her a knowing look. "Boone. Every time I glance over, his eyes are finding you in the crowd."

Laura felt heat rising to her cheeks. "I'm sure he's just being protective. He feels responsible for me since the rescue."

"Mmm-hmm," Hannah hummed skeptically. "Is that why you keep looking for him, too?"

"I don't—" Laura began, then stopped at Hannah's raised eyebrow. "Is it that obvious?"

"Only to someone looking for it," Hannah assured her with a smile. "Don't worry, I don't think anyone else has noticed. Except maybe Ms. Patterson, but that woman notices everything."

As if summoned by her name, Louella appeared beside them, carrying a plate of cookies. "Here you are, dears. Try one of these before they're all gone. The men devour them like locusts."

She thrust the plate forward, and Laura obediently took a cookie, biting into the buttery sweetness.

"Delicious," she complimented sincerely.

"Family recipe," Ms. Patterson nodded with satisfaction. "Now, are you two planning to help with the social preparations this afternoon? We could use extra hands setting up."

"Of course," Hannah agreed immediately. "We'd be happy to help."

Laura nodded her agreement, though she wondered briefly if she should check with Boone first. The thought brought her up short. Why would she need his permission? It wasn't as though they were actually... anything. The very idea that she'd started thinking that way unsettled her.

"Excellent," Ms. Patterson beamed. "We'll meet at the community hall at two o'clock. That gives everyone time to go home for dinner and change if they wish." Her sharp eyes flicked to Laura's dress approvingly. "Though you, my dear, look lovely as you are."

"Thank you. This is Hannah's dress," Laura explained. "I'm afraid I don't have anything suitable for dancing, and this dress will do just fine."

"I have just the thing," Ms. Patterson declared. "A pale green dress that my niece left behind when she visited last summer. Never came back for it, and it would fit you perfectly. You stop by the boarding house before the social, and we'll have you fixed up in no time."

Before Laura could protest, Ms. Patterson was whisked away by another parishioner with a question about the social, leaving Laura and Hannah exchanging amused glances.

"There's no point arguing with her once she's got an idea in her head," Hannah laughed. "Believe me, I've learned that the hard way."

"I'm beginning to see that," Laura agreed with a smile.

The crowd in the churchyard had begun to thin as families headed home for their Sunday dinner. Laura spotted Zeb chatting with Reverend Tanner near the church steps, but Boone was nowhere to be seen. A flicker of disappointment passed through her, quickly suppressed. She had no claim on his time or attention.

"There you are."

The deep voice behind her made her start. She turned to find Boone standing there, hat in hand, the morning sun casting his features in sharp relief.

"I was just talking to Hannah about helping with the social preparations this afternoon," she explained, surprised at her own urge to justify her whereabouts.

"Good idea," he nodded. "I'll bring you to town after dinner."

"You don't need to trouble yourself," Laura said quickly. "I'm sure Hannah—"

"It's no trouble," he interrupted, his tone matter-of-fact. "Need to speak with Elijah about some work at the forge, anyway."

Hannah glanced between them, a smile playing at the corners of her mouth. "Well, that settles that. I'll see you at two, Laura." With a meaningful look that Laura chose to ignore, Hannah excused herself to join her father.

Left alone with Boone, Laura found herself uncharacteristically tongue-tied. The easy conversation they'd shared on the wagon ride from town seemed to have deserted her.

"Reverend Tanner's sermon was quite moving," she offered finally.

Boone nodded, his gaze drifting to where the minister still stood speaking with Zeb. "He has a way of... speaking to what needs hearing."

There was something in his tone that suggested the sermon had affected him personally. Laura wondered if he too had felt that the words about trust and open hearts had been meant specifically for him.

"Pa's ready to head back," Boone said, gesturing toward where Zeb was now making his way to the wagon. "Unless you wanted to stay in town?"

"No, I'll come back with you," Laura decided.

They walked side by side to the wagon, where Zeb was already waiting. The old man's eyes twinkled as he took in their approach.

"Mighty fine sermon today," he commented as Boone helped Laura up to the seat. "Seemed like the reverend had specific folks in mind."

"Always does," Boone replied neutrally, though Laura caught the quick glance he shot his father.

The ride back to the ranch was quiet, each lost in their own thoughts. Laura found her mind returning to the reverend's words about trust and vulnerability, about walls built too high to allow blessings in. She'd built such walls around her heart after the turmoil with Jasper, convinced that independence and self-reliance were her only path forward.

Yet in the few short weeks at the Callahan Ranch, those walls had begun to crumble. She'd found herself caring for these men, for this place. Worse, she'd begun to imagine what it might be like to stay, to belong here not as a temporary helper but as something more permanent. The very thing she'd sworn to avoid—dependency—now called to her with surprising strength.

The ranch came into view, the buildings solid and welcoming against the backdrop of distant mountains. In the bright midday sun, it looked like a scene from a painting—the kind of place that represented home and safety in the truest sense. Something tugged painfully in Laura's chest at the sight. How easily she could love this place if she allowed herself to.

Chapter 19

Dinner was a simple affair of leftover stew and fresh bread. Zeb announced his intention to rest during the afternoon, claiming that church always tired him out, though the wink he gave Laura suggested other motives for giving her and Boone time alone in town.

After helping clean up, Laura changed into her own serviceable dress, leaving Hannah's blue dress carefully laid out on the bed. She plaited her hair freshly and washed her face, studying her reflection in the small mirror above the washstand. Her cheeks held more color than they had in years, she realized, and the haunted look that had shadowed her eyes since leaving Jasper had begun to fade.

Boone was waiting by the wagon when she emerged from the house. His own clothes changed from Sunday best to everyday wear, though he still looked freshly groomed. He offered his hand to help her up, and she took it, trying to ignore the now-familiar flutter in her stomach at his touch.

The ride to town was easier than their journey to church had been, conversation flowing more naturally between them. Boone asked about her impressions of the townspeople she'd met, and Laura shared stories of the introductions, earning a rare chuckle from him when she recounted Ms. Patterson's insistence about the green dress.

"She's determined to see you properly outfitted," he commented.

"She's very kind," Laura agreed. "Everyone has been."

Boone's expression sobered slightly. "Small towns can be... curious about newcomers. But the good folks of Lone Valley are decent people. I figure they like what they see in you."

The simple compliment warmed her more than it should have. "They've welcomed me far more than I expected."

"Why wouldn't they?" Boone asked, genuinely puzzled.

Laura hesitated, unsure how to explain. "In my experience, people are often quick to judge a woman traveling alone. They assume... things."

Understanding dawned in Boone's eyes, followed by a flash of something harder, protective. "Anyone gives you trouble, you tell me."

The fierce certainty in his voice sent a shiver through her that had nothing to do with fear. "I can handle myself," she reminded him, though the offer of protection touched her deeply.

"I know you can," he replied, his gaze meeting hers directly. "Doesn't mean you have to."

The simple statement hung in the air between them, loaded with meaning beyond the words themselves. It was an offer of support, of partnership, of shared burdens—everything Laura had convinced herself she neither needed nor wanted.

They reached town before she could formulate a response. The community hall—a large, sturdy building adjacent to the church—already showed signs of activity, with several wagons parked outside and people moving in and out, carrying supplies.

"I'll be at the forge with Elijah. Then I will return home to change into my Sunday clothing," Boone said as he helped her down. "Come find me when you're finished, or if you need anything."

"I will," Laura promised. "Thank you."

He nodded, hesitating as though he might say something more, then simply touched the brim of his hat and headed toward the blacksmith's shop down the street.

Inside the community hall, preparations were well underway. Tables had been arranged around the perimeter of the large open space, leaving the center clear for dancing. Women bustled about with tablecloths and decorations, while men worked on setting up a small platform where the musicians would play.

Hannah spotted Laura immediately and waved her over. "Just in time! We need help with these garlands."

Laura spent the next hour working alongside the women of Lone Valley, stringing together pine boughs and ribbons to decorate the hall. The work was pleasant and the company even more so, with conversation flowing easily among the group. For the first time in longer than she could remember, Laura felt a sense of belonging, of community.

"So, Laura," Mary from the church group began as they worked on a particularly long garland, "how are you finding life at the Callahan Ranch?"

The question seemed innocent enough, yet Laura detected an undercurrent of curiosity that went beyond polite interest.

"It's been very pleasant," she replied carefully. "Mr. Callahan and his father have been exceedingly kind to take me in while I recover from the ordeal of the blizzard."

"Mmm," Mary hummed, exchanging glances with another woman. "Boone Callahan being kind. Imagine that."

"He's always been kind," Hannah defended quickly. "Just because he's not one for casual socializing doesn't make him cold."

"Oh, I didn't mean anything by it," Mary backpedaled unconvincingly. "It's just that since Eliza left, he's kept pretty much to himself. Barely says two words at these socials, never dances. Now suddenly he's bringing a pretty young woman to church and the social. People notice these things."

Laura's hands stilled on the garland. "Eliza?" she asked, unable to help herself.

Mary opened her mouth to explain, but Ms. Patterson chose that moment to sweep in, clapping her hands for attention.

"Ladies, you're doing beautifully with those garlands! Let's get them hung before the men finish with the platform. Laura, dear, don't forget to stop by the boarding house before the social for that dress I mentioned."

The moment for explanation had passed, and Laura found herself both frustrated and relieved. Part of her desperately wanted to know who Eliza was and what had happened between her and Boone. Another part feared the knowledge might somehow change how she thought of him.

As the preparations continued, Laura found her mind returning to the name. Eliza. It explained so much about Boone's reticence, his careful distance. There had been someone, and it hadn't ended well. The insight both clarified and complicated her understanding of the man who had rescued her from the blizzard.

By the time the decorating was nearly complete, Laura had managed to push the questions to the back of her mind. She bid goodbye to Hannah and the others, promising to return for the social, and made her way to the boarding house as instructed.

Ms. Patterson was waiting for her, practically vibrating with excitement. "There you are! Come upstairs, I've laid out the dress for you. It's going to be perfect, you'll see."

Laura followed her to a neat bedroom on the second floor, where a dress of pale green cotton lay across the bed. It was simple but pretty, with delicate embroidery at the collar and cuffs.

"It's lovely," Laura said sincerely, running a hand over the soft fabric.

"Try it on," Ms. Patterson insisted, already helping with the buttons of Laura's current dress without waiting for permission.

Surrendering to the woman's enthusiasm, Laura changed into the green dress, surprised to find that it fit almost perfectly. The color brought out the golden highlights in her hair and complemented her complexion in a way that made her look healthier, more vibrant.

"I knew it!" Ms. Patterson crowed triumphantly, circling Laura with critical eyes. "Fits like it was made for you. My niece is a bit shorter, but we can turn up the hem just a touch. Sit, sit! I'll have it fixed in no time."

As Ms. Patterson knelt with pins and needle, expertly adjusting the hem, she kept up a steady stream of chatter about the town, the social, and who would be attending. Laura listened with half an ear, her mind still caught on the mysterious Eliza.

"Ms. Patterson," she ventured during a brief lull, "may I ask you something?"

"Of course, dear," the woman replied, pins held between her lips as she worked.

"I overheard someone mention a woman named Eliza in connection with Boone. I was just... curious about her."

Ms. Patterson's hands stilled momentarily before resuming their work. "Ah. I wondered when that would come up. Small towns, you know. Can't keep anything quiet for long."

She adjusted another section of the hem before continuing. "Eliza Stratford was Boone's fiancée, oh, about two years ago now. Pretty girl, ambitious. She broke their engagement quite suddenly when the news of gold strikes in California became too tempting to resist. Left him standing there with a wedding planned and everything."

The pins in her mouth didn't seem to impede her ability to share the story. "Broke his heart, that girl did. He'd built the new section of the ranch house for her, had everything prepared to start their life together. After she left, he threw himself into the ranch work, barely came to town except for supplies and church. Didn't speak about it, not once that I ever heard. But everyone knew."

Laura absorbed this information with a strange mixture of emotions—sympathy for Boone's pain, anger at this Eliza who had hurt him so deeply, and an unsettling flutter of hope that she quickly tamped down.

"I see," she said quietly. "That explains a great deal."

Ms. Patterson looked up from her work, studying Laura's face with shrewd eyes. "It does, doesn't it? The man's built walls around his heart high enough to keep out an army. But walls can come down, given the right circumstances."

The knowing look that accompanied this statement made Laura's cheeks warm. "I'm only staying temporarily," she reminded the older woman. "Until I start work here."

"Mmm-hmm," Ms. Patterson hummed, in exactly the same skeptical tone Hannah had used earlier. "There, that should do it. Stand up, let me see the length."

Laura stood, grateful for the change of subject. The dress now hung perfectly, the hem just above her ankles, the fit flattering without being too snug.

"Perfect!" Ms. Patterson declared with satisfaction. "You'll be the belle of the social, mark my words. Now, let's see what we can do with your hair."

Despite Laura's protests that she was perfectly capable of arranging her own hair, Ms. Patterson insisted on helping, deftly creating a style that was both elegant and practical. Soft curls framing Laura's face and the rest swept up in a simple but flattering arrangement.

"There," she said finally, stepping back to admire her handiwork. "Boone Callahan won't know what hit him."

"Ms. Patterson, really, there's nothing between—"

"Save your breath, dear," the older woman interrupted with a knowing smile. "I've been watching men and women circle each other in this town for years. I know what I see."

Before Laura could formulate a response, a voice called up the stairway.

"That'll be him now," Ms. Patterson said with satisfaction. "Go on, I'll clean up here."

Still slightly dazed by the whirlwind of preparations and revelations, Laura made her way downstairs to find Boone, hat in hand, now dressed again in his Sunday best—clean dark trousers, a crisp white shirt, and a vest that emphasized the breadth of his shoulders.

His eyes widened slightly as he took in her appearance, his gaze traveling from her arranged hair to the green dress before quickly returning to her face.

"You look... beautiful," he said with intensity in his eyes.

"Thank you," Laura replied, suddenly shy under his scrutiny. "Ms. Patterson was very insistent about the dress and hair."

"She usually gets her way," Boone acknowledged with the hint of a smile. "Ready for the social?"

They stepped out onto the porch and closed the door behind them. The late afternoon sun cast a warm light over the town, and the air had a festive feel, with people already making their way toward the community hall.

They walked side by side, close but not touching. Laura was acutely aware of the glances they received, the nods and smiles that seemed to hold extra meaning. Word traveled fast in a small town, Ms. Patterson had said. Laura wondered what word was traveling now about her and Boone.

Chapter 20

The community hall had been transformed in the hours since Laura had helped with the preparations. Lanterns glowed warmly, casting a soft light over the decorated space. The garlands she had helped create hung festively from the beams, and tables laden with food lined one wall. At the far end of the hall, several men were tuning instruments on the small platform—guitars, a fiddle, and what appeared to be a small portable organ.

The hall was already half full, with more people arriving by the minute. Hannah spotted them immediately and hurried over, her face alight with excitement.

"There you are! And that dress—Ms. Patterson was right. It is perfect for you. Much better than the blue one I loaned you." She greeted Boone with a respectful nod. "Mr. Callahan."

"Miss Edwards," he returned politely.

"The Millers just arrived with their punch," Hannah informed them. "You should try some before it's gone. It's famous in these parts."

"Sounds like a good idea," Boone agreed, looking to Laura for confirmation.

She nodded, and they made their way toward the punch bowl, greeting the townsfolk as they went. Laura was surprised by how many people she now recognized, how many friendly faces welcomed her with genuine warmth. It was a stark contrast to the years of anonymity with Jasper, moving from town to town without forming connections.

The musicians began to play a lively tune that immediately drew several couples to the dance floor. Laura watched, enjoying the sight of people young and old joining in the fun, their faces animated with pleasure.

"Laura! Boone!" Zeb's voice surprised them both. The older Callahan made his way toward them, looking spry and cheerful.

"Thought you might be resting still," Boone said, raising an eyebrow.

"And miss the beginning of the first social of the season? Not likely." Zeb chuckled. "Besides, Doc says a little dancing is good for keeping these old bones limber."

As if on cue, the music shifted to a slightly slower tune. Zeb's eyes twinkled mischievously.

"Miss Laura, would you do an old man the honor of partnering him for this dance?" he asked with an exaggerated bow.

Laura laughed, charmed by his gallantry. "I'd be delighted, Mr. Callahan."

She allowed Zeb to lead her onto the dance floor, casting one glance back at Boone, who watched with an expression that might have been amusement or something else entirely.

Zeb proved to be a surprisingly spry dancer, guiding Laura confidently through the steps of the waltz. "You dance well," he commented approvingly.

"My mother taught me," Laura explained, a bittersweet memory surfacing of her mother counting steps in their small kitchen, her father providing vocal accompaniment since they owned no instruments.

"A worthwhile skill," Zeb nodded. "My Mary insisted all our children learn. Said it was a mark of civilization in the wilderness."

Laura's gaze involuntarily sought Boone, standing now in conversation with Reverend Tanner by the punch bowl. "She sounds like a remarkable woman."

"That she was," Zeb agreed, his voice softening with memory. "Would have liked you, I think. She had a good eye for character." He studied Laura's face with surprising perception. "Boone isn't much for these gatherings, you know. He comes honoring his Ma... she always insisted our children attend every social event."

Laura wasn't sure how to respond to the implied meaning in his words. "He seems well-respected by everyone here," she offered.

"Respected, yes. But holding people at arm's length doesn't invite close friendship." Zeb skillfully guided her through a turn. "He's changed since you arrived, though. Opening up bit by bit. It's good to see."

Before Laura could formulate a response to this startling observation, the music ended. Zeb bowed again, thanking her for the dance, and escorted her back to where Boone waited.

"She's a fine dancer," Zeb informed his son with a wink. "Don't let her spend the evening standing around, boy."

With that parting advice, he wandered off toward a group of older men, leaving Laura and Boone in awkward silence.

The musicians struck up another tune, this one livelier than the last. Laura watched the dancers, trying to ignore the tension that had suddenly sprung up between them.

"Would you like to dance?" Boone asked abruptly, the words coming out stiffly, as though forced.

Laura looked up at him in surprise. She'd assumed from his demeanor and Zeb's comments that dancing wasn't something he enjoyed. "Only if it pleases you," she replied carefully.

Something shifted in his expression—a softening around the eyes, a slight relaxation of his jaw. "I wouldn't ask otherwise."

The simple honesty in his statement warmed her. "Then yes, I'd like that very much."

Boone offered his arm, and Laura placed her hand lightly upon it, allowing him to lead her to the dance floor. As they took their positions—his hand at her waist, hers on his shoulder, their free hands clasped—Laura was struck by how natural it felt to be in his arms, despite the formality of the dance.

The music washed over them as they began to move, and Laura discovered that Boone was indeed a capable dancer. He guided her with the same confidence he showed in all physical tasks, his movements sure and surprisingly graceful for such a large man.

"Your father said your mother insisted on dance lessons," Laura commented as they smoothly navigated around other couples.

"She did," Boone confirmed, the corner of his mouth lifting slightly. "Said no son of hers would clod around a dance floor like a newborn calf."

The image made Laura laugh, and Boone's expression lightened further at the sound. For a moment, the carefully maintained distance between them seemed to diminish, replaced by a warm familiarity that felt both new and somehow inevitable.

"And how did you learn to dance?" he asked, genuinely curious about her past.

"My mother taught me in our kitchen," Laura replied, the memory washing over her with unexpected clarity. "My father would whistle or sing while she counted steps. We had no instruments, but they made do with what we had."

"Sounds like resourceful people," Boone observed.

"They were," she agreed softly. "After they passed, there wasn't much opportunity for dancing. Jasper wasn't one for social gatherings."

Boone's hand tightened slightly on her waist. "You've had to be resourceful too."

It wasn't a question, but Laura nodded anyway. "Life demanded it."

The music shifted tempo, and Boone adjusted their steps seamlessly. All around them, other couples twirled and stepped, faces flushed with pleasure and exertion. The lantern light caught the sheen of polished boots, the swirl of skirts, the gleam of a watch chain.

"You never speak much about your life before coming to Lone Valley," Boone remarked, his voice pitched low enough that only she could hear.

Laura hesitated. "It wasn't a life I care to remember in detail."

"Fair enough." He nodded, respecting her boundary. "What about happy memories? There must have been some."

The question touched her. It had been so long since anyone had cared enough to ask about her past joys rather than her hardships.

"There were," she confirmed, thinking back. "Summer evenings when my father would whittle on the porch and tell stories. My mother teaching me to bake bread, her hands guiding mine through the dough. A Christmas when Jasper—" She broke off, surprised by the memory. "When Jasper saved for months to buy me a book of poetry. He was different then."

Boone absorbed this, his expression thoughtful. "People change, for better or worse."

"They do," Laura agreed. "What about you? What happy memories do you hold on to?"

His eyes met hers, steady and reflective. "Riding with my father as a boy, learning about the land. My mother's singing in the evenings. The ranch in spring, when the calves are new and everything feels fresh with possibility." A pause, then: "Adding onto my home, plank by plank, knowing it would stand for generations."

Something in his tone made Laura wonder if he was thinking of Eliza, of the home he'd added on to for a bride who walked away. But before she could dwell on it, the music ended, and Boone stepped back, releasing her waist but keeping her hand in his as they left the floor.

They made their way to the refreshment table, where Jude was enthusiastically ladling punch into cups. "Boone! Miss Hartley! Have some of this year's batch—best yet, if I do say so myself."

Boone accepted two cups, handing one to Laura. "High praise, considering last year you said the same thing."

Jude grinned, unperturbed. "A man can improve his craft year by year, can't he? Just like ranching."

"Fair point," Boone conceded with the ghost of a smile.

Laura sipped the punch, finding it sweet and fruity, with a hint of something tart beneath. "It's delicious, Mr. Miller."

"Secret family recipe," Jude winked. "Been in the Miller family for generations. Speaking of family, your brother Marcus sends his regards, Boone. Saw him when I was in Denver last month."

"How's he faring?" Boone asked, genuine interest in his voice.

"Well enough. That mill of his is turning a profit now. He mentioned bringing the family to visit come summer."

"Be good to see them," Boone nodded. "His boy must be walking by now."

"Running, more like," Jude laughed. "Chasing after his big sister everywhere she goes. Cute little tykes, both of them."

As they continued their conversation, Laura observed Boone's face soften at the mention of his niece and nephew. There was a tenderness there, a hint of the man beneath the rugged exterior.

The evening progressed pleasantly, filled with more dancing, conversations with townspeople, and simple but delicious refreshments. Laura relaxed into the warmth of the community, savoring the sense of belonging that had eluded her for so long.

As the musicians took a brief rest, Boone led her toward the door. "Could use some air," he explained. "Care to join me?"

Outside, the night was clear and crisp, with stars scattered across the velvet sky like diamonds on black cloth. Lanterns hung from posts around the building, creating pools of golden light amidst the darkness. A few other couples had had the same idea, dotting the area with quiet conversations.

Boone guided her to a bench set against the side of the building, slightly apart from the others. Voices from inside drifted out softly, accompanied by the occasional burst of laughter.

"It's beautiful here," Laura said, looking up at the sky. "In the cities, you never see the stars so clearly."

"One of the benefits of country living," Boone agreed, following her gaze upward. "My ma used to say that stars were windows into heaven, places where the light of God's glory shines through."

"What a lovely thought," Laura smiled. "Mine said much the same, though she called them angel's footprints."

Boone turned to look at her, his expression curious. "You speak of your parents with such fondness, yet losing them so young... that must have been difficult."

"It was," Laura acknowledged quietly. "But I was fortunate to have had them at all, even for the short sixteen years I did. They gave me a foundation—faith, values, memories to sustain me through harder times."

"A strong foundation is essential," Boone nodded, his gaze steady on her face. "For a life, for a home."

"Yes," Laura agreed. "Though I've learned that even the strongest foundations sometimes need repairs."

Something flickered in Boone's eyes—recognition, perhaps, or acknowledgment of her insight. "What repairs has your foundation needed?"

The question was deeply personal, yet asked with such genuine interest that Laura found herself answering honestly. "Learning to trust again, after Jasper's... troubles. Finding my faith when life seemed determined to test it. Believing that stability could be more than just a distant dream."

She hesitated, then continued more softly, "And yours? What repairs have you made to your foundation?"

For a long moment, Laura thought he might not answer. Then Boone's gaze shifted to the distant mountains, barely visible in the moonlight.

"Learning that plans don't always unfold as expected," he said finally. "That sometimes what seems like the end of a dream is just... a redirection." His eyes returned to hers, intense in their directness. "That walls built to protect can also imprison."

The honesty of his response touched something deep within Laura. Here was a man who understood loss, who had faced disappointment and continued forward, who recognized his own barriers even as he maintained them. She felt a sudden, overwhelming connection to him—not despite their different paths, but because of the similar scars those paths had left.

"Do you ever wonder," she asked softly, "what might have happened if life had taken different turns? If the walls had never needed building?"

"Sometimes," Boone admitted. "But then I remember that different turns might have led places I wouldn't want to be." His gaze held hers steadily. "Might never have led to a blizzard, and a stagecoach, and a woman who needed rescuing."

Laura's breath caught at the implication. "I've wondered the same," she confessed. "Whether all the difficult paths were somehow... necessary. Leading me here."

"To Lone Valley?" Boone asked quietly.

"To this moment," she clarified, her voice barely above a whisper.

The space between them seemed to contract, charged with unspoken emotions. Boone's gaze dropped briefly to her lips, then back to her eyes. A question in their depths. Laura felt herself leaning slightly forward, drawn by something more powerful than conscious thought.

Boone mirrored her movement, the distance between them shrinking incrementally. The sounds of the social faded away, leaving only the rapid beating of her heart and the soft whisper of their shared breath.

Just as Laura thought he might close the final distance between them, a burst of raucous laughter erupted nearby as a group of young men rounded the corner of the building. The moment shattered like glass, and both she and Boone drew back reflexively.

"Mr. Callahan! Miss Hartley!" one of the young men called out, oblivious to what he had interrupted. "The music's starting up again. They're calling for the Virginia Reel!"

"Thank you, Timmy," Boone replied, his voice remarkably steady despite the intensity of the moment before. "We'll be right in."

As the group continued on, chattering excitedly, Boone rose from the bench and offered Laura his hand. She took it, feeling the warmth of his palm against hers, the strength in his fingers as they curled around her own.

"Shall we?" he asked simply.

Laura nodded, unable to trust her voice just yet. As they walked back toward the entrance, Boone kept her hand in his, a small intimacy that spoke volumes in the wake of their interrupted moment.

The Virginia Reel was in full swing when they reentered, couples forming two long lines facing each other. They joined at the end, taking their positions across from one another. The lively music filled the hall, and soon Laura found herself caught up in the energetic patterns of the dance—moving forward to meet Boone in the middle, circling back to back, joining hands to spin, separating to weave down the line.

Each brief touch, each meeting of their eyes across the formation, sent a thrill through her that had nothing to do with the exertion of the dance. When their hands clasped and they promenaded down the center of the lines to take their place at the foot, Laura felt as though she were floating rather than walking.

As the evening drew to a close, with the last dance called and final refreshments served, Laura was both exhilarated and wistful. The social had been unlike any event she'd experienced before—not because of its grandeur, but because of the sense of community, of belonging, and most of all, because of the man who had shared it with her.

Later, as she prepared for bed in the quiet of her room, Laura caught sight of her reflection in the small mirror. The woman who gazed back at her seemed different somehow—flushed with life, eyes bright with emotion, a small smile playing at the corners of her mouth.

She stood very still, letting the realization wash over her like a warm tide. It was no use pretending anymore, no use trying to maintain the careful distance she had thought necessary for her independence, for her protection.

She was falling in love with Boone Callahan.

The thought should have terrified her. Love meant vulnerability, dependency, the risk of heartbreak. Everything she had sworn to avoid after the turmoil with Jasper.

Yet as she climbed into bed and pulled the quilt up around her shoulders, Laura found that terror was the furthest thing from her mind. Instead, she felt a strange peace, as though her heart had been quietly making its decision all along, waiting only for her mind to catch up.

Chapter 21

Laura woke before dawn, her mind still swirling with thoughts of the previous night's social. She dressed quickly in the dim light filtering through her curtains, eager to start the day. The memory of almost kissing Boone under the stars sent a flutter through her stomach that was both thrilling and terrifying.

Rather than wait for breakfast, she slipped quietly from her room. The house was still, with only the ticking of the grandfather clock breaking the silence. She wrapped her shawl tightly around her shoulders and stepped outside into the crisp morning air.

The ranch was beautiful at this hour—peaceful in a way that touched something deep in her soul. The sky was lightening in the east, though the sun hadn't yet appeared over the mountains. A thin layer of frost covered the ground, glistening in the predawn light. The barn door stood partially open, a warm light spilling out into the yard.

Laura made her way across the frosted ground, her footsteps crunching softly. As she approached the barn, she heard the low murmur of Boone's voice, followed by a horse's gentle nickering. She paused at the entrance, suddenly uncertain.

What was she doing? Seeking him out so early, before the household was even awake? After last night's almost-kiss, wouldn't it be wiser to maintain some distance?

Before she could decide whether to advance or retreat, Boone's deep voice carried clearly through the gap in the door.

"Easy there, Rusher. You always were impatient for breakfast."

The affection in his tone made her smile. Taking a deep breath, Laura pushed the door wider and stepped inside.

Boone stood in one of the stalls, brushing down the big bay gelding. He wore only a simple flannel shirt despite the morning chill, his suspenders visible over broad shoulders. He looked up at her entrance, surprise flickering across his features before settling into something warmer.

"You're up early," he said, setting the brush aside.

"I couldn't sleep," Laura admitted, moving further into the barn's warmth. The scent of hay, horses, and leather surrounded her. "I saw the light."

Boone nodded, patting Jupiter's neck before stepping out of the stall. "I like the quiet of morning. Time to think."

"What were you thinking about?" The question slipped out before she could consider its boldness.

Instead of deflecting, Boone met her gaze directly. "You."

The single word hung in the air between them, simple and profound. Laura's heart began to race, and she gripped her shawl tighter.

"Oh," she managed, suddenly finding it difficult to meet his eyes.

Boone took a step closer, then paused, as if giving her space to retreat if she wished. When she didn't move, he continued, "Last night, before we were interrupted..."

"Yes?" Laura looked up at him, finding his expression uncharacteristically vulnerable.

"I nearly kissed you," Boone stated plainly, his directness both startling and refreshing.

Laura nodded, her throat dry. "I know."

"I've been wondering if you would have let me."

The question was so honest, so devoid of pretense, that Laura couldn't help but respond in kind. "Yes," she whispered. "I would have."

Something shifted in Boone's expression—relief, perhaps, or determination. He closed the distance between them slowly, giving her every opportunity to step away. But Laura remained rooted in place, her heart pounding so loudly she was certain he must hear it.

He stopped just before her, close enough that she could feel the warmth radiating from him, could see the flecks of gold in his hazel eyes.

"Laura," he said, her name like a prayer on his lips. "I've been fighting this since the day I found you in that blizzard."

"Fighting what?" she asked, though she already knew the answer.

"How I feel about you." His voice was low, almost rough with emotion. "I told myself you were just passing through. That after Eliza, I couldn't risk—" He broke off, then continued more softly. "But some things are worth the risk."

He reached out, his calloused fingers gently brushing a strand of hair from her face. The touch sent a shiver down her spine that had nothing to do with the morning chill.

"I care for you, Laura. More than I thought possible to care for someone again."

The words washed over her like warm water, melting the ice she'd built around her heart. Yet, a lifetime of caution couldn't be discarded in a moment.

"Boone," she began carefully, "I care for you too. But my life has been... unstable. I came here seeking independence, a chance to build something for myself."

"I know," he nodded, his hand dropping back to his side. "And I admire that about you. Your strength, your determination."

"What I'm trying to say," Laura continued, finding courage in his understanding, "is that I'm afraid of losing myself in someone else again. With Jasper, I became so focused on his needs, his problems, that I nearly disappeared."

Boone's expression grew serious. "I don't want you to disappear, Laura. I want you to flourish." He gestured around them. "Here, in town, wherever you choose. I'm not asking you to give up your independence."

"Then what are you asking?" Laura whispered.

"Just a chance," he said simply. "A chance to see if what's growing between us might be strong enough to support both our dreams, not diminish them."

The honesty in his eyes, the respect in his words, touched Laura deeply. This was not Jasper's desperate need or selfish demands. This was something altogether different—an offer of partnership, of shared strength.

"I'd like that chance," she admitted softly. "I'm just... afraid."

Boone nodded, understanding in his gaze. "Fear isn't always a bad thing. Keeps us careful about what matters."

"And this matters," Laura said, not a question but a realization.

"Yes," Boone confirmed, his voice deepening. "It does."

He reached for her hand, giving her time to pull away. Instead, Laura met him halfway, her fingers sliding against his palm until their hands were intertwined. The simple connection felt more intimate than any embrace.

"May I kiss you, Laura?" Boone asked, his voice barely above a whisper.

In answer, Laura took a small step forward, closing the remaining distance between them. She tilted her face up to his, her free hand coming to rest lightly on his chest, feeling the steady thump of his heart beneath her palm.

Boone leaned down, his eyes never leaving hers until the last moment. Then his lips met hers, gentle and questioning at first, then with growing certainty as she responded. The kiss was tender, unhurried, a beginning rather than a culmination. His hand released hers to curve around her waist, drawing her slightly closer without overwhelming her.

When they finally parted, Laura felt both steadied and shaken. Boone's eyes were warm as they gazed down at her, a smile playing at the corners of his mouth.

"Been wanting to do that since I carried you out of that blizzard," he admitted, his voice a low rumble that she felt as much as heard.

Laura couldn't help but laugh softly. "Even when I was half-frozen and unconscious?"

"Well, maybe not exactly then," Boone conceded, his smile widening. "But soon after, when you opened those determined eyes and asked where you were, like you were ready to take on the world no matter what the answer."

"I'm not sure that's entirely accurate," Laura said, thinking back to her disoriented state upon waking at the ranch.

"It is from where I was standing," Boone insisted gently. "You've got more strength in you than you realize, Laura Hartley."

Before she could respond, Jupiter nickered impatiently from his stall, breaking the moment. Boone glanced over with a rueful expression.

"Seems breakfast can't wait, even for important conversations," he noted dryly.

Laura stepped back slightly, though her hand remained on his chest. "I should probably head back to the house before Zeb wonders where I've gone."

Boone nodded, though reluctance showed in his eyes. "We'll continue this talk later?"

"Yes," Laura agreed, finally letting her hand fall. "I'd like that."

As she turned to leave, Boone caught her hand once more, bringing it briefly to his lips in a gesture that was both old-fashioned and deeply touching.

"Thank you," he said simply.

"For what?" Laura asked, puzzled.

"For taking a chance. For being brave enough to meet me halfway."

The words stayed with her as she made her way back to the house, her lips still tingling from his kiss, her heart fuller than it had been in years.

Chapter 22

The kitchen was warm and fragrant with the scent of coffee and frying bacon when Laura entered. Zeb looked up from the stove, his knowing gaze taking in her flushed cheeks and bright eyes.

"Mornin', Laura," he greeted, returning his attention to the pan before him. "Thought I heard someone slip out earlier."

"Good morning," she replied, moving to help with breakfast preparations. "I went for a walk. The ranch is beautiful at dawn."

"That it is," Zeb agreed amiably. "Anything interesting catch your eye on this morning stroll?"

There was something in his tone that made Laura suspect he knew exactly where she'd been. She busied herself with setting the table, hoping her face didn't betray her.

"The frost made everything look magical," she offered, which was true enough.

"Mmm," Zeb hummed noncommittally. "Boone's usually in the barn this time of morning. Did you happen to run into him?"

Laura paused in placing a fork, then decided honesty was the better course. "Yes, I did."

Zeb turned from the stove, spatula in hand, his expression gentle rather than teasing. "Laura, I hope you know that I consider you family now, whether or not..." He trailed off, then continued more directly. "What I mean is, you've brought light back to this house. However, things develop between you and my son. You'll always have a place here."

Touched by his words, Laura set down the silverware and faced him. "Thank you, Zeb. That means more than I can say."

The older man nodded, a twinkle returning to his eye. "Course, I wouldn't object to grandchildren before I'm too old to bounce 'em on my knee."

"Zeb Callahan!" Laura exclaimed, her cheeks flaming.

He chuckled, turning back to the stove. "Just thinking ahead. It's what old men do."

Before Laura could formulate a response, the front door opened and Boone entered, bringing with him the crisp morning air. Their eyes met briefly, a current of awareness passing between them before Boone greeted his father.

"Smells good," he commented, moving to the washbasin to clean his hands.

"Should be ready in a few minutes," Zeb replied. "Laura here was just telling me about her morning walk. Said the frost was particularly fine today."

Boone glanced at Laura, the corner of his mouth twitching slightly. "Was it?"

"Beautiful," Laura confirmed, holding his gaze a moment longer than necessary.

Zeb looked between them, a satisfied expression crossing his weathered features. "Well, now, I think breakfast is ready. Let's eat before it gets cold."

The meal passed pleasantly, with conversation flowing easily between the three of them. If Zeb noticed the lingering glances between his son and Laura, or the way Boone's hand occasionally brushed hers when passing the biscuits, he made no comment beyond a smile that crinkled the corners of his eyes.

After breakfast, Boone announced he needed to ride out to check the north pasture fence line. "That last storm might have brought down some trees on it," he explained. "Thought I'd take Jupiter for the exercise."

"I could come with you," Laura offered impulsively. "If you think I wouldn't be in the way."

Boone's expression brightened. "You wouldn't be in the way at all."

Laura nodded, excitement building at the prospect of exploring the ranch beyond the immediate surroundings of the house.

"Better bundle up," Zeb advised.

Half an hour later, Laura was in the barn once more, this time being introduced again to the dappled gray mare named Willow.

"She's steady as they come," Boone assured her, adjusting the stirrups on a smaller saddle he'd selected for Laura.

Laura stroked the mare's velvet nose, receiving a gentle nudge in return. "She's beautiful."

"She suits you," Boone observed, his eyes warm as they took in the picture Laura made beside the horse.

He helped her mount, his hands strong and sure at her waist as he lifted her into the saddle. Laura settled herself, adjusting to the familiar but long-forgotten feeling of sitting astride a horse.

"How does that feel?" Boone asked, standing at Willow's shoulder.

Laura gathered the reins as he'd shown her, sitting up straighter. "Good. Strange, but good."

"We'll take it slow," he promised, moving to mount Rusher.

The big bay pranced sideways as Boone swung into the saddle, eager to be moving. Boone controlled him with an easy confidence that spoke of years of horsemanship.

They set out from the barn at a walk, Boone keeping Rusher reined in beside Willow's more sedate pace. The ranch spread out before them, bathed in winter sunshine that did little to warm the crisp air.

As they rode, Boone pointed out features of the land—the creek that ran along the eastern boundary, the hills where the cattle were wintered, the distant line of trees that marked the beginning of forest land.

"It's larger than I realized," Laura commented, taking in the vastness of Callahan Ranch.

"My grandfather started with just fifty acres," Boone explained. "My father expanded it to three hundred. I've added another three hundred since taking over."

"You love this land," Laura observed, hearing the pride in his voice.

"It's in my blood," Boone nodded. "Every hill, every stream, has a history. Stories my grandfather told my father, who told me." He glanced at her. "Land like this becomes part of you after a while."

"I've never had that," Laura said quietly. "A place that felt like it was truly mine, that I was connected to."

Boone was silent for a moment, then said carefully, "You could have it. If you wanted."

The implication was clear, hanging in the air between them. Before Laura could respond, Rusher tossed his head impatiently, and Boone chuckled.

"He's tired of this slow pace. Want to try a gentle trot? Might help warm us up."

Laura nodded, grateful for the momentary reprieve from the weight of the conversation. "I think I remember how."

"Just move with her," Boone advised. "Let your body follow her rhythm."

He clicked to Rusher, who immediately stepped into a smooth trot. Laura did the same to Willow, who obediently followed. For the first few strides, Laura bounced uncomfortably, then muscle memory began to return, and she found herself settling into the mare's pace.

The sensation was exhilarating—the crisp air on her face, the rhythmic movement beneath her, the open land stretching around them. She laughed aloud from sheer pleasure, earning a grin from Boone.

"Ready to try a canter?" he asked, eyes bright with shared enthusiasm.

Laura hesitated only briefly before nodding. "Show me how."

Boone demonstrated the cue, then let Rusher move ahead to give Laura space. She took a deep breath, then squeezed her legs as he'd shown her, leaning slightly forward. Willow responded immediately, smoothly shifting into a rocking canter that felt like flying.

For several glorious minutes, they galloped across an open meadow, Laura's fear giving way to pure joy. When Boone finally slowed Rusher, Laura followed suit, her cheeks flushed and her eyes sparkling.

"That was wonderful!" she exclaimed breathlessly as they walked the horses side by side once more.

"You're a natural," Boone said, watching her with undisguised admiration. "Most people who haven't ridden in years wouldn't take to cantering so quickly."

"It all came back once we started moving," Laura explained, patting Willow's neck affectionately. "Thank you for suggesting it."

"My pleasure," Boone replied, his voice warm. "There's something about sharing this land with someone who appreciates it..."

He trailed off, but Laura understood. "It makes it even more beautiful," she finished for him.

Their eyes met, and Laura felt that now-familiar connection spark between them—stronger for having been acknowledged, for having been given a voice in the barn earlier that morning.

They continued toward the north pasture, riding mostly in comfortable silence, occasionally broken by Boone pointing out a landmark or Laura asking a question about the ranch. The easy companionship felt as natural as breathing, as though they had been riding together for years rather than hours.

When they reached the fence line, Boone dismounted to inspect a section where several branches had indeed fallen across the wire. Laura slid down from Willow's back, her legs slightly wobbly after the unaccustomed exercise.

"Let me help," she offered, moving to hold the branches while Boone lifted them clear of the fence.

They worked together efficiently, Boone cutting away the larger sections with an ax he'd brought in his saddlebag, Laura dragging the smaller pieces clear. The physical labor in the cold air was invigorating, and Laura found herself enjoying the simple, shared task.

"You're stronger than you look," Boone commented when they'd finished, regarding her with a mixture of surprise and respect.

Laura brushed pine needles from her skirt. "Years of practical work will do that. I may not have ranch experience, but I'm no stranger to labor."

"I didn't mean it as an insult," Boone clarified quickly. "Just the opposite."

"I know," Laura assured him with a smile. "And I'm taking it as a compliment."

He returned her smile, then gestured to a large flat rock nearby. "Care to rest a bit before we head back? I brought coffee in that flask."

The rock overlooked a small valley, offering a view of rolling hills disappearing into the distance. Boone spread a small blanket he's gathered from his saddlebag over the stone's cold surface, then retrieved a flask and two tin cups as well.

They sat side by side, steaming cups in hand, surveying the winter landscape. A hawk circled lazily overhead, riding thermals in the still air.

"I've been thinking about what you said earlier," Laura began after a comfortable silence. "About fear not always being a bad thing."

Boone nodded, attentive but allowing her to continue at her own pace.

"I've spent so long being afraid," she admitted. "Afraid of Jasper's moods, of never finding stability, of losing what little independence I managed to carve out for myself." She turned to face him more directly. "But this morning I realized there are different kinds of fear. The fear I've known was stifling, limiting. But what I feel now—with you—it's different."

"How so?" Boone asked quietly.

Laura considered her words carefully. "It's the kind of fear that comes with possibility, with hope. Like standing at the edge of something vast and beautiful, knowing that stepping forward means leaving the familiar behind." She smiled slightly. "It's frightening, but in a way that makes me feel alive rather than diminished."

Boone's expression softened as he gazed at her. "I know that feeling," he said. "After Eliza left, I promised myself I wouldn't risk that kind of pain again. Built walls, focused on the ranch, convinced myself it was enough." He set his cup down, turning to face her fully. "Then you appeared in that blizzard, and suddenly those walls felt like a prison instead of protection."

He reached for her hand, his touch warm despite the cold air. "I'm not asking you to give up anything, Laura. Not your independence, not your plans for working in town. But I am asking if you might consider building something new alongside those plans. Something we could create together."

The sincerity in his voice, the openness of his expression, touched Laura deeply. This was not the desperate need that had characterized her relationship with Jasper, nor was it the stifling protection that had left her feeling small and powerless. This was an invitation, freely given, to a partnership of equals.

"I'd like that," she said softly. "To see what we might build together."

Boone's smile was like the rising, warm and full of promise. He leaned forward slowly, his eyes seeking permission, and when Laura nodded almost imperceptibly, he kissed her with a tenderness that made her heart ache in the most wonderful way.

This kiss was different from their first—deeper, more certain, a seal on the words they had exchanged. Laura's free hand came up to rest against his cheek, feeling the slight roughness of stubble beneath her palm. When they finally parted, Boone rested his forehead against hers, his breath visible in the cold air between them.

"I've been alone a long time," he murmured. "Convinced myself it was better that way."

"So have I," Laura admitted. "Easier to rely solely on myself."

"Easier, maybe," Boone agreed. "But not better."

He drew back slightly, his expression thoughtful. "Laura, I know you've accepted Ms. Patterson's offer to work at the boarding house, and I respect that. Your independence matters to me because it matters to you."

"But?" Laura prompted, sensing there was more.

"But I find myself selfishly wishing you wouldn't move to town," Boone admitted with a rueful smile. "Though I understand why you feel you should."

Laura considered this, her thoughts conflicted. On one hand, moving to town had been her plan from the beginning—a way to establish herself independently, to create the stability she craved on her own terms. On the other hand, the thought of leaving the ranch, of seeing Boone only during visits rather than sharing daily life with him, left an unexpected ache in her chest.

"It wouldn't be proper for me to stay at the ranch now," she said carefully. "Not with things changing between us."

"I know," Boone acknowledged. "And I wouldn't ask you to compromise your reputation. But perhaps there's a middle path we haven't considered yet."

"Such as?" Laura asked, curious.

"I'm not sure," Boone admitted. "But we can think on it together." He squeezed her hand gently. "Whatever comes, we'll find our way through it. One step at a time."

The simple promise, free of demands or expectations, reassured Laura more than elaborate declarations might have. Boone was offering partnership, not possession; support, not control.

"One step at a time," she agreed, returning the pressure of his hand.

They finished their coffee in companionable silence, watching the hawk's graceful circles against the clear blue sky. The cold had begun to seep through Laura's layers, but she was reluctant to suggest returning to the ranch and ending this moment of perfect understanding.

As if reading her thoughts, Boone eventually stood, offering his hand to help her up. "We should head back before you catch a chill. But we can ride this way again soon, if you'd like."

"I would," Laura said, taking his hand and rising to her feet. "Very much."

He packed away the blanket and cups with efficient movements, then helped her mount Willow once more. As they turned the horses toward home, Laura felt a profound sense of contentment wash over her. For perhaps the first time in her adult life, she was moving toward something rather than simply away from something else. The distinction felt important, meaningful in ways she was only beginning to understand.

Chapter 23

Matt burst through the door of the Callahan ranch house, his usual easygoing demeanor replaced by urgent intensity. "Boone! You need to come into town right now."

Boone looked up from the ledger where he'd been recording the ranch's expenses, his brow furrowing at Matt's tone. "What's happened?"

"There's a fella at Louella's asking all kinds of questions about a Laura. Causing quite a stir—drunk as a skunk and looking like he's seen the wrong end of several fights." Matt shook his head. "Not the friendly sort, if you take my meaning."

Laura, who had been mending a tear in one of her dresses by the window, froze at the mention of her name. The blood drained from her face as the needle slipped from her suddenly numb fingers.

"Jasper," she whispered, the name barely audible.

But Boone heard. His head turned sharply toward her, eyes narrowing as he registered her reaction. "Your brother?"

She nodded, her throat too tight to speak. The peaceful routine they'd established—the quiet breakfasts, the riding lessons, the tender moments when their hands or eyes would meet—suddenly felt like a fragile dream dissolving in morning light.

"What does he look like, Matt?" Boone asked, his voice taking on a hardness Laura hadn't heard before.

"Tall, dark hair, badly in need of a shave and a bath. Got a nasty scar across his left cheek. He's making quite an impression on the ladies of Lone Valley, and not the favorable kind."

Laura stood, her half-mended dress forgotten. "I should go to him."

"No." Boone's response was immediate, definitive. He rose from his chair, closing the ledger with a decisive snap. "You'll stay here. I'll handle this."

"Boone, he's my brother. I know how to—"

"Do you?" Boone interrupted, his expression unreadable. "Because from what little you've told me, your methods of 'handling' your brother haven't worked out particularly well for you."

The words stung all the more for their accuracy. Laura felt herself shrink inward, arms crossing protectively over her middle. "That's not fair."

Boone's jaw worked as though he was restraining himself from saying more. Finally, he turned to Matt. "Saddle Rusher. I'll be out in five minutes."

Matt nodded, casting a sympathetic glance toward Laura before heading back out the door.

Once they were alone, Boone took a deep breath, visibly collecting himself. When he spoke again, his voice was calmer but still strained. "Laura, I don't know precisely what kind of man your brother is, but from your reaction and Matt's description, I don't think you should be the first person he sees."

"I know Jasper better than anyone," Laura insisted, though her voice trembled. "He wouldn't hurt me."

"Maybe not intentionally," Boone conceded. "But a drunk man looking for his sister doesn't sound like someone thinking clearly."

Laura wanted to argue further, to insist that despite everything, she knew how to manage Jasper's moods and outbursts. But the weariness of those years washed over her—the constant vigilance, the careful navigation of his temper, the endless cycle of hope and disappointment. And she realized, with a clarity that surprised her, that she didn't want to go back to that life. Not even for a moment.

"At least let me come with you," she said instead.

Boone shook his head. "I need to assess the situation first. I'll come back for you if it seems appropriate." He hesitated, then added, "I promise."

The space between them felt wider than the few feet separating them. Just yesterday, they had ridden side by side, sharing confidences and gentle kisses beneath the winter sun. Now Boone's posture was rigid, his expression guarded, as though he were already preparing to face an adversary.

"Alright," Laura agreed reluctantly. "But please don't judge him too harshly. Jasper wasn't always like this. Before the drinking took hold, he was a good brother. Kind, even."

Something flickered in Boone's eyes—skepticism, perhaps, or simply concern. But he nodded. "I'll remember that."

He moved toward the door, then paused, turning back. For a brief moment, Laura thought he might offer some reassurance, might cross the room to embrace her or at least take her hand. Instead, he simply said, "Stay here. I'll return as soon as I can."

Then he was gone, the door closing firmly behind him. Laura stood in the silence of the room, listening to his footsteps cross the porch, followed by the sound of booted feet on frozen ground as he and Matt headed toward the barn.

She sank back into her chair, the half-mended dress lying forgotten in her lap. The bright thread she'd been using to repair the tear seemed to mock her with its cheerfulness. Just minutes ago, she had been content, even happy, planning what to wear to Sunday services tomorrow, wondering if Boone might formally court her now that they had acknowledged their feelings for each other.

Now Jasper had arrived, bringing with him all the chaos and uncertainty Laura had fled. And already, she could see the effect on Boone—the walls coming up, the warmth receding behind a mask of protective distance.

Zeb entered from the kitchen, a mug of coffee in his hand, his weathered face creased with concern. "I heard the commotion. Your brother's found you, it seems."

Laura nodded, blinking back tears that threatened to spill. "I knew he might, eventually. I just hoped..."

"That he wouldn't," Zeb finished for her, settling into the chair across from her. "Or that if he did, it would be different somehow."

"Yes," Laura admitted. "Foolish of me."

"Not foolish to hope," Zeb said gently. "Just human."

Outside, Laura heard the rhythmic hoofbeats as Boone and Matt rode toward town, the sound growing fainter until it disappeared altogether.

"What will happen now?" she asked, her voice small in the quiet room.

Zeb considered the question, taking a thoughtful sip of his coffee. "That depends on many things. What your brother wants. What you want. What Boone decides to do."

"What I want hasn't mattered much to Jasper in the past," Laura said, unable to keep the bitterness from her voice.

"And what is it you want, Laura?" Zeb asked, his eyes kind but searching.

Laura looked around the comfortable room that had become more of a home to her in weeks than any place had been in years.

"I want to stay," she said simply. "I've found peace here. Purpose. And with Boone..." She trailed off, uncertain how to express the tender, growing feelings between them.

"My son cares for you deeply," Zeb said, filling the silence. "More than I've seen him care for anyone since his mother passed. Including Eliza."

"But now he's pulling away," Laura observed sadly. "I could see it in his eyes when Matt mentioned Jasper. As if he were already preparing for me to leave."

Zeb sighed, setting his coffee mug on the small table beside him. "Boone protects himself from pain. Always has, even as a boy. When his mother died, he threw himself into ranch work, as if physical labor could somehow fill the hole her passing left. With Eliza, it was the same. Buying more land, expanding the herd—anything to avoid feeling the loss."

"And now he thinks I'll leave too," Laura realized, her heart aching for the man who'd begun to mean so much to her.

"It's easier for him to pull back first," Zeb confirmed. "To be the one doing the leaving, even if it's just emotionally. Old habits die hard, especially those formed in pain."

Laura twisted the fabric of her dress between her fingers. "What should I do?"

"That depends on what you want, as I said." Zeb leaned forward, his elbows on his knees. "If you want to go with your brother, there's nothing anyone here can do to stop you. If you want to stay but think Jasper needs help, well, that's a different matter. And if you want to build a life here, with or without Boone's involvement, that's yet another path."

"I don't want to go back to the life I had with Jasper," Laura said firmly, surprising herself with her certainty. "But I can't simply abandon him if he truly needs me."

"There's a difference between helping someone and enabling them," Zeb observed. "Took me years to learn that with my own brother. He had a similar weakness for the bottle."

Laura looked up in surprise. "I didn't know you had a brother."

"Jedidiah," Zeb nodded. "Younger than me by four years. Smartest of the Callahan boys, but with a thirst that could never be quenched. I spent years trying to save him from himself. Nearly lost this ranch doing it."

"What happened to him?" Laura asked softly.

"He died in '64. Froze to death in a Denver alley after being thrown out of a saloon." Zeb's voice was matter-of-fact, but Laura could hear the old pain underneath. "I hadn't seen him in almost a decade by then. Had to cut him off to save myself and my family."

"I'm sorry," Laura said, reaching across to touch his weathered hand.

"It was a hard lesson," Zeb acknowledged. "But a necessary one. You can't save someone who doesn't want saving, Laura. Not without destroying yourself in the process."

They fell silent again, the weight of his words settling around them. Laura thought of all the times she'd tried to help Jasper—hiding his bottles, cleaning up after his rages, making excuses to landlords and employers, sacrificing her own needs and dreams to accommodate his addiction. And where had it gotten either of them?

"I don't know if I'm strong enough to turn him away," she admitted. "Especially if he's in trouble."

"Nobody said it would be easy," Zeb replied. "But remember—you're not alone anymore. Whatever you decide, you have people here who care about you. People who'll stand with you."

Laura nodded, trying to draw comfort from his words. But as the minutes stretched into an hour, and then two, with no sign of Boone returning, doubt began to creep in. What if Jasper's appearance had changed everything? What if Boone, seeing the reality of her troubled family, decided she wasn't worth the complications she brought with her?

The fear gnawed at her, growing stronger with each tick of the grandfather clock.

Chapter 24

Louella establishment was unusually crowded for a Saturday afternoon. Word had spread quickly about the stranger asking after Laura, and it seemed half the town had found some reason to visit the café, eager for a glimpse of the man causing such a stir.

Jasper sat at a corner table, a half-empty bottle of whiskey before him, his posture slumped but tense. Even from the doorway, Boone could see that Matt's assessment had been accurate. Jasper looked like a man on the edge—unshaven, unwashed, his clothes showing the wear of hard travel and harder living. The scar across his left cheek stood out against his pallid skin, and his eyes held the feverish, unfocused look of a man who'd been drinking for days.

Louella approached Boone as soon as he entered, wiping her hands on her apron. "Thank the Lord you're here," she murmured. "He's been asking about Laura for the past hour. Wouldn't take 'I don't know' for an answer."

"Has he caused any trouble?" Boone asked quietly, his eyes never leaving Jasper.

"Not yet, but it's just a matter of time," Louella replied. "He's on his second bottle, and getting louder by the minute. I was about to send for the sheriff when Matt said he was fetching you."

Boone nodded, thanking her before making his way across the room. Conversations hushed as he passed, the townsfolk watching with undisguised interest. He was acutely aware of their scrutiny, of the whispers that would surely follow whatever happened next.

He stopped at Jasper's table, standing silently until the other man looked up. Recognition flashed in Jasper's bloodshot eyes, though Boone was certain they'd never met before.

"You're him, aren't you?" Jasper slurred, his voice carrying in the suddenly quiet café. "The rancher. The one who took her in."

"I'm Boone Callahan," Boone confirmed, his tone neutral despite the instinctive dislike he felt for the man before him. "I understand you're looking for your sister."

Jasper's laugh was harsh and without humor. "Looking? I've been searching for days. Followed her trail all the way from Elk Ridge. Town to town, always a step behind." He took another swig directly from the bottle. "Laura's gotten clever. Never used to be so deceitful."

Boone's jaw tightened at the accusation, but he kept his voice level. "Perhaps she had reasons for not wanting to be found."

Something dangerous flickered in Jasper's eyes. "What's that supposed to mean? She's my sister. My responsibility."

"From what I've gathered, she's been the one taking responsibility for quite some time," Boone replied, unable to completely mask his disapproval.

Jasper pushed himself to his feet, swaying slightly. He was tall—nearly Boone's height—but thinner, with none of the solid muscle that came from daily ranch work. Still, desperation and alcohol could make a dangerous combination.

"You don't know anything about us," Jasper hissed. "About me and Laura. We're family. We look out for each other."

"Is that what you call it?" Boone asked, his patience wearing thin. "Because from where I'm standing, it looks like you drove her to flee in the middle of a bitter Montana winter, alone and with barely enough money to live on."

Jasper's face contorted with anger, and for a moment, Boone thought he might lunge across the table. Instead, he slumped back into his chair, something like shame crossing his features.

"I wasn't myself then," he muttered. "Been trying to make it right. To find her and explain."

Boone studied the man before him, trying to reconcile this broken figure with the brother Laura had described—the one who had once been kind, who had saved to buy her a book of poetry. It was difficult to see any trace of that man in the wreck before him.

"What do you want from her, Jasper?" Boone asked directly.

"Want? I want my sister back," Jasper replied, as if it were obvious. "We're a team, Laura and me. Have been since our parents died. She knows I need her."

And there it was—not concern for Laura's wellbeing, not remorse for how he had treated her, but simply his own need. Boone thought of Laura's quiet strength, her determination to build a life on her own terms, her flourishing in the short time she'd been at the ranch. The idea of her returning to a life dominated by this man's selfish demands made something hard and protective rise in Boone's chest.

"Laura is safe and well," he said carefully. "She has work, a place to live, people who care about her welfare."

"She belongs with me," Jasper insisted stubbornly. "We're family. Blood."

"Family doesn't treat each other the way you treated her," Boone countered, keeping his voice low despite his rising anger. "Family doesn't drive each other away through selfishness and cruelty."

Jasper's hand slammed down on the table, rattling the bottle and sending a few drops of whiskey splashing onto the worn wood. "Who do you think you are to judge me? Some high-and-mighty rancher who thinks he can buy whatever he wants—including my sister?"

The accusation hung in the air, ugly and insinuating. Boone was suddenly aware of every ear straining to catch the conversation, of the speculative looks being exchanged around the room. He thought of Laura back at the ranch, her reputation now being questioned by the very community she'd begun to feel a part of.

"You're drunk, Hartley," Boone said coldly. "And making a spectacle of yourself isn't helping your cause or your sister's standing in this town."

"Then take me to her," Jasper demanded. "Let me see for myself that she's alright. That she hasn't been...taken advantage of."

The implication was clear, and Boone had to clench his fists at his sides to keep from grabbing the man by his filthy collar. "Laura will decide if and when she wants to see you," he stated flatly. "In the meantime, you need to sober up and clean yourself up. Louella has rooms available if you can afford one."

"Already paid for three nights," Jasper muttered, some of the fight going out of him as quickly as it had flared up. "Been traveling hard. Need rest before I see her, anyway."

Boone nodded, relieved at this small concession. "I'll let Laura know you're here. The decision to see you will be hers to make."

Jasper looked as though he wanted to argue further, but exhaustion seemed to overtake him. He slumped lower in his chair, reaching for the bottle again. "Tell her I'm sorry," he said, his voice suddenly smaller. "Tell her I've changed."

Boone made no promises. He caught Louella's eye as he turned to leave, communicating silently that she should keep an eye on their troublesome guest. She nodded her understanding, her expression concerned.

As he made his way back through the café, Boone was uncomfortably aware of the conversations that had ceased at his approach, only to resume in hushed tones as he passed. He recognized the signs of gossip already taking root—the speculative glances, the huddled conference between Mrs. Miller and the blacksmith's wife, the way Reverend Tanner looked at him with a troubled expression.

Outside, Matt was waiting with the horses, his face expectant. "Well? Is it really her brother?"

"It is," Boone confirmed grimly. "And he's exactly what I feared."

"Trouble?" Matt asked.

"The kind that follows a man like a shadow," Boone replied, mounting Rusher with a fluid motion. "Let's ride. I need to speak with Laura."

They rode in silence for several minutes, Boone's thoughts churning. The peaceful existence he'd begun to imagine with Laura at the ranch seemed suddenly threatened, not just by Jasper's physical presence, but by the complications he brought with him. Boone had worked hard to build his reputation in Lone Valley—as a fair employer, a dependable neighbor, a man whose word could be trusted. Now, through no fault of her own, Laura's association with her brother cast a shadow that extended to him as well.

"You're awful quiet," Matt observed as they approached the ranch.

"Thinking," Boone replied tersely.

"About Laura?"

"About everything." Boone sighed, slowing Rusher to a walk. "Jasper is...a mess. Drunk, desperate, making insinuations loud enough for half the town to hear. You know how people talk."

Matt nodded sagely. "Already started before we left. Heard Mrs. Dunmore wondering aloud why Laura never mentioned having a brother until he showed up looking for her."

Boone felt a flare of irritation at the town's gossips. "It's none of their business."

"Maybe not," Matt agreed. "But you know how some folks in Lone Valley can be. Folks are protective of their own. And suspicious of strangers who might bring trouble."

"Laura isn't a stranger anymore," Boone said firmly. "She's earned her place here."

"I know that. You know that. But her brother showing up like this raises questions. People will wonder what else she hasn't told them." Matt shook his head. "Not saying it's right, just saying it's how things are."

Boone fell silent again, recognizing the truth in Matt's words. He thought of Laura, of how hard she'd worked to build connections in Lone Valley, to create a place for herself. The tentative roots she'd begun to put down were now threatened by the very past she'd tried to escape.

And what of their own connection? The fragile, beautiful thing growing between them? Could it withstand this test, or would it wither beneath the weight of community suspicion and family complications?

As they approached the ranch house, Boone caught sight of Laura standing on the porch, her slender figure tense with anticipation. She'd wrapped a shawl around her shoulders against the winter chill, but even from a distance, he could see that she was shivering.

An unfamiliar feeling of uncertainty washed over him. For the first time since they'd acknowledged their feelings for each other, Boone wasn't sure what to say to her, how to bridge the distance that Jasper's arrival had already begun to create between them.

Chapter 25

Laura watched Boone and Matt ride into the yard, her hands clutching her shawl tightly around her shoulders. The sun was beginning its descent toward the mountains, casting long shadows across the frozen ground. She'd spent the afternoon alternating between anxious pacing and sitting by the window, watching for any sign of Boone's return.

Now that he was here, the expression on his face as he dismounted sent a chill through her that had nothing to do with the winter air. His features were composed into the same mask of careful neutrality he'd worn when she first arrived at the ranch—distant, guarded, revealing nothing of his thoughts.

Laura descended the porch steps as he approached, searching his face for any hint of what had transpired in town. "Did you find him? Is he alright?"

Boone nodded once, his jaw tight. "He's at Louella's. Paid for a room for three nights."

Relief and apprehension warred within her. "Is he...was he..."

"Drunk?" Boone supplied flatly. "Yes. And making quite an impression on the good people of Lone Valley."

Laura winced, imagining all too clearly the scene Jasper must have created. "I'm sorry. He doesn't usually—"

"Doesn't he?" Boone interrupted, a thread of skepticism running through his voice. "Because from what little you've told me, and what I saw today, this seems to be exactly who your brother is."

The judgment in his tone stung. "You don't know him," Laura protested weakly. "He wasn't always like this."

"So you've said." Boone's expression softened slightly at her distress, but his posture remained rigid. "Laura, he wants to see you. Says he's been tracking you for days, following your trail from Elk Ridge."

A chill ran down Laura's spine.

"Did he say what he wants?" she asked, though she already knew the answer.

"He says he wants you back. That you're 'a team' and that you belong with him because your family." Boone's tone made it clear what he thought of this reasoning. "He also asked me to tell you he's sorry, and that he's changed."

Laura's laugh held no humor. "He always says that. Always believes it, too, for a while."

"I told him that seeing you would be your decision," Boone continued. "That I wouldn't force you either way."

"Thank you for that," Laura said.

An awkward silence fell between them, filled with unspoken questions and concerns. Laura could sense Boone holding back, choosing his words carefully. It was a stark contrast to the easy openness they had shared just yesterday, when they'd ridden side by side across his land, their futures beginning to intertwine in both their minds.

"There's something else you should know," Boone finally said, his voice low. "Jasper was...vocal about his concerns for you. Made some insinuations about your situation here."

Laura felt her cheeks burn with embarrassment. "What kind of insinuations?"

"The kind that questions a young woman living alone on a ranch with two men," Boone replied bluntly. "The kind that were loud enough for half the town to hear."

"Oh," Laura breathed, mortification washing over her. She thought of Hannah, of Reverend Tanner, of all the people in Lone Valley who had begun to accept her. What would they think now?

"I'm so sorry, Boone. I never meant to bring this kind of trouble to your doorstep."

"It's not your fault," Boone said, but there was a distance in his voice that belied his words. "You're not responsible for your brother's behavior."

"But I am responsible for the consequences of my connection to him," Laura countered. "For the way his actions reflect on me—and now on you."

Boone didn't argue the point, which only confirmed Laura's fears. She wrapped her arms more tightly around herself, suddenly feeling cold to her core.

"What should I do?" she asked, hating the uncertainty in her voice.

Boone hesitated. "That's not for me to decide, Laura. Jasper is your brother. Only you can determine what obligation, if any, you have toward him."

His careful neutrality was worse than any criticism. Laura found herself longing for the Boone of yesterday—the one who had held her close and promised that they would find their way together, one step at a time. This Boone felt like a stranger, withdrawn behind walls of propriety and caution.

"Would you take me to see him?" she asked, needing to fill the growing silence between them.

"If that's what you want," Boone agreed, his expression unreadable. "Though it might be better to wait until morning. Give him time to sober up."

Laura nodded, acknowledging the wisdom in this suggestion. "Tomorrow, then."

"Tomorrow," Boone confirmed, his tone neutral.

Another silence fell, this one heavier than before. Laura could feel their newfound closeness fracturing, hairline cracks spreading like ice breaking beneath too much weight. The easy companionship, the tender glances, the shared confidences—all seemed suddenly fragile in the face of Jasper's arrival and the complications he brought with him.

"I should check on Willow," Laura said finally, grasping for any reason to escape the growing awkwardness between them. "I promised her an apple after our ride yesterday."

"Of course," Boone replied, stepping aside to let her pass. As she moved past him, their arms brushed briefly, and Laura felt him stiffen slightly at the contact. It was a small thing, barely perceptible, but it sent a wave of desolation through her.

In the barn, surrounded by the comforting scents of hay and horses, Laura finally allowed her tears to fall. Willow nickered softly, pushing her velvety nose against Laura's shoulder, as though sensing her distress.

"Everything's changed," Laura whispered, burying her face in the mare's warm neck. "In just a few hours, everything's changed."

She thought of the looks that would greet her in town tomorrow, the whispers behind hands, the speculation about her character and her past. She'd experienced it before, in other towns, where Jasper's behavior had marked them both as outsiders. But this time was different. This time, she had begun to believe she might belong, might build a real life here.

The cost of Jasper's arrival wasn't just her own reputation, but Boone's as well. He had worked his entire life to build his standing in this community, to be respected and trusted. Now, through her connection to him, that reputation was threatened. How could she expect him to risk everything he'd built for a woman whose troubled past had followed her right to his doorstep?

"He's pulling away already," she murmured to Willow, who flicked an ear in response. "And I don't blame him. Why would he want to be associated with the kind of scandal Jasper brings wherever he goes?"

The mare nudged her gently, and Laura managed a watery smile, reaching into her pocket for the promised apple. "At least you don't care about gossip, do you?"

As Willow happily crunched the treat, Laura tried to marshal her thoughts. She needed a plan. If Jasper was determined to "take her back," as he'd apparently told Boone, she needed to make it clear that wasn't an option. She had built the beginnings of a life here, and despite today's setback, she wasn't willing to abandon it. Not even for her brother.

Yet, she couldn't simply turn her back on him, either. For all his faults, Jasper was the only family she had left. And there had been times in between the drinking and the rages, when glimpses of the brother she'd loved would shine through. The boy who had taught her to skip stones across a pond, who had held her hand at their parents' funeral, who had once gone hungry himself to make sure she had enough to eat.

"There has to be a way to help him without destroying myself in the process," she told Willow, echoing Zeb's earlier wisdom.

But what that way might be remained frustratingly unclear. And as the sun dipped below the mountains, casting the barn into shadow, Laura felt more alone than she had since the day she'd left Elk Ridge.

Chapter 26

The morning dawned gray and sullen, a perfect match for Laura's mood as Boone's wagon rolled into Lone Valley. She sat stiffly beside him on the bench, the space between them feeling wider than the few inches that separated their bodies. Neither had spoken much during the journey from the ranch, their conversation limited to practical matters—the weather, the time they should return, whether Laura needed her coat buttoned against the winter chill.

Boone guided the horses down the main street with ease, his expression unreadable. As they approached Louella's boarding house, Laura noticed curtains twitching in windows, faces peering out from shops. Word of Jasper's arrival had clearly spread through the small community like wildfire.

"Are you certain you want me to come in with you?" Boone asked, bringing the wagon to a halt. It was the most direct question he'd asked her all morning.

Laura nodded, swallowing against the dryness in her throat. "Please. I'd rather not face him alone."

Something flickered across Boone's features—concern, perhaps, or resignation—before he secured the reins and jumped down from the wagon. He came around to her side, offering his hand to help her descend. Even now, despite the tension between them, his touch was steady and sure. Laura clung to that small reassurance as her boots touched the ground.

Louella was waiting for them just inside the entrance, her normally cheerful countenance pinched with concern. "Thank goodness you're here," she murmured, drawing them away from the curious gaze of the two elderly men sipping coffee at a nearby table. "He's upstairs in room three."

"Has he been... troubled?" Laura asked, dreading the answer.

"Agitated," Louella replied diplomatically. "Pacing. Asking when you'd arrive. He seems sober enough this morning, though I'd wager he's feeling the effects of yesterday's indulgence."

"Thank you for keeping an eye on him," Boone said, removing his hat with formal politeness. "We won't impose on your hospitality any longer than necessary."

Louella waved away his words. "Nonsense. Take whatever time you need." She lowered her voice. "Though you should know, there's been talk. Mrs. Miller was in early for her bread order, full of questions about your brother, Laura. And Reverend Tanner stopped by, concerned about your safety."

Laura felt her cheeks warm with shame. "I'm sorry to have brought this trouble to your doorstep, Louella."

The older woman's expression softened. "Honey, I've seen more scandal than this in my years running this place. Don't you worry about me." She patted Laura's arm. "Just take care of yourself. And remember, you've made friends here who won't be swayed by idle gossip."

Gratitude flooded Laura, unexpected and overwhelming. She blinked back sudden tears. "Thank you," she whispered.

Louella nodded, then gestured toward the stairs. "Up you go, then. I'll make sure you're not disturbed."

The stairs creaked beneath their weight as Laura led the way, Boone following close behind. Outside room three, she hesitated, her hand poised to knock. Doubt assailed her. Would Jasper be angry? Remorseful? Demanding? All were possibilities she'd seen before.

As if sensing her uncertainty, Boone stepped closer. "I'm right here," he said quietly, and for a moment, it felt like the distance between them narrowed.

Laura drew a steadying breath and knocked.

The door swung open almost immediately, revealing Jasper's haggard face. He looked worse than Laura had imagined—thinner, with shadows beneath his bloodshot eyes and a gauntness to his cheeks that spoke of more than just hard travel. For an instant, brother and sister stared at each other in silence, years of shared history and separate pain hanging between them.

"Laura," Jasper finally breathed, her name half whisper, half prayer.

"Hello, Jasper," she replied, her voice steadier than she felt.

His gaze flickered past her to Boone, his expression hardening. "I see you brought your protector."

"I asked him to come," Laura said firmly, unwilling to let Jasper dictate the terms of their meeting. "May we come in?"

Jasper stepped back, gesturing with exaggerated courtesy. "By all means. Mi casa es su casa, as they say down in Texas."

The small room was in disarray—the bed unmade, clothes strewn about, an empty bottle lying on its side near the washstand. Jasper had clearly been here for less than a day, but had already managed to leave his chaotic mark.

Laura remained standing, noting that Boone positioned himself near the door, his posture alert and watchful. Jasper noticed too, a sneer twisting his lips.

"No need to stand guard, Callahan. I'm not going to abduct my own sister."

"Let's not start this way, Jasper," Laura interjected, before Boone could respond. "You wanted to see me. I'm here. What is it you want to say?"

Jasper's bravado faltered, something vulnerable and almost boyish crossing his features. "I wanted to see that you were alright," he said, his voice losing its edge. "You disappeared, Laura. Do you have any idea what that did to me?"

Laura felt a flicker of guilt, quickly suppressed by memories of why she'd felt the need to leave so abruptly. "I couldn't stay anymore, Jasper. You know why."

"Because of one bad night?" he challenged, a defensive note entering his voice.

"It wasn't just one night, and you know it," Laura countered, forcing herself to meet his gaze directly. "It was months—years—of watching you destroy yourself and dragging me down with you. It was waking up wondering if today would be the day you'd finally push too far, drink too much, anger the wrong person."

Jasper's face flushed, his eyes darting toward Boone and back to Laura. "So you've been telling tales about me, have you? Painting me as the villain to your new friends?"

"No," Laura said truthfully. "I've shared very little about our past. I was trying to start fresh."

"Without me," Jasper said bitterly. "Cutting me out of your life like I meant nothing to you."

"That's not fair," Laura protested, her composure beginning to crack. "You were the one who made choices that drove me away. You were the one who came home drunk night after night, who lost job after job, who frightened me with your rages. You left me no choice but to leave."

"I was in pain!" Jasper shouted, his voice breaking. "Don't you understand? Everything I did—everything I've become—it's because I couldn't bear the pain anymore. Mother, Father, all of it... The drink helps. It's the only thing that helps."

Laura shook her head, a familiar ache spreading through her chest. They'd had this conversation so many times before, running in the same circles, never reaching resolution. "I lost them too, Jasper. But I didn't turn to the bottle to escape my grief."

"No, you turned to running away instead," he shot back. "Abandoning the only family you have left in the world."

From the corner of her eye, Laura saw Boone shift, his jaw tightening at Jasper's accusation. She wished she could explain to him how this pattern played out—Jasper's anger, his accusations, his eventual remorse, followed by promises that were always, always broken.

"I didn't come here to argue, Jasper," she said wearily. "I came because Boone said you were asking for me. So tell me, what do you want?"

The directness of her question seemed to throw Jasper off balance. He ran a hand through his unkempt hair, beginning to pace the small room like a caged animal. "I need help, Laura," he admitted, his voice lower now, a tremor of something like fear threading through it. "I'm in trouble. Bad trouble."

Laura felt her stomach clench. "What kind of trouble?"

Jasper glanced at Boone again, his expression calculating. "The kind that's private. Family business."

"Mr. Callahan stays," Laura stated firmly. "Whatever you have to say can be said in front of him."

Jasper's mouth twisted in displeasure, but after a moment, he nodded curtly. "Fine. Have it your way." He resumed his pacing, seeming to gather his thoughts, or perhaps his courage. "Remember McCready back in Elk Ridge? The fellow who ran the card games behind the Silver Dollar Saloon?"

Laura nodded, a sense of foreboding settling over her.

"Well, I had a streak of bad luck. Lost more than I should have," Jasper continued, his words coming faster now. "McCready's not the kind of man who extends credit, if you know what I mean. But he made an exception for me. Said I had an honest face." He laughed bitterly. "Turns out his idea of 'credit' comes with steep interest and painful reminders when payments are missed."

"How much do you owe him?" Laura asked, her voice flat.

Jasper named a sum that made her inhale sharply. It was more than she would earn in a year of honest work, maybe two.

"And now he wants his money," she guessed.

Jasper nodded, his expression growing desperate. "He sent some men after me. Mean ones, Laura. I barely got out of Elk Ridge ahead of them. Been moving ever since, trying to stay one step ahead."

"Yet you caught wind of me being here," Laura concluded, the pieces falling into place.

"I heard talk of a young woman matching your description heading west on the stage," Jasper confirmed. "Followed the trail, asking questions. When I heard about a woman named Laura taken in by a rancher in Lone Valley..." He shrugged, spreading his hands. "Here I am."

Laura closed her eyes briefly, attempting to process this revelation. The familiar weight of Jasper's troubles settled across her shoulders like an old, unwelcome burden. Of course, he hadn't come seeking reconciliation, or out of concern for her welfare. He'd come because he needed something—money, protection, a place to hide.

"And now McCready's men are likely on your trail," she said, opening her eyes to find him watching her intently. "Leading them straight to me. To Lone Valley."

"They won't find me here," Jasper insisted. "It's too small a town, too far off the main routes."

"Don't fool yourself," Boone spoke up for the first time since entering the room, his voice hard with certainty. "Men like that are persistent. If they want to find you badly enough, they will."

Jasper shot him a resentful look. "What would you know about it, rancher? Ever had men hunting you down for a debt?"

"No," Boone acknowledged coolly. "Because I don't gamble with money I don't have, and I don't borrow from men who use violence as a collection method."

"Well, aren't you just perfect?" Jasper sneered. "Sitting in judgment from your high horse."

"Jasper, stop it," Laura said sharply. "Boone is right. If these men are as determined as you say, they'll follow your trail just as you followed mine."

Fear flashed across Jasper's face, quickly masked by bravado. "That's why I need your help, Laura. I need money to pay off Mc-Cready. Enough to settle the debt and get him off my back for good."

Silence fell in the room, heavy and charged. Laura felt a curious detachment, as though observing the scene from a distance. How many times had she been here before? Different towns, different troubles, but always Jasper with his hand out, his eyes pleading, his promises empty.

"I don't have that kind of money, Jasper," she said finally. "Even if I did..." she trailed off, unwilling to finish the thought aloud: *even if I did, why should I give it to you?*

"But he does," Jasper said, nodding toward Boone. His expression turned wheedling, a tone Laura recognized with sinking dismay. "A successful rancher like yourself, Callahan. You must have access to funds. If you care for my sister as she seems to think you do, surely you can see your way to helping her only brother out of a tight spot?"

Laura's cheeks burned with humiliation. "Jasper, no! How dare you—"

"It's not about the money," Boone interrupted, his voice cold with anger. "It's about you coming here, bringing your troubles to Laura's door, trying to drag her back into the very life she fled."

Jasper's face flushed with an ugly color. "She's my sister! My blood! Whatever life we had, we had together. You're just some man who took her in, who thinks he can replace family with a few weeks of shelter."

"He's not trying to replace anyone," Laura broke in, stepping between the two men as tension crackled in the small room. "Boone offered me work and a place to stay when I had nowhere else to turn. That doesn't give you the right to come here demanding his money or making insinuations about our relationship."

"Relationship?" Jasper seized on the word, his eyes narrowing. "So there is something going on between you two. I knew it! Living alone together on that ranch, what else would people think?"

"That's enough," Boone said, his voice dangerously quiet. "You've insulted me in my own community, questioned your sister's character, and now you're attempting to extort money for a debt of your own making. I think this conversation is over."

He moved toward the door, clearly expecting Laura to follow. But Jasper reached out, catching Laura's wrist in a desperate grip.

"Laura, please," he begged, all pretense of anger falling away. "I know I've been a terrible brother. I know I drove you away. But these men will kill me if they find me before I can pay McCready. I'm not asking for myself—I'm asking because I want to live long enough to make things right between us."

Laura looked into his face—the face she'd known all her life, now ravaged by drink and hard living but still, beneath it all, her brother. The only family she had left in the world. She saw genuine fear in his eyes, and beneath that, a flicker of the boy he'd once been. The brother who had taught her to skip stones, who had held her hand at their parents' funeral.

"Let go of her," Boone commanded, moving forward with menace in his stance.

Jasper released her immediately, raising his hands in surrender. "I'm not hurting her. I'd never hurt Laura. She knows that."

But did she? Laura rubbed her wrist, remembering other times, other grips that had left bruises. Jasper had never struck her, true, but his drunken rages had frightened her more than once. The line between threatening and harming was thinner than he seemed to realize.

"I need time to think, Jasper," she said, stepping back toward the door. "I can't—I won't decide anything right now."

Disappointment and anger warred on Jasper's face. "Time is the one thing I don't have, Laura. If McCready's men find me—"

"Then perhaps you should have considered that before gambling with money you didn't have," Boone interrupted coldly. "Laura said she needs time. You'll respect that if you truly care for her welfare."

For a moment, Laura thought Jasper might lunge at Boone, such was the fury that flashed across his features. But then his shoulders slumped, defeat replacing the anger.

"Fine," he muttered. "Time. But not too much, Laura. Please."

"I'll return tomorrow," she promised, not meeting Boone's eyes. She knew he would disapprove, but she couldn't simply walk away from Jasper while his life might genuinely be in danger. "We'll talk more then."

Jasper nodded, something like relief crossing his face. "Tomorrow, then."

Laura turned and left the room without another word, aware of Boone close behind her. She could feel the tension radiating from him as they descended the stairs, could sense his disapproval in the rigid set of his shoulders.

Chapter 27

Louella was still at the front desk, her expression brightening when she saw Boone and Laura descend the stairs. "Everything alright?" she asked, taking in their grim faces.

"Fine, thank you," Laura managed, forcing a smile that felt brittle on her lips. "My brother will be staying another night, at least for now."

Louella nodded, her eyes kind but concerned. "He's welcome as long as he behaves himself. Though between you and me, dear, he looks like a man who needs more than a good night's sleep to set him right."

"Yes," Laura agreed softly. "I'm afraid he does."

Outside, the winter sun had broken through the morning clouds, casting pale light across the main street. Laura inhaled deeply, grateful for the cold, fresh air after the stifling atmosphere of Jasper's room.

Boone's hand at her elbow guided her toward the wagon, his touch impersonal and light. Once seated, with Boone taking up the reins beside her, Laura waited for the inevitable reckoning. She didn't have to wait long.

"You can't seriously be considering giving him money," Boone said as the wagon pulled away from the boarding house, his voice pitched low but intense.

Laura stared ahead, watching the buildings of Lone Valley slide past. "He's my brother, Boone. If his life is truly in danger—"

"His life is in danger because of his own bad choices," Boone interrupted, his knuckles white on the reins. "Choices he'll keep making as long as someone is there to bail him out of the consequences."

The words stung, not least because Laura recognized their truth. How many times had she covered for Jasper, paid his debts, made excuses for his behavior? And what had it achieved, besides enabling him to sink deeper into his destructive patterns?

"I know that," she said quietly. "But I can't simply turn my back if he's in real trouble."

"Can't you?" Boone challenged, glancing at her with an expression that made her heart sink. "Or won't you? There's a difference, Laura."

She bristled at his tone. "You don't understand. He's my family. My only family."

"Family isn't just blood," Boone countered. "It's actions. It's choices. It's trust and support and caring for one another. Has Jasper been that kind of family to you? Or has he used that bond to manipulate you into enabling his worst behaviors?"

Laura felt tears prick behind her eyes, but she blinked them back resolutely. "It's not that simple."

"Isn't it?" Boone's voice softened slightly, but the tension remained in his posture. "Laura, I saw your face when he grabbed your wrist. That wasn't just surprise I saw there. It was fear."

She looked away, unable to deny the observation. "He's never hurt me," she said, hating the defensive note in her voice. "Not physically."

"But he's frightened you," Boone pressed. "Made you feel unsafe. Driven you to flee in the dead of winter with barely enough money to survive."

Laura remained silent, the truth of his words hanging in the air between them. The wagon rattled past the outskirts of town, the open country stretching before them, the mountains a jagged line against the horizon.

"Even if his story is true," Boone continued after a moment, "giving him money won't solve the underlying problem. Men like Jasper don't change because someone pays their debts. They see it as confirmation that they can continue as they have been, that someone will always be there to clean up their messes."

"I know," Laura whispered, the words pulled from her reluctantly. "But what if these men really are looking for him? What if they harm him because I refused to help?"

Boone sighed, some of the hardness leaving his expression. "Then that would be tragic. But it wouldn't be your fault, Laura. It would be the result of Jasper's choices, and his alone."

They rode in silence for several minutes, each lost in their own thoughts. The sound of the horses' hooves on the frozen ground and the creak of the wagon were the only interruptions to their mutual contemplation.

"I don't understand," Boone said finally, breaking the silence. "You're one of the strongest women I've ever met. You left everything behind to build a new life on your own terms. You've worked hard on the ranch, never complained, never asked for special treatment. You're brave and determined and capable." He shook his head, frustration evident in the gesture. "But when it comes to your brother, it's like watching a different person emerge. Someone who doubts herself, who accepts treatment no one should have to endure."

Laura's throat tightened with emotion. He had seen more clearly than she realized, had recognized the transformation that occurred whenever Jasper entered her life.

"It's complicated," she said, knowing how inadequate the explanation was. "When you grow up with someone, share loss and grief and hardship...it creates a bond that's not easily broken. And Jasper wasn't always like this. There was a time when he was my protector, my hero even. After our parents died, he was the one who held us together, who found work and made sure we had a roof over our heads."

She paused, memories flooding back of a younger, sober Jasper, his face unlined by dissipation, his eyes clear and determined. "It wasn't until later, when the burden became too much for him, that he turned to drink. By then, our roles had reversed. I became the caretaker, the one trying to hold things together. And somehow, once that pattern was established, we couldn't break free of it."

Boone listened without interruption, his expression thoughtful. When she finished, he was quiet for so long that Laura began to wonder if he would respond at all.

"I understand loyalty," he said at last. "And I understand not wanting to abandon someone who's struggling. Those are admirable qualities, Laura." He glanced at her, his eyes troubled. "But there comes a point where loyalty becomes self-destruction. Where helping becomes hurting—both yourself and the person you're trying to save."

The words echoed Zeb's advice about not being able to save someone who didn't want to be saved. Laura wondered if father and son had had similar conversations about Zeb's alcoholic brother.

"I don't know what to do," she admitted, the confession costing her pride but offering a strange relief. "I don't want to abandon Jasper if he's truly in danger. But I don't want to enable him either. And I don't want…" She hesitated, then forced herself to continue. "I don't want to lose what I've found here. The peace. The sense of belonging. The connections I've made."

You, she wanted to add, but didn't. I don't want to lose you.

Boone's expression softened marginally, but his next words carried a caution that made Laura's heart sink. "Those connections are important to me, too. But I have responsibilities, Laura. To my father, to my ranch, to the community that's known me all my life. I can't—" He broke off, seeming to struggle with how to phrase what came next. "I can't allow Jasper's troubles to put all of that at risk."

The unspoken implication hung in the air between them: I can't allow you to put all of that at risk.

Laura felt a cold certainty settle over her. Boone was pulling away, creating distance between them. Whatever tender feelings had been growing between them were now overshadowed by his concerns about Jasper and the complications he brought. She couldn't blame him, not really. He had worked his entire life to build his reputation and his ranch. Why would he jeopardize that for a woman whose troubled past had followed her right to his doorstep?

"I understand," she said softly, turning to look out across the winter landscape. "And I wouldn't ask you to."

She felt rather than saw Boone's sharp glance, but he didn't respond immediately. When he did speak, his voice held a careful neutrality that told Laura more about his emotional withdrawal than any heated words could have.

"We'll need to consider our options," he said, as if they were discussing a business arrangement rather than the fragile beginnings of what Laura had hoped might be love. "If these men are truly looking for Jasper, and if they follow his trail to Lone Valley, it could create problems for everyone."

"Yes," Laura agreed, matching his neutral tone, though it cost her dearly. "I wouldn't want to bring danger to the town or to your ranch."

"My concern is for your safety as well," Boone added, almost as an afterthought. "If these men are as dangerous as Jasper claims, they might use you to get to him."

Laura hadn't considered that possibility, and the thought sent a chill through her that had nothing to do with the winter air. She'd been so focused on Jasper's immediate predicament that she hadn't fully processed the wider implications.

"Perhaps I should leave," she said, the words emerging before she'd fully formed the thought. "Go somewhere else, at least until this situation is resolved."

Boone's head turned sharply toward her, surprise evident in his features. "That's not what I was suggesting."

"Isn't it?" Laura challenged quietly. "You just said you couldn't allow Jasper's troubles to put your responsibilities at risk. If I stay, those troubles stay with me."

"Laura—" Boone began, but she cut him off.

"It's alright, Boone. I understand. You've been more than generous, taking me in, giving me work, allowing me to become part of your household. I can't expect you to extend that generosity to include my brother's problems as well."

Boone's jaw tightened, a muscle working beneath the skin. "That's not fair, and you know it. This isn't about generosity. It's about safety—yours included."

"And reputation," Laura added softly. "Your standing in the community. The ranch's good name. Those matter too, and they should."

Boone didn't deny it, which only confirmed Laura's suspicion that he was indeed concerned about how Jasper's presence—and by extension, her connection to him—might affect his position in Lone Valley.

"The community respects you," she continued when he remained silent. "They trust you. But a rancher harboring a man who's running from gambling debts and the men sent to collect them? That could change how people see you. How they see your father and your ranch? I wouldn't want to be the cause of that."

"So you'd just leave?" Boone asked, an edge entering his voice. "Walk away from everything you've started building here? From the people who care about you?"

From me, his eyes seemed to say, though his voice didn't form the words.

"If it protected those same people? Yes," Laura answered honestly. "I've started over before. I can do it again."

The ranch came into view as they crested a small rise, the house and outbuildings nestled in the valley below, smoke rising from the chimney against the winter sky. Laura felt a pang of longing so sharp it took her breath away. This place had become home to her in a way nowhere had since her parents' death. The thought of leaving it—leaving Boone—filled her with a grief almost physical in its intensity.

"Running away doesn't solve problems," Boone said, his voice gruff. "It just postpones them."

"Sometimes it's the only option left," Laura countered. "Sometimes staying would cause more harm than good."

They fell silent again as Boone guided the wagon down the slope toward the ranch. Laura could sense that he was wrestling with something, words, or feelings he wasn't ready to express. She waited, hoping against hope that he might offer some reassurance, some indication that he wasn't giving up on the fragile connection between them.

But when he finally spoke, his words were practical, distant. "Let's get through today. Tomorrow, you can speak with Jasper again. Perhaps after a night's reflection, he'll see reason."

The hope that had flickered briefly in Laura's chest guttered and died. Boone was retreating behind walls of practicality and caution, exactly as Zeb had warned he might. Whatever warmth had been growing between them was now overshadowed by doubt and concerns about Jasper and the complications he represented.

"Yes," she agreed, her voice empty of emotion. "Perhaps he will."

But they both knew, though neither said it aloud, that Jasper seeing reason was the least likely outcome of all.

Chapter 28

T he afternoon passed in a haze of routine tasks, each of them finding reasons to work apart. Laura threw herself into household chores—scrubbing floors that didn't need scrubbing, polishing silverware until it gleamed, kneading bread dough with such force that Zeb commented on her apparent determination to subdue it into submission.

Boone, for his part, remained outside long after the sun began its descent toward the mountains. Boone found work in the barn, the corral, anywhere but the house where Laura moved about like a ghost of her former self, quiet and withdrawn.

By evening, when they gathered around the supper table, the silence between them had hardened into something almost tangible. Zeb looked from his son to Laura and back again, his weathered face creased with concern.

"I take it the meeting with Jasper didn't go well," he observed as he passed the plate of biscuits.

Laura stared at her barely touched food. "Not particularly, no."

"He's in trouble," Boone elaborated when it became clear Laura wouldn't say more. "Gambling debts. Claims there are men after him who mean to collect one way or another."

Zeb's eyebrows rose. "Serious trouble, then."

"Yes," Laura confirmed softly. "And he wants me—us—to help him pay it off."

"Ah," Zeb said, understanding dawning in his eyes. "And did you agree to this?"

"No," Boone answered before Laura could speak. "No decisions were made. Laura plans to speak with him again tomorrow."

Laura felt a flare of irritation at Boone answering for her, but she suppressed it. What did it matter now? The distance between them was already widening with every passing hour.

"I see," Zeb said, glancing between them again. "And in the meantime, you two have decided that not speaking to each other is the best approach to the situation?"

Laura's cheeks flushed at the direct challenge. Across the table, she saw Boone's jaw tighten.

"We've spoken plenty," Boone said, a defensive note in his voice.

"Hmm," Zeb hummed skeptically. "Funny because from where I'm sitting, it looks like you're both retreating to opposite corners, waiting for the other to make the first move."

"It's complicated, Zeb," Laura murmured, discomfort making her push her food around her plate rather than meet his penetrating gaze.

"Most worthwhile things are," the older man observed mildly. "But complications don't resolve themselves through silence."

"There's nothing to resolve," Boone stated flatly. "Jasper's problems are his own making. Laura knows my thoughts on the matter."

"And Laura is sitting right here," she retorted, stung by his dismissive tone. "Capable of speaking for herself."

Boone's eyes met hers across the table, surprise flashing briefly in their depths before his expression closed again. "By all means, then. Speak."

The challenge hung in the air between them, daring her to articulate the complex tangle of emotions swirling inside her. Laura set down her fork, drawing a steadying breath.

"Jasper is my brother," she began, her voice growing stronger as she continued. "He's made terrible choices, and I won't pretend otherwise. But he's also the only family I have left in this world. I can't simply turn my back on him if his life is genuinely in danger."

"Even if helping him now only ensures he'll come back for more help later?" Boone challenged. "Even if it puts you—puts all of us—at risk?"

"I didn't say I would give him money," Laura clarified, frustration coloring her words. "I said I wouldn't turn my back on him. There might be other ways to help, solutions we haven't considered yet."

"Such as?" Boone's skepticism was evident in his tone.

Laura hesitated, then admitted, "I don't know yet. That's why I need time to think, to pray about it. But dismissing the problem outright isn't the answer, either."

"No one's suggesting dismissing it," Boone countered, leaning forward intently. "But we need to be clear-eyed about who Jasper is and what he's capable of. From what little you've told me, and what I saw today, he's manipulative, self-centered, and willing to use your bond to get what he wants, regardless of the cost to you."

The assessment was harsh but not inaccurate, which only made it sting more. "He wasn't always like that," Laura insisted, though the defense felt hollow even to her own ears.

"Maybe not," Boone conceded. "But he is now. And pretending otherwise won't help him or you."

Laura felt tears threatening again and blinked them back furiously. She wouldn't cry, not here, not now. "So what would you have me do? Abandon him? Tell him his life means nothing to me because he's made mistakes?"

"Of course not," Boone's voice softened fractionally. "But there's a world of difference between abandoning someone and enabling them. Between offering genuine help and allowing yourself to be manipulated by guilt and family obligation."

Zeb, who had been listening intently to their exchange, cleared his throat. "If I might offer an observation?"

Both Laura and Boone turned to him, perhaps grateful for the momentary interruption of their increasingly heated discussion.

"It seems to me," Zeb said carefully, "that you're both so focused on Jasper's problems that you're overlooking what's happening between the two of you."

Laura looked down at her plate, uncomfortable with the accuracy of his assessment. Across the table, she heard Boone shift in his chair but offer no denial.

"Since Jasper arrived, you've both been retreating," Zeb continued, his voice gentle but firm. "Pushing each other away, making assumptions about what the other is thinking or feeling rather than simply asking. That's no way to handle a crisis—or a relationship."

"We don't have a relationship," Boone stated flatly, the words like a blow to Laura's heart. "Not in the way you're implying."

Laura couldn't stop the small, audible intake of breath at his declaration. She kept her eyes fixed on her plate, not trusting herself to look up. Just days ago, they had ridden together across the ranch, sharing hopes and gentle touches that had suggested the beginnings of something meaningful. Now, with a few terse words, Boone had dismissed it all.

Zeb's eyebrows rose as he studied his son. "Is that so?" he asked mildly, though Laura detected a note of disappointment in his voice. "Seems to me that two people who care enough to argue this passionately have some kind of relationship, whether they're ready to name it or not."

"Pa, this isn't about—" Boone began, but Zeb raised a hand, cutting him off.

"Let me finish, son." The older man turned his gaze to Laura, who reluctantly met his eyes. "Laura, I understand your loyalty to your brother. Family bonds are powerful things, and they shouldn't be broken lightly. But loyalty doesn't mean allowing someone to drag you down with them."

"I know that," Laura said softly.

"Do you?" Zeb challenged gently. "Because from where I sit, it looks like you've spent years trying to save Jasper from himself, at great cost to your own happiness and well-being."

The truth of his words struck deep, and Laura found herself unable to offer a rebuttal.

"And you," Zeb continued, turning to Boone, "are so afraid of being hurt again that you're pushing away someone who matters to you at the first sign of complication. Eliza left you for gold and an easier life. Laura is facing a difficult situation with strength and integrity. They're not the same thing, son."

Boone's expression darkened. "This isn't about Eliza."

"Isn't it?" Zeb countered. "You've been different since Laura arrived—lighter, happier. I've seen the way you look at her when you think no one's watching. But now trouble's come knocking, and instead of standing together, you're both ready to walk away."

An uncomfortable silence fell over the table. Laura felt exposed, vulnerable, as if Zeb had laid bare feelings she'd barely acknowledged to herself.

"I'm not walking away," Boone finally said, his voice low. "I'm being practical. Jasper's trouble could bring danger to this ranch, to this family. I can't ignore that."

"No one's asking you to," Zeb replied. "Being cautious is wise. But building walls between yourself and Laura won't make the danger any less real. It'll just ensure you face it alone instead of together."

Laura looked up then, finding Boone's eyes on her. She glimpsed uncertainty in his gaze, a crack in his carefully constructed armor.

"I would rather not bring trouble to your door," she said quietly. "That was never my intention."

"Trouble has a way of finding us whether we invite it or not," Zeb observed. "The question is how we meet it when it comes."

Boone pushed back from the table, standing abruptly. "I need some air," he announced, avoiding Laura's gaze. Without another word, he strode from the room, the front door closing firmly behind him.

Laura sat frozen, the echo of his departure seeming to reverberate through her entire being. Part of her wanted to follow him, to force the conversation to its conclusion. But another part, the part that had learned to protect herself through years of disappointment, held her in place.

"He'll come around," Zeb said after a moment, his voice gentle. "Boone's got a good heart, but he can be as stubborn as a mule when he's afraid."

"Afraid?" Laura echoed, surprised. "Boone doesn't seem afraid of anything."

Zeb's smile was sad and knowing. "Everyone's afraid of something, Laura. For Boone, it's losing what he loves. After his mother died, after Eliza left... well, he decided it was easier not to risk his heart at all."

Laura absorbed this, thinking of Boone's guarded demeanor when she'd first arrived, how gradually he had begun to open up to her. "I understand that feeling," she admitted.

"I expect you do," Zeb agreed. "The difference is, you're still willing to try, despite your fears. Boone needs to remember how to do that, too."

"And if he can't?" Laura asked, voicing the fear that had been growing in her heart since their return from town.

Zeb reached across the table, patting her hand with his weathered one. "Then that's his loss, my dear. But I have faith in my son. He just needs time to sort through his thoughts."

Laura nodded, wishing she shared Zeb's confidence. "Thank you," she said, managing a small smile. "For understanding about Jasper, and for... everything."

"Family's not always about blood," Zeb reminded her, rising from the table. "Sometimes it's about who stands beside you when times get hard."

As he gathered the dishes, refusing her offer of help with a gentle shooing motion, Laura sat alone at the table, his words echoing in her mind. Family's not always about blood. The concept was foreign to her after years of Jasper insisting that blood was the only bond that truly mattered.

Yet here in this house, with Zeb's quiet wisdom and Boone's complicated care, she had begun to understand family differently. Even Matt, with his good-natured teasing and protective instincts, had become something like the brother she wished Jasper could be.

The thought of walking away from them all made her heart ache. But could she stay if her presence brought danger to their door? Could she build a life here, knowing Jasper might return again and again, bringing his troubles with him?

And what of Boone? His withdrawal hurt more than she wanted to admit. In just a few short weeks, he had become central to her thoughts, her hopes. The possibility that he might retreat permanently behind his walls of caution left her feeling hollow.

Laura rose from the table, needing movement, action, anything to quiet the tumult of her thoughts. She made her way to the front door, stepping out onto the porch. The night was clear and cold, stars scattered like diamond dust across the vast Montana sky. She wrapped her arms around herself, scanning the yard for any sign of Boone.

At first, she saw nothing, but then movement near the barn caught her eye. Boone stood leaning against the corral fence, his posture rigid even from this distance. She watched him for a moment, debating whether to approach or retreat.

In the end, courage won out over caution. Drawing her shawl more tightly around her shoulders, Laura stepped off the porch and made her way toward him, her footsteps crunching softly on the frozen ground.

Boone turned at the sound, his expression unreadable in the moonlight. He didn't speak as she approached, but he didn't walk away either. Laura took that as permission to join him.

They stood in silence for several minutes, side by side at the fence, looking out over the sleeping ranch. Steam rose from the horses' nostrils as they dozed in the corral, peaceful despite the cold.

"Your father is a wise man," Laura finally said, her voice soft in the night stillness.

Boone's short laugh held little humor. "He has his moments."

Another silence stretched between them, less comfortable than before. Laura could feel words building inside her, pressing against her ribs like physical things.

"I'm sorry," she said eventually. "For bringing this trouble to you. To your ranch."

Boone sighed, the sound weary and frustrated. "You didn't bring anything, Laura. Jasper did."

"But I'm connected to him," she pointed out. "As long as I'm here, that connection remains."

Boone turned to face her then, his expression serious in the pale moonlight. "Is that why you suggested leaving? Because you think you're somehow responsible for Jasper's actions?"

Laura wrapped her arms more tightly around herself. "Partly," she admitted. "And partly because I saw how quickly things changed between us when Jasper arrived. How quickly you..." She trailed off, not wanting to sound accusatory.

"How quickly I pulled away," Boone finished for her, his voice low. "You're right. I did."

The admission surprised her. She had expected denial, perhaps even anger. His honesty left her momentarily speechless.

"I've spent two years rebuilding my life after Eliza left," Boone continued after a moment. "Making this ranch successful, earning back the community's trust after the scandal of a broken engagement. When I saw how easily Jasper's arrival threatened all of that..." He shook his head. "It was easier to retreat than to face the possibility of losing everything again."

"I understand," Laura said softly. "Your ranch, your reputation—they matter. They should matter."

"They do," Boone agreed, turning to face her fully. "But today, watching you with Jasper, seeing how he manipulated you, how he tried to use our... connection to his advantage... I realized something."

"What?" Laura asked, hardly daring to breathe.

"That I care more about your welfare than I do about gossip or reputation," Boone admitted. "When he grabbed your wrist, when I saw that flash of fear in your eyes..." His expression hardened. "I wanted to protect you, not from what others might think, but from him. From the pain he causes you."

A lump formed in Laura's throat. "Boone—"

"Let me finish," he said gently. "I was wrong earlier, at supper. We do have a relationship. I don't know exactly what to call it yet, but it's there, growing between us. And I've been fighting it because I'm afraid."

"Of what?" Laura whispered.

"Of caring for someone who might leave," he admitted, his voice rough with emotion. "Of opening myself up only to be hurt again. Of trusting and being betrayed."

Laura's heart ached at the vulnerability in his admission. "I understand fear," she said. "I've spent years being afraid—of Jasper's next outburst, of never finding stability, of trusting the wrong person. But since coming here..." She paused, gathering her courage. "Since meeting you, I've started to believe that maybe some things are worth the risk."

Boone's eyes searched hers in the moonlight. "Even with all the complications? Jasper's troubles, the town's gossip, my own stubborn fears?"

A small smile curved Laura's lips. "Especially with those. Your father was right—worthwhile things are rarely simple."

Boone's hand reached for hers, his calloused fingers warm against her skin. "I can't promise I won't struggle with this. With Jasper, with opening up, with all of it."

"I don't need promises," Laura replied, her fingers curling around his. "I just need to know we're facing these challenges together instead of pulling apart."

Boone's expression softened, and for the first time since their return from town, Laura saw a glimmer of the warmth that had been growing between them. "Together, then," he agreed. "Starting with Jasper."

"We need a plan," Laura acknowledged. "One that doesn't involve simply giving him money."

"Yes," Boone nodded. "And tomorrow, we'll figure one out. But tonight..." He hesitated, then seemed to make a decision. Gently, he drew her closer, his arm encircling her waist. "Tonight, I just want to stand here under these stars with you and remember what matters."

Laura leaned into his embrace, feeling some of the day's tension drain from her body. Against all odds, in the midst of complication and trouble, they had found their way back to each other. Whatever came next—Jasper, his gambling debts, the town's gossip—they would face it together.

For now, that was enough.

Chapter 29

Laura woke before dawn, her mind already racing with thoughts of the day ahead. She slipped quietly from her bed, careful not to wake anyone, as she made her way to the kitchen. The house was silent, save for the occasional creak of the winter-chilled timbers contracting in the night air.

She stoked the banked fire in the stove and set water to boil, finding comfort in the familiar routine. As she measured coffee into the pot, her conversation with Boone from the previous night replayed in her mind. The memory of his arm around her waist, the gentle pressure of his body next to hers as they stood beneath the stars, brought both warmth and uncertainty. They had taken a step forward, acknowledging whatever was growing between them, but Jasper's presence in Lone Valley still cast a long shadow over their fragile understanding.

"You're up early."

Laura turned to find Zeb in the doorway, his weathered face creased with a gentle smile.

"Couldn't sleep," she admitted, reaching for another cup. "Coffee?"

"Never been known to refuse," he said, easing himself into a chair at the table. "Thinking about your brother?"

Laura nodded as she poured the steaming liquid into two cups. "We're going back to town today. I need to talk to him again, try to figure out a solution that doesn't involve giving him money or abandoning him entirely."

"Not an easy balance to find," Zeb observed, accepting the cup she offered with a nod of thanks.

"No," Laura agreed, settling across from him. "It never has been with Jasper."

They sat in companionable silence for a moment, the kitchen gradually brightening with pre-dawn light.

"I'm going to tell you a little more about my brother?" Zeb asked suddenly as his fingers traced the rim of his cup, his eyes distant with memory. "Jedidiah was four years younger than me. Bright as a new penny and twice as quick. Could charm the birds from the trees when he set his mind to it."

Laura recognized the familiar mixture of love and resignation in Zeb's voice—the same feelings that surfaced whenever she spoke of Jasper.

"What happened to him?" she asked.

"Same story you've lived, I expect," Zeb said. "The drinking started after his wife died in childbirth. Just a drink or two at first, to help him sleep. Then more, to help him forget. Before long, he couldn't get through a day without it."

He paused, taking a sip of his coffee before continuing. "I tried everything—reasoning with him, threatening him, offering him work here on the ranch where I could keep an eye on him. Nothing took.

He'd make promises, stay sober a week, maybe two, then be right back at it."

"How did you handle it?" Laura asked, desperate for any wisdom that might help her navigate her own situation.

Zeb's smile held a world of sadness. "Poorly, at first. Covered for him, paid his debts, made excuses to anyone who'd listen. Near bankrupted this ranch doing it, too."

"But you stopped?"

"Had to," Zeb nodded. "Mary was the one who made me see I wasn't helping him. I was just making it easier for him to keep destroying himself."

Laura absorbed this, seeing the parallels in her own situation with painful clarity. "What did you do?"

"Told him I loved him, but wouldn't contribute to his self-destruction anymore. Said he was welcome at this ranch anytime he was sober, but I wouldn't give him money, wouldn't pay his debts, wouldn't lie for him." Zeb's eyes met hers directly. "Hardest thing I ever did, watching him walk away, knowing he might not survive on his own."

Laura felt tears prick behind her eyes. "Do you regret setting those boundaries? Letting him go?"

"Every day and never," Zeb answered with the paradoxical wisdom of age. "I regret that I couldn't save him. But I don't regret refusing to help destroy him. And I don't regret protecting my family from the chaos he brought with him."

The kitchen had filled with morning light as they talked, the sun now clearing the eastern mountains. Laura heard movement from the other parts of the house—Boone rising, most likely.

"I don't know if I have your strength," she admitted.

Zeb reached across the table, patting her hand. "Strength isn't something you have or don't have, Laura. It's something you find when you need it, one decision at a time."

The sound of boots in the hallway announced Boone's approach. He appeared in the doorway, hair still damp from washing, his expression softening when he saw Laura.

"Good morning," he said, his gaze lingering on her face with a warmth that made her pulse quicken despite her worries. "You're up early."

"Couldn't sleep," Laura replied, rising to pour him coffee. "Your father has been keeping me company."

"Telling tales, no doubt," Boone said, accepting the cup with a grateful nod.

"Just sharing some family history," Zeb said mildly. "Thought it might be relevant to the day's challenges."

Boone's expression sobered as he took a seat. "Speaking of which, what time do you want to head into town?"

"After breakfast, I think," Laura answered. "I'd like to get there before Jasper has a chance to—" She hesitated, unwilling to explicitly say "start drinking."

"Before he gets restless," Boone supplied diplomatically. "Makes sense."

"I've been thinking about what to tell him," Laura continued, returning to her seat. "About how to help without enabling."

"And?" Boone prompted, his tone gentler than it had been the previous day when discussing Jasper.

Laura wrapped her hands around her coffee cup, drawing strength from its warmth. "I won't give him money for the gambling debts. That would only reinforce that I'll bail him out when he makes bad decisions."

"He won't like that," Boone observed.

"No," Laura agreed. "But I've been bailing him out for years, and he's only gotten worse."

Zeb nodded approvingly. "What will you offer instead?"

Laura took a deep breath. "A place to stay—not here," she added quickly, seeing Boone tense, "but somewhere he can be safe while he sobers up. And help finding honest work, if he's willing to take it."

"And if he refuses?" Boone asked, though his tone suggested he already knew the answer.

"Then I'll have to let him make that choice," Laura said, the words difficult but necessary. "I can't force him to accept help he doesn't want."

The courage in her quiet declaration wasn't lost on either man. Boone's eyes reflected a mixture of respect and concern, while Zeb's held understanding, born of having walked a similar path.

"It won't be easy," Boone warned. "From what I saw yesterday, Jasper's not the type to accept limitations gracefully."

"I know," Laura acknowledged. "But I have to try. For him and for myself."

Boone reached across the table, covering her hand with his.

The simple touch and reassurance eased something tight in Laura's chest. After their strained interactions the previous day, Boone's support meant more than she could express.

Zeb cleared his throat. "Well, if you two are heading to town after breakfast, I'd best start cooking. Can't face the day's battles on an empty stomach."

As Zeb busied himself at the stove, Boone kept his hand on Laura's, his thumb tracing small circles on her skin. The gesture was both comforting and distracting, a tangible reminder of the tentative understanding they had reached the night before.

"Are you sure about this?" he asked.

Laura nodded. "I can't keep doing what I've always done and expect different results. Jasper needs to face the consequences of his choices if he's ever going to change."

"And if these men really are looking for him?" Boone pressed. "If his life is genuinely in danger?"

"Then we'll figure something out," Laura said, determination in her voice. "Something that doesn't involve paying his debts or leaving him to face them alone. There has to be a middle path."

Boone's expression suggested he wasn't entirely convinced, but he nodded. "We'll find it together."

As they ate breakfast, the conversation shifted to more practical matters—which horses to take, when they expected to return, what needed attention on the ranch in their absence. Laura was grateful for the normalcy of these discussions, the sense that despite the complications Jasper had brought, life here continued.

After breakfast, as Laura was pulling on her coat, Zeb pressed something into her hand. She looked down to find a small, worn Bible.

"Mary's," he explained softly. "She used to say it gave her courage when she needed it most. Thought you might want it today."

Laura's throat tightened with emotion. The gift represented more than just a book—it was acceptance, inclusion, a tangible sign that Zeb considered her part of their family despite the trouble her blood relative had brought to their door.

"I'll take good care of it," she promised, slipping it into her pocket.

Zeb nodded, patting her shoulder before turning to Boone. "And you, son—remember that level heads prevail where hot ones fail."

Boone gave his father a wry smile. "Now you sound like Reverend Tanner."

"Man occasionally speaks sense, even if he takes the long way round to it," Zeb replied with a chuckle. "Be careful, both of you."

The journey to town passed more comfortably than their tense ride the previous day. Laura and Boone spoke of small things—the hawk circling overhead, the fresh dusting of snow on the distant peaks, plans to expand pasture fences. Beneath these mundane topics ran a current of mutual understanding. Today would be difficult, but they would face it together.

As they entered Lone Valley, Laura noticed curious glances from townspeople going about their morning business. News of Jasper's dramatic arrival had clearly spread, and she felt the weight of speculation in each passing look. Boone seemed to sense her discomfort, moving his horse closer to hers in a silent show of support.

"Ignore them," he said quietly. "Small towns run on gossip, but they forget just as quickly when something new comes along."

Laura managed a small smile. "Speaking from experience?"

"Unfortunately," Boone admitted. "After Eliza left, I couldn't walk down this street without feeling every eye on me, wondering why I wasn't good enough to keep her here."

The candid admission surprised Laura. Boone rarely spoke of Eliza or the pain her departure had caused him.

"That must have been difficult," she said.

Boone shrugged, though the casual gesture didn't disguise the lingering hurt in his eyes. "It was. But eventually, someone's cow got loose in Reverend Tanner's garden, and suddenly my romantic disappointment wasn't nearly as interesting as watching the good reverend chase a Holstein through his prized rosebushes."

The image startled a laugh from Laura, easing some of the tension that had been building as they approached Louella's boarding house.

Louella herself was sweeping the front steps when they arrived, her face brightening at the sight of them.

"Good morning!" she called, setting her broom aside. "I was hoping you'd be by early. Your brother's been up and pacing since dawn, Laura. Asked three times already if I'd seen you."

"Has he been..." Laura hesitated.

"Sober?" Louella supplied with characteristic directness. "So far as I can tell. Though he didn't touch the breakfast I sent up, which isn't a good sign for a man his age. Too thin by half, if you ask me."

Laura exchanged a glance with Boone as they dismounted. Jasper's refusal to eat was a familiar warning sign—usually an indication that he was too anxious or too focused on his next drink to bother with food.

"Is he in his room?" Boone asked, securing their horses to the hitching post.

"Was when I checked thirty minutes ago," Louella confirmed. "Room three, same as yesterday. I'll bring up some coffee in a bit."

Laura thanked her, then took a deep breath, steeling herself for the confrontation ahead. As if sensing her need for reassurance, Boone's hand found the small of her back, the light pressure a silent reminder that she wasn't alone.

They climbed the stairs in silence, Laura's heart pounding harder with each step. Outside room three, she hesitated, her hand raised to knock. Doubt assailed her again. Would Jasper accept her terms? Or would he react with the volatile anger she had seen so many times before?

"I'm right here," Boone murmured, echoing his words from the previous day, but with a warmth that had been missing then.

Laura nodded gratefully and knocked. Seconds stretched into a minute with no response. She knocked again, louder this time.

"Jasper?" she called. "It's Laura."

Silence greeted her, broken only by the muffled sounds of the boarding house—a door closing somewhere down the hall, voices from the dining room below. Uneasiness prickled along Laura's spine.

"Jasper, open the door," she tried again. "We need to talk."

When no answer came, Boone stepped forward. "Stand back," he instructed quietly. At Laura's nod, he tested the door handle, finding it unlocked. He pushed the door open slowly, one hand moving instinctively to position himself between Laura and whatever awaited them inside.

The room was empty. The bed was unmade, as it had been the day before, but Jasper's few belongings were gone. The only evidence of his presence was an empty whiskey bottle on the floor and a folded piece of paper on the pillow.

"He's gone," Laura whispered, a confusing mixture of relief and concern washing over her.

Boone moved cautiously into the room, confirming, "Completely gone."

Laura approached the bed, picking up the folded paper with trembling fingers. Her name was scrawled across the front in Jasper's untidy hand. She unfolded it, Boone coming to stand beside her as she read aloud:

Laura,

By the time you read this, I'll be gone. Don't bother looking for me   I won't be found unless I want to be. I came to ask for your help, but I can see your rancher has turned you against me. Family used to mean something to you. Remember when it was you and me against the world? Seems you've forgotten that since finding your cozy new life.

McCready's men won't stop looking for me, and the debt won't disappear on its own. I've got a plan to get the money, don't worry about that. You've made your choice, and now I'm making mine. Don't come after me. I'll contact you when I've sorted this mess out.

Your brother (since you seem to need reminding),
Jasper

Laura's hand fell to her side, the letter clutched tightly in her fingers. The familiar mix of guilt, anger, and concern that Jasper always managed to evoke swirled within her.

"He's trying to manipulate you," Boone observed quietly. "Making you feel guilty for not giving him what he wanted."

"I know," Laura said, surprised by the steadiness in her voice. "It's his favorite tactic when he doesn't get his way."

"Any idea what he meant by having a plan to get the money?" Boone asked, concern evident in his tone.

Laura shook her head. "Nothing good, I'm sure. Jasper's 'plans' usually involve gambling, drinking, or both."

"I don't like this," Boone muttered, moving to the window to scan the street below. "If McCready's men really are after him..."

"Then Jasper has put himself in more danger by running," Laura finished. "And potentially brought that danger closer to Lone Valley."

Boone turned back to her, his expression grave. "We need to tell Sheriff Hayes. If there are dangerous men headed this way, he should be prepared."

Laura nodded, still clutching Jasper's letter. "Yes, of course."

They found Louella at the bottom of the stairs, coffee tray in hand. Her expression fell as she took in their grim faces.

"He's gone, isn't he?" she guessed.

Boone nodded.

Louella shook her head. "Jenny Burnham mentioned seeing a stranger heading east out of town when she was opening the post office. Said he looked like he was in a hurry."

"East?" Laura echoed, trying to make sense of this. "There's nothing much east of here except other small towns..."

"The train station at Elk Ridge," Boone concluded.

Laura's mind raced, trying to understand Jasper's plan. The train could take him anywhere—farther east to more populated towns, or west toward the coast. Had he truly given up on getting money from her? Or was this another of his dramatic gestures, designed to make her feel guilty enough to come after him?

"Sheriff Hayes first," Boone reminded her gently, seeing her confusion. "Then we can decide what we should do."

Chapter 30

The sheriff's office was a small building on the far end of the main street, distinguished only by the weathered sign hanging over its door. As they approached, Laura saw a tall man with iron-gray hair and a neatly trimmed mustache sweeping the boardwalk in front of the entrance.

He looked up at their approach, keen eyes taking in Boone's grim expression and Laura's tense posture. "Boone," he greeted, setting his broom aside. "Miss Hartley, isn't it? Heard you were staying out at Callahan Ranch."

"Sheriff Hayes," Boone nodded. "We need to speak with you. It's important."

The sheriff gestured them inside without further questions. His office was spare but neat—a desk with two chairs before it, a potbellied stove in one corner, and a row of three cells along the back wall, all currently empty.

"What brings you to me on this fine morning?" Hayes asked, settling behind his desk and motioning for them to take the chairs opposite.

Boone glanced at Laura, silently asking if she wanted to explain. She nodded, drawing a steadying breath.

"My brother, Jasper Hartley, arrived in Lone Valley yesterday," she began. "He came looking for me, but he also came running from trouble back in Elk Ridge."

Sheriff Hayes leaned forward, his expression turning serious. "What kind of trouble?"

"Gambling debts," Laura explained, embarrassment heating her cheeks despite her resolve to be forthright. "He claims there are men looking for him—dangerous men sent by someone named McCready, who runs card games in Elk Ridge."

"Lyle McCready?" The sheriff's eyebrows rose. "He's got quite a reputation. Not a man to cross, especially when money's involved."

"You know of him?" Boone asked sharply.

Hayes nodded, his expression grim. "By reputation only. He operates all through this territory—illegal gambling, some say worse. If your brother owes him money, Miss Hartley, then his concerns about being followed aren't exaggerated."

Laura felt a chill run through her at the confirmation. She had hoped, in some small corner of her heart, that Jasper might be exaggerating the danger to gain her sympathy.

"Jasper left sometime this morning," she continued, handing the sheriff his letter. "We think he might be headed for the train station at Elk Ridge."

Sheriff Hayes read the letter quickly, his frown deepening. "Says here he has a plan to get the money. Any idea what that might entail?"

Laura shook her head. "Nothing specific. But Jasper's 'plans' have never been particularly law-abiding."

"I see," the sheriff said, returning the letter. "And you're concerned these men might follow him to Lone Valley?"

"Yes," Boone confirmed. "If they tracked him from Elk Ridge, they could easily follow his trail here. We wanted you to be aware of the potential danger."

Sheriff Hayes stood, moving to a map pinned to the wall. "Elk Ridge is the nearest train stop, but there's also Bailey Junction to the north and Fort Collins much farther south. If he's smart, he'll buy a ticket to one place and get off somewhere else entirely."

"If he's smart," Laura echoed, not bothering to hide her doubt. Jasper's decisions were rarely guided by intelligence, especially when he was desperate.

"How much does he owe this McCready?" Hayes asked, turning back to them.

Laura named the sum that Jasper had mentioned. The sheriff let out a low whistle.

"That's a significant amount," he observed. "Enough that Mc-Cready won't simply write it off. And if he's sent men after your brother, they'll be professionals—not the type to give up easily."

"What would you advise?" Boone asked, his hand finding Laura's in a gesture of support that didn't go unnoticed by the sheriff's keen eyes.

Hayes considered for a moment. "I'll send telegrams to the sheriffs in Elk Ridge, Fort Collins, and Bailey Junction, alerting them to watch for your brother and any men who might be following him. Beyond that, I'll keep an eye out for strangers in town. Lone Valley's small enough that newcomers stand out."

"And if they come here looking for Jasper?" Laura pressed.

"Then I'll handle them," Hayes stated with quiet authority. "But Miss Hartley, you should know—men like the ones McCready employs don't typically care about legal niceties. If they believe you know where your brother is, they might not be gentle in their questioning."

The warning sent another shiver through Laura. Boone's grip on her hand tightened.

"She won't be alone," he said firmly. "And the ranch isn't an easy target."

Sheriff Hayes nodded, acknowledging Boone's implied promise of protection. "Still, take precautions. Both of you. Don't travel alone. Keep your doors locked at night, and report any strangers immediately."

They thanked the sheriff for his advice and headed back into the street. The morning had advanced while they were inside, the town now bustling with its usual activities. Laura felt exposed suddenly, scanning each unfamiliar face with new wariness.

"We should head back to the ranch," Boone suggested, his voice low. "We can stop at the general store for supplies on the way, but I don't want to linger in town longer than necessary."

Laura nodded her agreement, but as they turned toward where they had left their horses, a familiar voice called Boone's name. They turned to see Reverend Tanner approaching, his kind face creased with concern.

"Boone, Miss Hartley," he greeted them. "I hoped I might catch you in town today."

"Reverend," Boone acknowledged with a nod. "Is everything alright?"

"That's what I was going to ask you," the reverend replied. "Word travels fast in Lone Valley, as you know. I heard about your brother's arrival, Miss Hartley, and his... colorful introduction to our town."

Laura's cheeks warmed with embarrassment. "I apologize for any disruption he caused, Reverend."

Tanner waved away her apology. "No need for that. We all have family members who challenge us." His eyes twinkled briefly. "You should hear about my brother-in-law sometime—the man once tried to sell my sister's cow while she was milking it."

The absurd image startled a small laugh from Laura despite her worries. Reverend Tanner had a gift for putting people at ease.

"I actually came to offer my help," the reverend continued, his tone turning more serious. "Family troubles can be a heavy burden to carry alone. And sometimes, an outside perspective can provide solutions we might not see ourselves."

Boone glanced at Laura, clearly leaving the decision to her whether to share more with the reverend. She hesitated only briefly before explaining about Jasper's departure and the potential danger his gambling debts had created.

Reverend Tanner listened without interruption, his expression thoughtful. When she finished, he nodded slowly.

"A difficult situation, to be sure," he acknowledged. "And one that requires wisdom beyond what any of us might possess alone."

"We've already spoken with Sheriff Hayes," Boone said. "He's taking precautions."

"Good, good," the reverend agreed. "Practical measures are important. But I was thinking of spiritual guidance as well." He turned his kind eyes to Laura. "Your brother is lost in more ways than one, Miss Hartley. His soul needs healing as much as his body needs protection."

Laura had never thought of Jasper's problems in such terms before. His drinking, his gambling, his manipulative behavior—she had viewed them as character flaws, bad habits, signs of weakness. But the reverend's framing of them as spiritual ailments offered a different perspective.

"What can I do?" she asked softly. "He won't listen to me. He won't accept help unless it's exactly what he wants, on his terms."

"Then we pray," Reverend Tanner said simply. "We pray for his protection, yes, but also for his enlightenment. For him to reach the end of himself and find God waiting there."

"Like the prodigal son," Laura murmured, remembering the parable.

"Exactly so," the reverend smiled. "Sometimes a person needs to hit bottom before they can look up. But in the meantime, we can pray, and we can be ready to welcome him home when he's ready to return."

The words echoed Zeb's earlier advice about his own brother. Both men had recognized what Laura was only beginning to understand—that sometimes love meant letting go, allowing the other person to face the consequences of their choices while remaining ready to help when they were truly ready to change.

"Thank you, Reverend," she said sincerely. "I would appreciate your prayers. For Jasper and... for me as well."

"Of course, my dear," he assured her. "And remember, the church is always open if you need a quiet place to gather your thoughts or seek God's guidance."

As they took their leave of the reverend, Laura felt a curious lightening of her spirit despite the circumstances. The burden of Jasper's problems hadn't disappeared, but somehow it felt more manageable now, shared as it was among people who genuinely cared—not just for her, but for Jasper's welfare as well.

"You're very fortunate in your friends here," she observed to Boone as they mounted their horses.

Boone's gaze swept the town—from the sheriff's office to the church steeple, from the general store where Jude Miller was arranging his display to Louella's boarding house where she stood chatting with a customer on the porch.

"We are," he agreed, the deliberate inclusion of Laura in that "we," not lost on her. "For all its faults and gossip, Lone Valley takes care of its own."

"And am I one of 'its own'?" Laura asked, the question escaping before she could reconsider it.

Boone's eyes met hers, warm and certain. "You are to me."

Chapter 31

Outside Miller's General Store, Laura noticed two unfamiliar men lounging against the opposite boardwalk. Something about their posture—too casual, too observant—sent a prickle of unease down her spine.

"Boone," she murmured, nodding subtly in their direction.

He followed her gaze, his expression hardening slightly. "I see them." His hand came to rest at the small of her back as they entered the store, a protective gesture that wasn't lost on Laura.

The bell jingled as they stepped inside, and Jude Miller looked up from where he was arranging a display of canned goods.

"Well, if it isn't Boone Callahan and Miss Hartley!" he exclaimed with characteristic enthusiasm. "Just the folks I was hoping to see today."

"Morning, Jude," Boone greeted, his posture relaxing slightly in the familiar environment. "We need a few supplies."

"Happy to help," Jude replied, but his eyes darted to Laura with barely concealed curiosity. "Heard your brother made quite an entrance yesterday, Miss Hartley."

Laura stiffened, feeling Boone tense beside her. News traveled fast indeed in Lone Valley.

"My brother was passing through," she said, keeping her voice even. "He's moved on now."

Jude's eyebrows rose. "Already? Well, that was a short visit."

"We need coffee, sugar, and flour," Boone interjected, his tone making it clear the subject of Jasper was closed.

Jude took the hint, moving behind the counter. "Of course, of course. Just got a fresh shipment yesterday." As he gathered their items, he continued with his usual chatter. "Did you hear about the Widow Abernathy? Found a whole family of raccoons living in her attic. Been there all winter, apparently. Said she thought it was ghosts making those scratching noises at night."

Laura found herself smiling despite her worries. Jude's gossip was harmless, focused on the small dramas of daily life rather than malicious speculation.

"Must have given her quite a fright," she commented.

"Oh, she was beside herself," Jude confirmed, weighing out the sugar. "Though not half as upset as those raccoons when Elijah Edwards and I smoked them out. Never seen a man move so fast as when that mama raccoon took exception to being evicted."

Boone chuckled, the sound warming Laura's heart. "I imagine so. Elijah's many things, but quick on his feet isn't one of them."

As Jude wrapped their purchases in brown paper, the bell above the door jingled again. Laura turned to see the two men she'd noticed earlier entering the store. Up close, they looked even more out of place—city clothes that had seen better days, unshaven faces, and eyes that moved too quickly around the space, assessing rather than browsing.

"Afternoon, gentlemen," Jude called, his salesman's instinct overriding any wariness. "Something I can help you find?"

The taller of the two men stepped forward, a tight smile not reaching his eyes. "Just passing through. Need some supplies for the road."

His voice carried an eastern accent, at odds with his rough appearance. As he moved closer to the counter, Laura felt Boone shift slightly, positioning himself between her and the newcomers.

"Where you headed?" Jude asked, unable to resist prying.

"East," the man replied without elaboration. His companion remained by the door, his stance casual, but his attention fixed on Boone and Laura.

"Plenty of folks passing through lately," Jude observed, his gaze flickering between the strangers and Laura. "Must be something in the air."

Laura could have kicked him for the unsubtle reference. The tall stranger's eyes narrowed, focusing more intently on her face.

"That so?" he asked. "Any interesting travelers come this way recently?"

Boone's hand found Laura's elbow, a gentle pressure urging her toward the door. "We should be heading back, Laura. Pa will be expecting us."

The second man shifted his position, blocking their path to the exit. "No hurry, friend. We're all just having a friendly conversation."

Tension crackled in the air. Laura felt her heart rate accelerate, a familiar fear taking hold—not for herself, but for what might happen if the situation escalated.

"Excuse us," Boone said, his voice carrying the quiet authority she had come to associate with him. "We have a long ride ahead."

The man by the door didn't move. "You folks live around here?"

"They're from the Callahan Ranch," Jude supplied helpfully, oblivious to the undercurrents. "Biggest cattle operation in the valley. Boone here runs it with his pa."

Laura could have strangled the storekeeper for his loose tongue.

The tall man approached, studying Laura more openly now. "And you, miss? You from around these parts too?"

Before she could answer, the door opened again, this time admitting Sheriff Hayes. The atmosphere in the store shifted immediately, the two strangers adopting more relaxed postures.

"Afternoon, Jude," Hayes greeted, nodding to Boone and Laura before turning his attention to the newcomers. "Don't believe we've met, gentlemen. Sheriff Thomas Hayes."

The tall man tipped his hat with forced casualness. "Just passing through, Sheriff. Stopping for supplies."

"Headed east, they say," Jude added.

Hayes nodded slowly. "East, is it? Unusual direction this time of year. Most folks head west for the milder weather."

"We go where the work is," the second man replied, his hand drifting toward his coat in a movement that made Laura tense.

Hayes noticed it too, his own hand shifting subtly toward his holster. "What line of work brings you to Lone Valley?"

"Collections," the tall man answered after a beat of hesitation. "We retrieve... outstanding debts for our employer."

The sheriff's eyes hardened. "That so? Sounds like interesting work. Your employer have a name?"

Another pause. "McCready. Lyle McCready."

Laura's blood ran cold. Boone's grip on her elbow tightened almost painfully.

"Well now," Hayes said, his tone deceptively casual, "that is interesting. I've heard that name before. Just this morning, in fact."

The tall man's gaze darted to Laura, a calculating look that confirmed her worst fears. They knew who she was, or at least suspected. They had followed Jasper's trail to Lone Valley, as Sheriff Hayes had predicted.

"Perhaps we should continue this conversation at my office," Hayes suggested, though his tone made it clear it wasn't a suggestion at all.

"No need for that, Sheriff," the tall man replied, his smile tight. "We're just passing through, like I said. No trouble here."

"I'll be the judge of that," Hayes countered. "And I'd feel a lot more comfortable discussing your... business... somewhere less public."

The tension in the store was thick enough to cut with a knife. Laura hardly dared breathe, sensing the precarious balance that might tip at any moment into violence.

Finally, the tall man nodded. "Lead the way, Sheriff. Always happy to cooperate with the law."

His companion looked less convinced, but followed his lead. As they moved toward the door, the tall man paused beside Laura.

"Interesting town you've got here, miss," he said quietly. "Might have to stay awhile, get better acquainted."

The threat in his words was unmistakable. Before Boone could react, Sheriff Hayes stepped between them.

"This way, gentlemen," he said firmly. "Miss Hartley, Boone—I suggest you finish your business and head on home."

As the sheriff escorted the two men from the store, Laura felt her knees weaken with relief and dread. Boone's arm came around her waist, steadying her.

"They know," she whispered, turning to face him. "They know who I am."

"They suspect," Boone corrected, though his expression remained grim. "But they don't know where Jasper is. Neither do we."

Jude was staring after the strangers, his usual chatter silenced by the encounter. "Friends of your brother?" he asked Laura, uncharacteristic concern in his voice.

"No," she replied firmly. "Not friends at all."

"We need to get back to the ranch," Boone said, gathering their packages. "Now, Jude, if anyone asks about Miss Hartley or where she might be staying—"

"I never saw her," Jude finished, surprising Laura with his quick understanding. "Never met the lady. Wouldn't know her from Eve."

Boone nodded, satisfaction in his eyes. "Good man."

They left the store quickly. Laura's mind raced as they rode out of town, scanning the road ahead and behind for any sign of pursuit.

Chapter 32

Zeb was splitting wood in the yard when Boone and Laura arrived, and he lowered his axe with a concerned frown as they dismounted.

"You two look like you've seen ghosts," he observed, wiping his brow with a kerchief. "What happened in town?"

Boone nodded for Laura to go ahead. "I'll take care of the horses and wagon. Tell Pa what happened."

As Laura explained the encounter in the general store to Zeb, his weathered face grew increasingly grave. By the time Boone joined them, Zeb was pacing the porch with agitation.

"McCready's men," he muttered, shaking his head. "Here in Lone Valley. Never thought I'd see the day."

"You know of him?" Laura asked, surprised.

"By reputation only," Zeb assured her. "But it's enough. Man's as cold-blooded as they come, from what I hear. Started as a small-time gambler in Kansas City, worked his way west setting up operations in every town big enough to have a saloon."

"Sheriff Hayes is holding the men for now," Boone said, "but he can't keep them indefinitely without cause."

"And when he releases them?" Laura asked the question that had been weighing on her since they left town.

Boone and Zeb exchanged a look that spoke volumes.

"They'll come looking," Zeb confirmed what she already knew. "For Jasper first, and for you if they think you know where he is."

Laura sank onto the porch step, the reality of their situation hitting her anew. "I've brought this danger to your door. To your home."

Zeb surprised her by chuckling, the sound incongruous with the tense atmosphere. "Wouldn't be the first time the Callahan Ranch has faced trouble, girl. Won't be the last, either. We don't scare easily."

"Pa's right," Boone agreed, though his expression remained serious. "But we do need to be prepared. I'll ride over to the north pasture and bring Matt back. Better to have another man here, just in case."

"I'll check the rifles," Zeb said, turning toward the house. "Make sure they're clean and loaded."

Laura stood, desperate to contribute something besides the problem itself. "I'll prepare supper. You'll all need to eat."

Boone caught her hand as she moved toward the door. "Laura."

She turned back, finding his eyes intent on hers.

"Together," he said.

She squeezed his hand, drawing strength from his steady confidence.

"Together," she echoed.

He held her gaze a moment longer, before releasing her hand and striding toward the barn to saddle a fresh horse.

Inside, Laura threw herself into cooking, finding comfort in the familiar routine. She prepared a hearty stew with vegetables from the root cellar and beef from their stores, and mixed dough for biscuits to accompany it. The physical activity helped calm her racing thoughts, channeling her anxiety into something productive.

She was pulling the golden biscuits from the oven when she heard riders in the yard. Her heart leapt to her throat before she recognized Matt's voice mingling with Boone's. Relief washed over her, followed quickly by guilt at the reason for his hasty return to the ranch house.

The kitchen door opened, and Matt entered, stomping snow from his boots. "Evening, Miss Laura," he greeted, removing his hat. "Heard we might have some unwelcome visitors."

Laura smiled weakly. "I'm afraid so. I'm sorry to pull you away from your work."

Matt waved off her apology. "Was getting tired of mending fences, anyway. Besides," he added with a grin that didn't quite hide his seriousness, "always did prefer human targets to fence posts."

"Matt," Boone admonished as he entered behind his ranch hand, though Laura caught the hint of a smile in his eyes.

"Just lightening the mood, boss," Matt replied unrepentantly. He sniffed the air appreciatively. "Something smells mighty fine, Miss Laura."

"Stew and biscuits," she said, grateful for his attempt to normalize the situation. "It's nearly ready."

"Best news I've heard all day," Matt declared, moving to wash his hands at the basin.

Zeb joined them shortly, and the four sat down to supper. Despite the circumstances, the meal wasn't the tense affair Laura had expected. Matt kept the conversation flowing with tales from the north pasture, and Zeb contributed stories of winters past when the ranch had been cut off by deep snows for weeks at a time.

"That winter of '62 was the worst," he recalled, reaching for another biscuit. "Snow so deep a man could walk right over the corral fence. Had to dig tunnels to the barn to feed the stock."

"Sounds like a tall tale to me, old man," Matt teased, earning a mock glare from Zeb.

"Who you calling old? I can still outride and out shoot you any day of the week."

"That so?" Matt challenged good-naturedly. "Care to wager on that?"

Laura glanced at Boone, expecting him to put an end to the banter given the seriousness of their situation. Instead, she found him watching her, a soft expression in his eyes. When their gazes met, he didn't look away, and Laura felt warmth spread through her chest despite their precarious circumstances.

After supper, they gathered in the main room to discuss strategy. Boone had brought out a map of the ranch and surrounding area, spreading it on the table.

"The main approach to the ranch is here," he said, tracing the road they had traveled earlier. "But there are other ways in—this old logging trail from the east, and the creek crossing to the south when the water's low."

"Too much ground to cover," Matt observed, studying the map. "Even with four of us."

"Which is why we won't try to watch all routes," Boone replied. "Instead, we'll set up warning systems. Trip wires with bells here and here." He indicated points on the map. "And we'll take watches through the night."

"What about Laura?" Zeb asked, voicing the question that had been weighing on her mind. "These men are after Jasper primarily, but they won't hesitate to use her if they think she knows where he is."

All eyes turned to her, and Laura straightened her spine, determined not to be the weakest link in their planning.

"I can shoot," she offered. "Papa taught me when I was young. I'm not an expert, but I can hit what I aim at."

A flash of surprise crossed Boone's face, followed by approval. "Good to know, but I'd prefer you weren't in a position to need that skill."

"I'm not hiding in the root cellar while the rest of you face danger on my behalf," Laura stated firmly.

Matt chuckled, earning a sharp look from Boone. "Sorry, boss, but she's got spirit. Reminds me of your ma when she'd get her dander up."

Something flickered in Boone's eyes at the comparison—surprise, perhaps, or a deeper emotion Laura couldn't quite identify.

"No one's suggesting you hide," Zeb assured her. "But we need to be smart about your safety."

"The most likely scenario," Boone said, returning to the map, "is that they'll come openly first. Try to intimidate us into telling them where Jasper is. When that fails, they might try more... direct methods."

The euphemism wasn't lost on Laura. McCready's men wouldn't be constrained by law or morality.

"So we present a united front," she said, thinking aloud. "Show them we're prepared and that harming any of us would be costly."

Boone nodded, something like pride in his expression. "Exactly. Men like that calculate risk versus reward. If the risk is too high, they'll look elsewhere."

"And if they don't?" Laura couldn't help asking.

Matt patted the revolver at his hip. "Then they'll learn why folks don't mess with the Callahan Ranch."

The blunt answer should have frightened her, but Laura found it oddly reassuring. These men—Boone, Zeb, even the usually jovial Matt—were prepared to defend their home and, by extension, her. The knowledge settled something within her, a foundation of security she hadn't realized she'd been missing.

As the evening wore on, they finalized their preparations. Matt would take the first watch, followed by Boone, then Zeb at dawn. Laura insisted on contributing and was assigned to keep coffee brewing through the night for whoever was on duty.

With the practical matters settled, a different kind of tension emerged—the awkward uncertainty of how to pass the remaining hours before they each took to their posts. Zeb solved the problem by retrieving a well-worn deck of cards from a drawer.

"Nothing settles the nerves like a good hand of poker," he declared, shuffling with surprising dexterity. "No stakes, mind you. Just to pass the time."

Matt grinned. "Afraid I'll clean you out, old timer?"

"Just sparing your pride, youngster," Zeb retorted.

Laura hesitated, memories of Jasper's gambling losses making her wary of the game. But this was different—a friendly pastime among people who cared for each other, not the desperate reaching for easy money that had characterized Jasper's play.

"I don't know how," she admitted as Zeb began to deal.

"We'll teach you," Boone offered, pulling out a chair beside him. "It's simple enough once you know the hands."

Under their patient tutelage, Laura quickly grasped the basics. She played cautiously at first, then with growing confidence as she won several small hands. The familiar banter between Zeb and Matt continued, with Boone occasionally joining in, and for brief stretches, Laura could almost forget the reason for their vigilance.

Almost, but not quite. Each creak of the house settling, each gust of wind rattling the windows, brought her attention sharply back to the danger that might be approaching through the darkness.

During one such moment, as Zeb was re-dealing the cards, Laura felt Boone's hand cover hers beneath the table. A simple touch, hidden from the others, but it spoke volumes. I'm here. We're safe. Together.

She turned her hand beneath his, their palms meeting, fingers intertwining. This small, secret connection anchored her, steadying her racing thoughts. When she glanced up, she found Boone watching her, his eyes conveying things his voice hadn't yet said.

The moment stretched between them, a private world existing alongside the card game and conversation. Laura felt her breath catch, aware of every place their skin touched, every subtle shift of his fingers against hers.

"Your turn, son," Zeb's voice broke through the bubble, and Boone reluctantly turned his attention back to the game, though his hand remained with hers beneath the table.

Later, as Matt prepared to take the first watch and Zeb retired to his room, Laura was alone with Boone in the kitchen. She was heating water for coffee while he checked the loading of a rifle he would take on his watch.

"You should try to get some sleep," he said, not looking up from his task. "At least until my watch. It's been a long day."

Laura knew he was right—exhaustion pulled at her limbs and clouded her thoughts—but the idea of lying alone in her room, straining to hear any unusual sound, held little appeal.

"I'm not sure I could sleep," she admitted, pouring the hot water over the ground coffee. "Too many thoughts spinning."

Boone set the rifle aside and approached, stopping close enough that she could feel the warmth radiating from him. "Laura."

She looked up, finding his expression softer than she had expected, concern eclipsing the vigilance that had marked it most of the evening.

"I meant what I said earlier," he told her. "We'll get through this. I won't let anything happen to you."

Laura's heart swelled at the promise, even as a part of her recognized he couldn't guarantee such a thing. Life had taught her that safety was always provisional, security always temporary.

"It's not just myself I'm worried about," she confessed. "It's you, Zeb, Matt... all of you in danger because of me."

"Because of Jasper," Boone corrected gently. "And we've faced trouble before. This ranch was built on the frontier when danger came in all forms. A couple of city men with guns doesn't change who we are or what we stand for."

"And what do you stand for?" Laura asked, genuinely curious about how he saw himself and his legacy.

Boone seemed to consider the question carefully. "Loyalty. Family. Doing what's right even when it's hard." His eyes met hers. "Protecting what matters."

The simplicity and sincerity of his answer moved Laura deeply. Here was a man who knew his values and lived by them, who had carved a place in the world through hard work and integrity. The contrast with Jasper's shifting, self-serving principles couldn't have been starker.

"Thank you," she said softly, "for including me in what matters."

Boone's expression shifted, intensity replacing with gentle concern. He took a half-step closer, his hand rising to cup her cheek. Laura held perfectly still, hardly daring to breathe as his thumb traced a gentle arc over her skin.

"You matter, Laura," he said, his voice low and rough with emotion. "More than I expected. More than I was prepared for."

The admission sent warmth cascading through her. She leaned into his touch, her own hand rising to rest against his chest, feeling the strong, steady beat of his heart beneath her palm.

"Boone..."

The space between them seemed to shrink of its own accord. His face lowering toward hers, her chin tilting up to meet him. Laura's eyes fluttered closed, anticipation sending her pulse racing.

His lips brushed hers with exquisite gentleness, a question more than a demand. She answered by leaning into the kiss, her hand sliding up to his shoulder for support as her knees weakened.

The contact was brief—soft, warm, and over too soon—but it left Laura breathless. Boone rested his forehead against hers, his hand still cradling her cheek, both of them suspended in the moment.

The sound of boots on the porch shattered the moment. They separated quickly, Boone reaching for the rifle as Matt entered, stamping snow from his boots.

"All quiet so far," he reported, oblivious to what he had interrupted. "But it's starting to snow harder. Could work for us or against us."

Boone nodded, his demeanor shifting back to alert watchfulness, though his eyes still held a warmth when they returned to Laura. "Fresh coffee's ready," he told Matt, gesturing to the pot.

"Much obliged," Matt replied, helping himself to a cup. "You two should get some rest while you can. No telling what tomorrow brings."

Laura knew he was right, yet the thought of separating from Boone now, with the memory of that kiss still tingling on her lips, seemed impossible. As if sensing her reluctance, Boone's hand found the small of her back, a reassuring pressure guiding her toward the hallway.

"I'll walk you to your room," he said, his voice pitched for her ears alone.

In the dim hallway, away from Matt's presence, they paused outside her door. Boone's expression was hard to read in the shadows, but his hand remained at her waist, unwilling to break contact.

"Try to sleep," he encouraged. "I'll wake you when it's my watch, if you still want to help with the coffee."

Laura nodded, reluctant to end the moment but aware of the practical necessities. "I will."

Boone hesitated, then bent to place another soft kiss on her lips, this one even briefer than the first but no less affecting. "Goodnight, Laura."

"Goodnight," she whispered, watching as he turned and walked back toward the main room.

Chapter 33

Inside her room, Laura prepared for bed mechanically, her mind replaying the kiss, analyzing every second of contact, every word spoken in that quiet moment in the kitchen. Despite the danger lurking outside, despite the uncertainty of Jasper's whereabouts and the men searching for him, her heart felt oddly light.

She slipped beneath the covers, certain she would lie awake for hours. Instead, exhaustion claimed her almost immediately, dragging her into a deep sleep.

The dream came without warning—Jasper, stumbling through the snow, pursued by shadowy figures. His face turned toward her, pleading, desperate. "Help me, Laura. They're coming. They're coming for both of us."

She tried to reach him, but her feet were rooted to the ground. The shadows closed in, and Jasper's face contorted with betrayal. "You abandoned me. Your own blood."

Laura jolted awake, heart pounding, momentarily disoriented in the dark room. Outside, the wind had picked up, rattling the window frame. Snow pattered against the glass, accumulating on the sill.

The remnants of the dream clung to her, Jasper's accusing face vivid in her mind's eye. Had it been merely a nightmare, or something more? Laura wasn't particularly superstitious, but the intensity of the vision left her uneasy.

She slipped from bed and moved to the window, peering out at the snowy landscape. The moon had emerged from behind the clouds, casting blue-white light across the freshly fallen snow. The ranch lay peacefully under its blanket of white, no sign of disturbance or danger.

A movement caught her eye—a figure walking the perimeter of the yard, rifle cradled in his arms. Boone, on his watch now. The sight of him brought both comfort and a flutter of remembered pleasure from their kiss.

As if sensing her gaze, he paused, looking toward her window. Laura raised a hand in greeting, knowing he could see her silhouette against the faint light from the moon. He returned the gesture, the simple acknowledgment warming her despite the cold glass beneath her fingers.

She stayed at the window, watching him complete his circuit of the property before disappearing into the barn to check on the horses. The dream had left her too unsettled to return to sleep immediately, and observing Boone's steady vigilance soothed her rattled nerves.

When he emerged from the barn, his gaze returned to her window, finding her still there. He gestured toward the house with a questioning tilt of his head. Laura hesitated only briefly before nodding.

She opened the front door to find him brushing snow from his coat, concern etched in his features.

"Couldn't sleep?" he asked quietly, mindful of Zeb sleeping down the hall.

"Bad dream," she admitted. "About Jasper."

Understanding dawned in his eyes. "Want to talk about it?"

Laura hesitated. "I should make coffee anyway," she decided. "For your watch."

Boone nodded, following her to the kitchen. As Laura busied herself with the coffeepot, he removed his coat and hat, hanging them by the door to dry.

"The dream?" he prompted gently when she didn't volunteer more.

Laura sighed, measuring grounds into the pot. "Jasper was running, being chased. He was calling for me to help him." She paused, remembering the accusation in her brother's eyes. "He said I abandoned him."

Boone was silent for a moment, watching her work. "It was just a dream, Laura. Not a vision or a message."

"I know," she agreed, though part of her wondered. "But what if he is in danger? What if these men find him before he can get far enough away?"

"Then he'll face the consequences of his actions," Boone said, not unkindly but with firm honesty. "Just as we all must."

Laura poured water over the coffee grounds, watching the dark liquid begin to filter through. "I know you're right. And I know Jasper brought this on himself." She looked up, meeting Boone's steady gaze. "But he's still my brother. I can't help worrying about him."

"That's because you have a good heart," Boone told her, moving closer. "One of the many things that..." He trailed off, seeming to reconsider his words.

"That what?" Laura pressed, her pulse quickening.

Boone's hand came to rest on the counter beside hers, their fingers nearly touching. "That draw me to you," he finished, the admission clearly costing him something in vulnerability.

Laura's breath caught. After their kiss, she had wondered if he might retreat again, rebuild the walls that had started to come down between them. Instead, he was moving forward, acknowledging what was growing between them despite the complications surrounding them.

"Even with all this chaos?" she asked, needing to be sure.

"Especially with it," he answered, surprising her. "Trouble reveals character, Laura. Yours has only grown brighter in my eyes with each challenge."

The simple sincerity of his words moved her deeply. She turned her hand, letting her fingers brush against his. "As has yours?"

They stood in companionable silence as the coffee finished brewing, neither feeling the need to fill the quiet with unnecessary words. When Laura poured a cup and offered it to Boone, their fingers touched in the exchange, a small contact that nonetheless sent warmth through her.

"I should get back to my watch," he said reluctantly.

Laura nodded, understanding the responsibility that came before personal desires. "I'll come with you, at least for a while. I'm too awake to go back to sleep now, anyway."

Boone looked as if he might object, then nodded. "Bundle up. It's cold out there."

They settled on the covered porch, Laura wrapped in a heavy blanket beside Boone. The night was peaceful; the snow falling steadily now, muffling all sound and creating a world of white stillness. Despite the circumstances that had brought them to this vigil, Laura found a curious contentment in sitting beside Boone, sharing coffee and quiet conversation as the hours passed.

"Do you think they'll come tonight?" she asked softly, watching the snow drift down in the moonlight.

Boone considered the question, his eyes scanning the white landscape. "Doubtful with this weather. Men like that prefer clear conditions and surprise. This snow would make their approach noisy, leave tracks."

Relief washed through Laura, though she knew it was merely a temporary reprieve. "So we have until the storm passes, at least."

"Most likely," he agreed. "Though we'll keep the watch, regardless."

They fell silent again, the only sounds the soft whisper of falling snow and the occasional creak of the house settling. Laura found herself studying Boone's profile in the dim light—the strong line of his jaw, the thoughtful set of his mouth, the steady vigilance in his eyes as he surveyed their surroundings.

"Tell me about your mother," she said suddenly, the question emerging from nowhere.

Boone glanced at her, surprise flickering across his face before softening into something warmer. "She was... remarkable. Strong but gentle. Could break a wild horse in the morning and bake the finest pie you ever tasted by afternoon."

Laura smiled, imagining such a woman. "Matt said I reminded him of her."

"You do," Boone confirmed, his voice dropping lower. "Not just in your determination, though there's that. It's your kindness alongside your strength. The way you face challenges without losing your compassion."

The compliment warmed Laura more than the blanket wrapped around her shoulders. "I wish I could have known her."

"She would have liked you," he said with certainty. "She always said a person's true character shows in how they handle adversity." A smile touched his lips, barely visible in the moonlight. "She'd approve of how you've handled yours."

Laura's throat tightened with emotion. "My own mother was similar in some ways. Papa always said she had 'steel in her spine and sunshine in her smile.'"

"A good combination," Boone observed. "One you inherited, it seems."

They shared memories then, exchanging stories of their childhoods—Laura's brief but loving years with her parents before their deaths, Boone's upbringing on the ranch with Zeb and Mary Callahan. The conversation flowed easily between them, building bridges of understanding across their different experiences.

"I've never spoken so freely about my parents," Laura admitted as a comfortable pause settled between them. "Not even with Jasper. It was always too painful."

Boone's hand found hers beneath the blanket. "And now?"

"It still aches," she acknowledged, "but differently. Like remembering brings them closer instead of emphasizing their absence."

"That's healing," he said softly. "When memories comfort rather than wound."

Laura turned to face him fully, struck by the wisdom in his words. "Is that how you feel about your mother now?"

Boone nodded slowly. "Most days. Though sometimes grief still catches me unawares." His thumb traced gentle circles on her hand. "The heart doesn't heal in straight lines."

The simple truth of this observation touched Laura deeply. Before she could respond, a sound from within the house drew their attention—the creak of a floorboard, followed by the soft closing of a door.

"Zeb's up early," Boone noted, glancing at the lightening eastern sky. Dawn was approaching, though the snow clouds obscured the horizon. "My watch is nearly done."

Laura felt a pang of disappointment that their quiet time together was ending. "I should prepare breakfast for everyone."

Neither moved immediately, reluctant to break the intimate bubble that had formed around them during the night. Boone's hand tightened briefly around hers.

"Laura," he began, his voice hushed, "when this is over—when we've dealt with McCready's men and Jasper is... wherever he ends up—we should talk about..."

"About?" she prompted when he hesitated.

"About us," he finished simply. "What's happening between us. What could happen, if you wanted it to."

Laura's heart quickened at the directness of his words. "I'd like that very much."

The door opened behind them, and Zeb stepped onto the porch, bundled against the cold. "Morning," he greeted, eyeing them knowingly. "Any visitors in the night?"

"Just the snow," Boone replied, standing and helping Laura to her feet. "It's been quiet."

Zeb nodded, scanning the white expanse beyond the porch. "Good weather for tracking if anyone does come." He glanced between them, noting their closeness but saying nothing about it. "Breakfast sounds mighty appealing after a cold night."

"I'll get started on it," Laura said, gathering her blanket around her shoulders.

As she turned to go inside, Boone caught her arm gently. "Thank you for keeping me company," he said, his eyes conveying much more than his words.

"Anytime," she replied softly, meaning it completely.

In the warm kitchen, as Laura bustled about preparing a hearty breakfast for the men who had stood guard through the night, she found herself humming softly. Despite the danger that still lurked outside, despite the uncertainty of Jasper's fate, her heart felt lighter than it had in quite some time.

As she worked, Laura sent up a silent prayer—for Jasper's safety, for protection for the Callahan ranch and all within it, and for whatever lay ahead between her and Boone to have the chance to grow into all it might become.

Chapter 33

The eggs sizzled in the cast-iron skillet as Laura worked at the stove. She glanced at the men gathered around the table—Boone watching the window between bites of toast, Matt methodically cleaning his revolver while his coffee cooled beside his plate, and Zeb studying a worn map of the surrounding countryside, marking potential approach routes with a stubby pencil.

Laura brought the platter of scrambled eggs to the table, setting it down alongside the plate of bacon she'd prepared earlier. Despite their vigilance, they all needed sustenance. Whatever the day might bring, they would face it better on full stomachs.

"Should be enough here to hold us through till supper," she said, trying to inject a note of normalcy into the morning. "Though I'm afraid we're down to our last few eggs."

"These'll do just fine," Zeb assured her, helping himself to a generous portion. He nodded appreciatively after his first bite. "Fine indeed. You've got a way with simple fare, Laura."

Boone looked up from his watchful stance, his eyes softening as they met hers.

Laura took her place at the table, though her appetite had abandoned her. She forced herself to take a small portion, aware that she, too, would need her strength.

"Weather's starting to clear," Matt observed, glancing toward the window. "Snow's letting up."

Boone nodded, the furrow between his brows deepening. "Which means better traveling conditions. For everyone."

The implication hung in the air. McCready's men would no longer be hampered by the storm.

"We stick to the plan," Zeb said firmly, folding the map and tucking it into his shirt pocket. "Regular perimeter checks. No one goes anywhere alone, and we keep the rifles loaded and ready."

"And Laura stays inside," Boone added, his tone leaving no room for argument.

Laura opened her mouth to protest, then closed it again. This wasn't the time for stubborn independence. These men knew what they were doing, and challenging their strategy would only add unnecessary complications.

"I'll keep watch from an upstairs window," she offered instead. "It has a good view of the approach road and the eastern trail."

Boone's expression softened with approval. "Good thinking. Extra eyes are always useful."

They ate in silence for a few minutes, the clink of forks against plates and the occasional crackle from the stove the only sounds. Laura found herself studying each of them in turn—Zeb's weathered face reflecting years of frontier wisdom, Matt's quiet competence belying his usual joviality, and Boone...

Boone caught her watching him and held her gaze, a world of unspoken feeling passing between them. The memory of their kiss and the quiet intimacy of their nighttime conversation on the porch seemed to hover in the air between them, a fragile, precious thing amid the threat of violence.

The sudden sound of hoofbeats approaching the ranch shattered the moment. All four froze, exchanging sharp glances before springing into action with efficiency.

Boone moved to the window in two quick strides, rifle already in hand. Matt positioned himself by the kitchen door, revolver drawn but held low. Zeb motioned for Laura to move away from the window line.

Laura's heart hammered in her chest as she pressed herself against the wall beside the stove, out of sight of any windows. The hoofbeats grew louder, then slowed to a walk as the rider approached the house.

"It's Hayes," Boone announced, the tension in his shoulders easing slightly. "Sheriff's alone, far as I can tell."

Relief washed through Laura, though she remained wary. The sheriff's arrival could mean many things, not all of them good.

"I'll go meet him," Boone said, moving toward the door. He paused, glancing back at Laura. "Stay inside until we know why he's here."

She nodded, watching as he stepped out onto the porch, rifle still in hand but pointed safely toward the ground. Through the window, she could see Sheriff Hayes dismounting, his expression serious but not alarmed.

The two men exchanged words Laura couldn't make out, then both turned toward the house. Boone opened the door, ushering the sheriff inside with a gesture that was both welcoming and cautious.

"Morning, folks," Sheriff Hayes greeted, removing his hat as he entered. Snow dusted his coat shoulders, melting quickly in the warmth of the kitchen. His eyes found Laura's, his expression unreadable. "Miss Hartley."

"Sheriff," she acknowledged, her voice steadier than she felt. "Would you like some coffee? We've just had breakfast, but there's plenty left if you're hungry."

A hint of a smile cracked his professional demeanor. "Coffee would be welcome. Been a long night."

Boone gestured toward an empty chair at the table. "Join us, then. Whatever news you're bringing can wait till you've warmed up."

Laura busied herself pouring a cup of strong black coffee for the sheriff, grateful for the simple task of occupying her trembling hands. The lawman's presence meant news—about Jasper, about McCready's men, about the danger that had been hanging over them since yesterday. Whether that news was good or bad remained to be seen.

"Thank you, Miss Hartley," Hayes said as she placed the steaming cup before him. He wrapped his hands around it gratefully, the chill of the morning ride evident in his reddened fingers.

An expectant silence fell over the kitchen as everyone waited for the sheriff to speak. He took a long sip of coffee, seeming to gather his thoughts before setting the cup down with deliberate care.

"I've got news that concerns you all," he began, his gaze moving around the table before settling on Laura. "Especially you, Miss Hartley. It's about your brother."

Laura's breath caught in her throat. "Jasper? Is he—" She couldn't finish the sentence, suddenly afraid of what the answer might be.

"He's alive," Hayes assured her quickly, seeing the fear in her eyes. "But he's in a fair bit of trouble. More than usual, I'd wager."

"What kind of trouble?" Boone asked, his hand finding Laura's shoulder in a gesture of support that didn't go unnoticed by the others.

Hayes took another sip of coffee before answering. "Got word late yesterday from Sheriff Donovan over in Piney Ridge. Seems your brother decided to try his hand at bank robbery."

The words hit Laura like a physical blow. "Bank robbery?" she echoed, disbelief coloring her voice. "That's not possible. Jasper's made poor choices, but he's never—he wouldn't—"

"I'm afraid he did," Hayes said, his tone gentle but firm. "Walked into the Piney Ridge Bank and Trust late yesterday afternoon, demanded money with a pistol. Didn't get far, though. Town marshal was getting his hair cut across the street and happened to look out the window at just the right moment."

Laura sank into the chair Boone pulled out for her, her legs suddenly unable to support her weight. "Is he hurt?"

"No, ma'am. Got himself a nasty knock on the head when they took him down, but nothing serious. He's in the Piney Ridge jail now, awaiting the circuit judge."

A strange mixture of relief and horror washed through Laura. Jasper was alive. Not dead in a snowdrift somewhere, not at the mercy of McCready's men. But bank robbery... The implications of such a serious crime were devastating.

"How much time will he face?" Boone asked the question Laura couldn't bring herself to voice.

Hayes sighed, rubbing a hand over his stubbled jaw. "Hard to say. Being it was his first attempt, and no one was hurt, and he didn't actually get away with any money... could be anywhere from five to fifteen years, I'd reckon. Judge Hollister isn't known for leniency with bank robbers, though."

Years. Jasper would spend years behind bars. The reality of it struck Laura with terrible clarity. Despite everything, despite his failings and the danger he'd brought to her door, he was still her brother. The only family she had left.

"There's more," Hayes continued, his expression softening as he took in Laura's distress. "And this part might actually be good news, of a sort. For you folks, anyway."

Zeb leaned forward. "How's that?"

"Those men who came to town yesterday—McCready's collectors—they left before dawn. Rode out in a hurry once word came to them about Jasper's arrest." Hayes directed his next words to Laura. "They came looking for your brother, Miss Hartley, not you. With him in custody and facing prison time, they've got no reason to stick around. McCready will get his due through the courts, most likely. Any debts your brother owed will be settled as part of his sentencing."

The weight that had been pressing on Laura's chest since the men appeared in Miller's store began to lift. "They're gone? Truly gone?"

Hayes nodded. "Headed east, from what my deputy could tell. They've got no business here now."

"Thank the Lord," Zeb murmured, the sentiment echoed in the relieved expressions around the table.

Matt holstered his revolver with a flourish. "Well, that's a sight better than the shootout I was expecting. Not that I wasn't ready for it, mind you."

"We noticed," Hayes said dryly, a hint of amusement in his eyes. "Saw your preparations as I rode up. Would've thought you were expecting an army, not just a couple of city thugs."

"Better prepared than surprised," Boone said, though the rigid tension had melted from his shoulders. He turned to Laura, his expression a complex mixture of relief and concern. "Are you all right?"

The simple question unlocked something in Laura. Tears welled in her eyes—not of grief exactly, but of release. The fear that had been her constant companion since fleeing Jasper's side days ago finally had an end point. She was safe. These people who had taken her in were safe. The danger had passed.

But Jasper... poor, broken, foolish Jasper was facing years in prison.

"I don't know," she answered honestly, a tear spilling down her cheek. "I'm relieved, but also... saddened, he's still my brother Boone. Despite everything."

Boone's hand covered hers on the table, a silent acknowledgment of the complicated emotions roiling within her. "I understand."

The sheriff cleared his throat gently. "There's one more thing, Miss Hartley. Your brother sent a message."

Laura's gaze snapped to Hayes, surprise momentarily displacing her other emotions. "A message?"

"When they processed him into the jail. Said if anyone could get word to his sister, to tell her he was sorry." Hayes shifted uncomfortably. "I can't speak to his sincerity, of course. Men in his position often say things they think might help their case."

"Or things they truly mean when faced with the consequences of their actions," Boone suggested quietly.

Laura closed her eyes briefly, processing this new information. Jasper, sorry. It was something she had longed to hear for years, through countless broken promises and disappointments. Now that the words had finally come, she wasn't sure what to do with them.

"Can I see him?" she asked, opening her eyes to find everyone watching her with varying degrees of concern.

Hayes hesitated. "It's a fair ride to Piney Ridge, and the weather—"

"Please," Laura interrupted, surprising herself with the intensity of her plea. "I need to see him. To speak with him face to face, at least once more."

The sheriff exchanged glances with Boone, some unspoken communication passing between them. "It could be arranged," Hayes finally conceded. "Though not today. Roads are still treacherous with the fresh snow. Day after tomorrow would be safest."

"I'll take her," Boone said, the statement both an offer and a decision. "We can leave at first light."

Laura turned to him, touched by his immediate support despite his complicated feelings about Jasper. "You don't have to—"

"I know," he cut her off gently. "I want to."

Zeb nodded approvingly. "Good. Wouldn't want either of you making that journey alone, weather being what it is."

Hayes drained the last of his coffee and stood. "I'll send word to Donovan that you'll be coming. He's a good man. He'll arrange the visit." He settled his hat back on his head. "I should be getting back to town. Glad to find you all safe and sound."

"We appreciate the ride out to tell us in person," Boone said, rising to walk the sheriff to the door. "Saved us a lot of worry."

"Just doing my job," Hayes replied, though the quirk of his mouth suggested he'd done a bit more than duty required. His eyes flickered to where Boone's hand had rested on Laura's shoulder, but he made no comment.

As the men stepped onto the porch, Laura remained at the table, trying to process the whirlwind of emotions Jasper's situation had stirred within her. Relief for her own safety warred with grief for her brother's fate. Could she forgive him after everything? Did she even want to?

Matt broke into her thoughts, his voice uncharacteristically gentle. "Family's a complicated business, Miss Laura. Even the disappointin' ones are still blood."

She looked up, finding unexpected wisdom in his weather-beaten face. "How did you—"

"Written all over your face," he said simply. "Been there myself. My younger brother took to the outlaw life when we were barely more than boys. Made his choices and paid for 'em. Didn't make it any easier to bear, though."

"What happened to him?" Laura asked softly.

Matt's eyes grew distant. "Died in a prison fight three years into his sentence. I never got to say goodbye properly, never got to tell him I forgave him for the pain he caused our ma." His gaze refocused on Laura. "Don't make my mistake. Say what needs saying while you can."

The advice struck Laura deeply, bringing clarity to her jumbled thoughts. Jasper had asked for her, had expressed remorse, however belated. Whatever came next, she owed it to both of them to hear him out, to seek closure if nothing else.

The door opened, and Boone returned, stamping snow from his boots. "Hayes is on his way back to town," he announced. "Said he'll arrange everything for our visit to Piney Ridge."

Laura nodded, gratitude warming her despite the lingering sadness. "Thank you, Boone. For being willing to take me."

His eyes held hers, steady and reassuring. "Of course."

The atmosphere in the kitchen had transformed with the sheriff's news. The vigilant tension was gone, replaced by a collective relief that manifested differently in each of them. Matt whistled as he returned to cleaning his revolver—a habit now rather than a necessity. Zeb pulled out his pipe, settling into his favorite chair by the stove with a contented sigh. And Boone...

Boone moved with new purpose, the weight of immediate danger lifted from his shoulders. He gathered the breakfast dishes, bringing them to the washbasin, where Laura had begun to clean up.

"You don't have to help," she protested halfheartedly as he rolled up his sleeves.

"I want to," he replied simply, reaching for a towel to dry as she washed.

They worked together, the domestic task grounding after the emotional tumult of the morning. Laura was hyperaware of his presence beside her—the brush of his arm against hers as he reached for a plate, the clean scent of soap and man, the controlled strength in his hands as he carefully dried each dish.

"Are you truly all right?" he asked quietly, pitching his voice for her ears alone.

Laura considered the question seriously. "I will be," she decided. "It's a lot to take in."

"About Jasper."

"Yes." She passed him a dripping cup, their fingers brushing in the exchange. "I've spent so many years trying to help him, trying to save him from himself. And now..."

"Now it's out of your hands," Boone finished for her.

She nodded, swallowing against the tightness in her throat. "It feels like failure, somehow. Like I should have done more."

Boone set down the cup he was drying and turned to face her fully, his expression earnest. "Laura, listen to me. You did everything humanly possible for your brother. More than most would have done. His choices were his own."

"I know that in my head," she admitted. "My heart is slower to accept it."

"That's because you care deeply. It's one of the things I…" He hesitated, a flash of vulnerability crossing his face. "One of the things I most admire about you."

The almost-confession hung between them, charged with possibilities. Neither was quite ready to voice in the kitchen with Zeb and Matt nearby. Laura's cheeks warmed under his intense gaze, and she returned her attention to the dishes before her emotions overwhelmed her completely.

They finished the task in silence, but it was a comfortable one, filled with unspoken understanding and the promise of conversations to come. As Laura dried her hands on her apron, Boone leaned close.

"Would you walk with me? To check on the horses," he clarified when she looked questioningly at him. "I'd like some time to talk. Just us."

Her heart skipped at the request, at the intentional privacy he was seeking. "Yes, I'd like that."

"Zeb," Boone called over his shoulder. "Laura and I are going to check on the horses. We won't be long."

Zeb waved an acknowledging hand, his attention on his pipe. "Take your time. Danger's passed, no need to rush about."

Matt's knowing grin followed them as they donned coats and gloves. Laura pretended not to notice, though she felt a telltale heat creeping up her neck.

Chapter 35

Outside, the world was transformed. The storm had left everything draped in fresh, pristine white, the snow sparkling in the late morning sunlight. Their boots crunched through the fresh powder as they made their way to the barn, the air crisp and clean in Laura's lungs.

"It's beautiful," she breathed, taking in the snow-covered landscape. "Like God washed everything clean."

Boone glanced at her, appreciation warming his gaze. "I was thinking the same thing."

The barn was warm and fragrant with the smell of hay and horses. The animals nickered in greeting as they entered, several heads poking inquiringly over stall doors. Boone moved methodically from stall to stall, checking water troughs and feed levels, while Laura stroked the velvet nose of a curious chestnut mare.

"Hello, lovely girl," she murmured as the horse lipped at her gloved hand. "Looking for treats, are you?"

"That's Marigold," Boone said, pausing in his chores to watch them. "She's usually standoffish with strangers. She must sense something special about you."

Laura smiled, flattered by the simple observation. "Animals know who truly appreciates them, I think."

"As do people," Boone replied, his meaning clear.

He finished checking the last stall, then came to stand beside her at Marigold's door. For a moment, they both simply petted the gentle mare, the repetitive motion soothing.

"Laura," Boone began, his voice lower, more intimate than before. "When the sheriff arrived this morning, I was afraid—"

"I know," she interrupted softly. "I was too."

"Not for myself," he clarified, turning to face her. "For you. For what his news might mean for you."

The admission touched her deeply. "And now? How do you feel about his news?"

Boone considered the question seriously, his eyes never leaving hers. "Relieved that you're safe. That we're all safe." He paused, choosing his next words carefully. "Concerned about how Jasper's situation affects you. And..."

"And?" she prompted when he hesitated.

"And selfishly glad that this chapter is closing," he admitted, a flash of guilt crossing his features. "That you're free of the burden you've carried for so long. Free to choose your own path without his shadow over you."

The words resonated within Laura, striking a chord of truth she hadn't fully acknowledged until that moment. She was free. For the first time since her parents' deaths, her future was truly her own to determine. The realization was both terrifying and exhilarating.

"I've never had that before," she whispered. "Freedom to choose."

Boone's expression softened. "What would you choose, Laura? If anything were possible?"

The question hung between them, heavy with implication. Laura's heart pounded as she considered her answer. In this moment of new-found liberty, what did she truly want?

"Connection," she said finally, her voice steady despite her racing pulse. "Belonging. A place to put down roots, people to love who love me in return. A home."

Boone stepped closer, close enough that she could feel the warmth radiating from him in the cool barn air. "And where would you find these things? These roots you want to put down?"

Laura gazed up at him, gathering her courage. "I think... I might have already found them."

The breath seemed to catch in Boone's throat. His hand rose to cup her cheek, the leather of his glove cool against her skin. "Laura..."

The moment stretched between them, taut with possibility. Marigold nickered softly, breaking the spell, and Boone dropped his hand with a rueful smile.

"Not here," he said, glancing around the barn. "Not like this. You deserve better than hay and horse blankets for what I want to say to you."

Curiosity and anticipation surged through Laura. "What do you want to say to me?"

Instead of answering, he took her hand. "Come with me. I want to show you something."

Intrigued, Laura allowed him to lead her from the barn and across the snow-covered yard. They bypassed the main house, heading in-stead toward a small rise that overlooked the property. The climb was short but steep, their boots slipping occasionally on the snow-covered slope.

At the top, Boone stopped, turning to face the vista before them. Laura followed his gaze and caught her breath.

The Callahan Ranch spread out below them, a patchwork of white fields and dark fences. The main house with its wisp of chimney smoke, the sturdy barn and outbuildings, the corrals where horses moved in lazy circles. Beyond, the pastures stretched toward distant mountains, their peaks sharp against the clear blue sky.

"It's magnificent," Laura said softly, genuinely moved by the beauty of the scene.

"My grandfather staked this claim years ago," Boone told her, pride evident in his voice. "Came west with nothing but a dream and determination. Built the first cabin with his own hands, right where the main house stands now."

Laura glanced at him, struck by the reverence in his tone. "You love this land very much."

"It's in my blood," he acknowledged. "Every tree, every hill, every inch of pasture—it's part of who I am." He turned to face her fully. "I never thought I'd want to share it. After Eliza left, I told myself the ranch was enough, that I didn't need anyone else."

Laura's heart quickened at the direction of his words. "And now?"

"Now I know better." Boone took both her hands in his, his expression more open, more vulnerable than she had ever seen it. "Laura, when you came into my life, I was... closed. Walled off. Convinced that was safer."

"I remember," she said softly, thinking of their first encounters, his gruff demeanor, the careful distance he had maintained.

"You changed that," he continued. "Not all at once, but day by day. Your strength, your kindness, the way you faced each new challenge... you woke something in me, I thought had died."

Emotion tightened Laura's throat, making speech impossible. She squeezed his hands, encouraging him to continue.

"I told myself it was temporary—that you'd move on once you found your footing. That it was better that way." A rueful smile touched his lips. "I was wrong. The thought of you leaving... it hollows me out."

"Boone," Laura managed, her voice thick with feeling.

"I'm not asking you to decide anything now," he said quickly. "You've just gained your freedom, and you deserve time to explore what that means. But I need you to know..." He took a deep breath, as if gathering courage. "I love you, Laura. I love your gentle heart and your stubborn spirit. I love how you hum when you cook and the way your eyes light up when you laugh. I love that you'd brave snow to comfort a man on watch duty."

Tears welled in Laura's eyes, blurring her vision of his earnest face. Her heart felt too full, overflowing with emotions she had scarcely allowed herself to acknowledge until this moment.

"When you go to see Jasper," Boone continued, "I'll be right beside you. Whatever comes after—whether you choose to stay in Lone Valley or seek your fortune elsewhere—I'll support you. But know this: if you want roots, if you want belonging, if you want a home... you have one. Here. With me."

The tears spilled over, tracking warm paths down Laura's cold cheeks. "Boone Callahan," she whispered, "are you asking me to stay?"

"I'm asking for more than that," he admitted, his voice dropping to match hers. "Much more. But not yet. Not until you've had time to be sure of your own heart."

Laura shook her head, a laugh bubbling up through her tears. "You wonderful, stubborn man. Do you think I haven't had time? Do you think I haven't been falling in love with you since the moment you carried me out of that blizzard?"

Hope blazed in Boone's eyes, transforming his face. "Laura..."

"I love you," she said clearly, the words ringing with certainty in the crisp air. "I love your strength and your tenderness. I love how you care for this land, for your father, for everyone under your protection. I love that you see me—truly see me—and still want me by your side."

Boone pulled her into his arms then, holding her as if she were the most precious thing in the world. Laura melted into his embrace, feeling the rightness of it down to her bones. This was what she had been seeking all along—not just safety or stability, but this profound connection, this sense of coming home.

"Stay," he murmured against her hair. "Stay with me, Laura. Not as my guest, not as someone passing through, but as..." He pulled back slightly, meeting her eyes. "As my wife, when you're ready. As my partner in everything."

The proposal, for that's what it was, stole Laura's breath. "Are you certain?" she asked, needing to be sure. "This isn't just relief speaking, or pity for my situation?"

Boone's laugh was soft but genuine. "Do I strike you as a man who would propose marriage out of pity?"

"No," she admitted, a smile tugging at her lips. "You're far too practical for that."

"Practical enough to know a good thing when I see it," he countered, his hands moving to frame her face. "Practical enough to grab hold of happiness with both hands when it appears." His expression grew serious again. "I've never been more certain of anything, Laura. I want you as my wife, if you'll have me."

The depth of emotion in his eyes banished any lingering doubts. This was real. This was true. This was the belonging she had sought for so long.

"Yes," she whispered, her heart so full she could scarcely breathe. "Yes, I'll stay. Yes, I'll be your wife."

Joy transformed Boone's face, years of caution and reserve falling away to reveal the full measure of his love. He bent his head, capturing her lips in a kiss that was both tender and fiercely passionate. Laura responded in kind, pouring all her newfound certainty, all her love and hope for their future, into the connection.

When they finally parted, both breathless, Boone rested his forehead against hers. "I was prepared to wait," he confessed. "To give you time, to court you properly."

"We've had our courtship," Laura replied, her fingers tracing the strong line of his jaw. "Through blizzards and danger and quiet conversations by firelight. I don't need more time to know my own heart."

"Even with Jasper's situation?" he asked gently. "You have much to process still."

Laura nodded, appreciating his concern. "I do. And I will need your strength when I face him. But that doesn't change what's between us. If anything, it makes me more certain." She gazed up at him, letting him see the full truth in her eyes. "You're my rock, Boone. My safe harbor in every storm."

He kissed her again, more briefly this time, but with no less feeling. "As you are mine."

They stood together on the hillside, the vast beauty of the ranch spread before them, the future stretching bright and promising ahead. Laura knew there would be challenges still—Jasper's imprisonment, her own adjustment to a new life, the everyday trials that came with building a life together. But for the first time in longer than she could remember, she wasn't afraid.

Here, in Boone's arms, with the land he loved surrounding them both, she had found what she had been searching for all along. Not an escape, not a temporary refuge, but a true home. A place to belong. A love to sustain her through whatever lay ahead.

"We should go back," Boone said eventually, though he made no move to release her. "Zeb and Matt will be wondering what's keeping us."

Laura smiled, imagining their knowing looks. "Let them wonder a little longer," she suggested, surprising herself with the boldness. "I'm not ready to share this moment just yet."

Boone's answering smile was tender and a little mischievous. "Mrs. Callahan-to-be makes a compelling argument."

The name sent a thrill through Laura. Mrs. Callahan. Laura Callahan. She would have a family name again, a true identity beyond 'Jasper Hartley's sister.' More importantly, she would have Boone, and he would have her partners in whatever the future might bring.

As they stood together on the hilltop, the winter sun warm on their faces despite the chill in the air, Laura sent up a silent prayer of gratitude. For the journey that had led her here, even through its darkest moments. For the man beside her, whose love had come to her like an unexpected gift. And for the promise of tomorrow, bright with possibilities neither of them could yet imagine.

In the valley below, smoke curled from the chimney of the house that would soon be her home. Their home. The thought filled Laura with a deep, abiding peace that surpassed all understanding.

She had found her place at last.

Epilogue

Laura stood in the small back room of the Lone Valley Church, her fingers trembling as she fastened the last pearl button at her throat. The wedding dress—a hand sewn gift from Hannah and several other women in town. The ivory fabric caught the light streaming through the small window, giving it a soft shimmer against her skin.

"Let me help you with that," Hannah said, stepping forward to secure the final button. "Your hands are shaking something fierce."

"Can you blame me?" Laura laughed, the sound breathless and buoyant with joy. "I'm getting married today."

Hannah grinned, stepping back to admire her handiwork. "And you look every bit the beautiful bride. Boone won't know what hit him when you walk down that aisle."

A knock at the door interrupted them. "Everyone decent in there?" Louella's voice called.

"Come in, Ms. Patterson," Laura answered, turning to face the door.

Louella entered, stopping short when she caught sight of Laura. Her hand fluttered to her chest, and for once, the talkative woman seemed momentarily speechless.

"Oh my," she finally managed. "If you aren't the prettiest thing I've seen in Lone Valley since... well, I can't rightly remember when."

Laura felt a blush warming her cheeks. "Thank you, Ms. Patterson."

"Louella, dear. We're well past formalities now." She bustled forward, carrying a small wooden box. "I've brought something for you. Every bride needs something borrowed, and I thought perhaps..." She opened the box, revealing a delicate silver hairpin with a small blue stone. "It was my mother's, and then mine, on my wedding day."

Emotion tightened Laura's throat. "It's beautiful."

"May I?" Louella asked, lifting the pin.

Laura nodded, turning, so Louella could secure a few stray curls with the hairpin. The older woman worked with deft fingers, tucking the pin into place with practiced ease.

"There now," Louella declared. "Perfect." She stepped back, her eyes suspiciously bright. "I knew from the moment you arrived that you belonged here in Lone Valley. Some people just fit a place, like they were always meant to be there."

The words touched Laura deeply. After years of drifting, of never belonging anywhere, the acceptance of these women—of this entire community—felt like a miracle.

"The church is filling up," Hannah reported, peeking through the door. "I think everyone in the county has come."

"Of course they have," Louella said with a satisfied nod. "It's not every day our most eligible bachelor gets himself hitched, and to such a lovely bride." She patted Laura's hand. "I'd better find my seat. Wouldn't want to miss a moment."

As Louella departed, Laura turned to the small mirror propped against the wall. The woman who looked back at her seemed transformed from the exhausted, frightened traveler who had arrived in Lone Valley weeks ago. Her eyes were bright, her cheeks flushed with happiness, her entire being radiating a quiet joy that came from deep within.

"It's time," Hannah said softly. "Are you ready?"

Laura took a deep breath, smoothing her hands over the simple but elegant dress. "More ready than I've ever been for anything in my life."

Boone stood at the altar of the small church, fighting the urge to tug at his collar. The new shirt felt stiff and formal, nothing like the comfortable work clothes he was accustomed to wearing. Beside him, Matt shifted from foot to foot, clearly no more comfortable in his Sunday best.

"Stop fidgeting," Boone muttered under his breath.

"Me?" Matt whispered back. "You look like you're about to jump out of your skin."

Boone forced himself to stand still, but his heart continued its relentless pounding. Not from doubt—never that—but from the overwhelming reality that in moments, Laura would be his wife. The scattered thoughts that had filled his mind all morning resolved into a single, crystal-clear certainty: this was right. This was meant to be.

Reverend Tanner caught his eye from his position at the pulpit, offering an encouraging smile. The church had been decorated simply but beautifully with evergreen boughs and white ribbons, the work of the women of Lone Valley, who had thrown themselves into wedding preparations with enthusiasm once the news had spread.

The pews were filled to capacity. Zeb sat in the front row, his weathered face clean-shaven for the occasion, his best suit pressed and neat. Behind him, it seemed the entire population of Lone Valley had turned out—Jude Miller from the general store, Elijah the blacksmith, Sheriff Hayes, and dozens of others whose lives had intersected with Boone's over the years.

The piano in the corner began to play, the familiar wedding march filling the small space. The congregation rose to their feet, turning toward the back of the church. Boone's breath caught in his throat as the doors opened.

Laura stood framed in the doorway, a vision in ivory, her hair arranged in soft curls, her face partially hidden behind a simple veil. She clutched a small bouquet of winter evergreens and dried flowers, her slender form illuminated by the light behind her.

Every other thought fled Boone's mind. There was only Laura, only this moment, only the miracle of finding love when he'd resigned himself to solitude.

She began to walk down the aisle, alone. They had discussed this—whether someone should give her away in her father's absence. Laura had decided against it, saying simply, "I'm giving myself to you, Boone. Freely and completely."

Now, watching her approach with steady steps and clear purpose in her eyes, Boone felt the rightness of that decision. She was choosing him with the same strength and determination she had shown throughout their acquaintance, walking toward their future with open eyes and an open heart.

When she reached him, she passed her bouquet to Hannah, who stood as her witness. Then she turned to face Boone, her eyes meeting his through the delicate veil. He could see the emotion shining there, could feel the slight tremor in her hands as he took them in his own.

"Dearly beloved," Reverend Tanner began, his resonant voice filling the church. "We are gathered here today in the sight of God and this company, to witness the joining of this man and this woman in holy matrimony..."

The words washed over Boone as he stood transfixed by the woman before him. He had heard countless wedding ceremonies before, had even stood as witness to friends, but never had the sacred promises seemed so profound, so deeply meaningful.

"Marriage is not to be entered into lightly," the reverend continued, "but reverently, discreetly, advisedly, and in the fear of God. It is a sacred union, blessed by our Lord, a covenant between a man and a woman that reflects Christ's own sacrificial love for His church."

Boone saw Laura's eyes soften at these words, faith and love intertwining in her expression. He squeezed her hands gently, overwhelmed by gratitude that this remarkable woman had chosen to share her life with him.

"Boone and Laura come before us today, having found in each other that special person with whom they wish to share their lives," Reverend Tanner said, looking between them with a warm smile. "They have journeyed through hardship and challenge to arrive at this moment, and their commitment has been tested and proven true."

A murmur of agreement rippled through the congregation. Everyone in Lone Valley knew something of their story—of Laura's arrival during the blizzard, of the danger that had followed her, of the love that had blossomed despite it all.

"Boone, will you take Laura to be your wedded wife, to live together in the holy estate of matrimony? Will you love her, comfort her, honor and keep her, in sickness and in health, and forsaking all others, keep yourself only unto her, so long as you both shall live?"

Boone's voice, when it came, was steady and sure. "I will."

"Laura, will you take Boone to be your wedded husband, to live together in the holy estate of matrimony? Will you love him, comfort him, honor and keep him, in sickness and in health, and forsaking all others, keep yourself only unto him, so long as you both shall live?"

"I will," Laura answered, the two simple words carrying the weight of absolute certainty.

Reverend Tanner nodded, then looked at Boone. "The couple has prepared their own vows. Boone, if you would."

Boone took a deep breath, grateful that he had committed his words to memory, for at this moment, he doubted he could read anything through the emotion blurring his vision.

"Laura," he began, his voice low and steady. "Before you came into my life, I thought I knew what strength was. I thought it meant standing alone, relying on no one. You taught me that true strength comes from opening your heart, from risking everything for love."

He heard a few sniffles from the congregation but kept his eyes fixed on Laura's, seeing tears gathering beneath her veil.

"I promise to be your shelter in every storm, your companion in every joy, your partner in every challenge. I promise to cherish you, respect you, and walk beside you in faith for all the days of our lives. With God as my witness, I give you my heart, my name, and my solemn vow to love you until my last breath."

A tear slipped down Laura's cheek, but her smile was radiant. When Reverend Tanner nodded to her, she took a moment to compose herself before speaking.

"Boone," she said, her voice clear despite her tears. "When I arrived in Lone Valley, I was searching for safety, for shelter from the storms of life. What I found was so much more. In you, I discovered not just protection, but understanding. Not just kindness, but deep and abiding love."

She squeezed his hands, her eyes never leaving his.

"I promise to stand by your side through every season—to share your burdens, celebrate your joys, and face whatever comes with unwavering faith and devotion. I promise to build a home with you filled with love, laughter, and the presence of God. I give you my trust, my loyalty, and my heart, now and forever."

Boone felt a tightness in his chest that had nothing to do with his stiff collar and everything to do with the depth of emotion her words evoked. This woman, who had known so much hardship, was offering him the precious gift of her heart, her future, her trust. He silently vowed to be worthy of it every day of their lives together.

"The ring is a symbol of eternity," Reverend Tanner said, "a circle unbroken, signifying the enduring nature of your vows. Boone, place the ring on Laura's finger and repeat after me."

Matt handed Boone the simple gold band he had purchased from Jude Miller's store just days before. Boone took Laura's left hand, his own surprisingly steady, as he prepared to place the ring on her finger.

"With this ring, I thee wed," he repeated after the reverend, "and with all my worldly goods, I thee endow. In the name of the Father, and of the Son, and of the Holy Spirit. Amen."

He slid the ring onto her finger, where it settled as if it had always belonged there.

Laura had no ring to give him today—there hadn't been time to procure one—but she took his left hand and pressed it between both of hers, her eyes conveying what material symbols could not.

"What God has joined together, let no man put asunder," Reverend Tanner declared. "By the authority vested in me by God and the territory of Montana, I now pronounce you husband and wife." He smiled widely. "Boone, you may kiss your bride."

With gentle hands, Boone lifted Laura's veil, revealing her face fully. The love shining in her eyes stole his breath all over again. He cupped her cheek tenderly, then bent to press his lips to hers in their first kiss as husband and wife.

The congregation erupted in cheers and applause. But for Boone, the world had narrowed to this one perfect moment—to Laura's lips against his, to the knowledge that she was now his wife, to the future stretching bright and promising before them.

When they finally parted, both were smiling so widely it almost hurt. Reverend Tanner raised his hands for quiet, then addressed the congregation once more.

"It is my great pleasure to present to you, Mr. and Mrs. Boone Callahan!"

Another round of cheers filled the church as Boone offered Laura his arm. Together, they walked back down the aisle, husband and wife at last, surrounded by the well-wishes and joyful faces of their community.

The celebration spilled from the church into the town hall, which had been transformed for the occasion with more evergreen garlands, lanterns, and tables laden with food. It seemed every household in Lone Valley had contributed something to the wedding feast—roasted meats, fresh bread, preserved fruits, and Louella Patterson's famous apple pie.

A small group of local musicians had assembled in the corner, filling the room with lively fiddle music that soon had folks tapping their feet and clearing space for dancing. Laura stood beside Boone, overwhelmed by the outpouring of generosity and genuine happiness on every face.

"Mrs. Callahan," Boone murmured near her ear, "may I have the honor of this dance?"

The name—her new name—sent a thrill through Laura. "You may indeed, Mr. Callahan."

He led her to the center of the impromptu dance floor, placing one hand at her waist while taking her other hand in his. As they began to move to the music, other couples joined them—Zeb with Louella, Matt with Hannah, and various other pairings from around the community.

"Are you happy?" Boone asked softly as they turned about the floor.

Laura looked up at him, unable to contain the joy bubbling within her. "Completely. More than I ever thought possible."

His eyes crinkled with answering happiness. "That makes two of us."

As the dance ended, they were surrounded by well-wishers eager to congratulate them. Jude Miller pumped Boone's hand enthusiastically.

"About time someone captured this one's heart," Jude declared, slapping Boone on the back. "We were beginning to think he'd spend his life married to that ranch of his."

"Fortunately, I don't have to choose," Boone replied with a smile, his arm slipping around Laura's waist. "I get to have both."

"And we get to keep you in Lone Valley," Mrs. Miller said to Laura. "Which is a blessing for us all. Your bread alone is worth having you settle here permanently."

Laura laughed, touched by the simple acceptance. "I'm looking forward to being part of this community for many years to come."

They moved through the crowd, accepting congratulations and well-wishes from everyone. Elijah the blacksmith presented them with a beautiful hand-forged door knocker for their home. Sheriff Hayes offered a bottle of fine whiskey "for special occasions." Hannah and several other young women had sewn linens for their household.

"You've got yourself a good man," Louella told Laura as they paused beside the refreshment table. "One of the best in the territory."

"I know," Laura agreed, her eyes finding Boone across the room where he stood talking with his father. As if sensing her gaze, he looked up, meeting her eyes with a smile that warmed her to her toes.

"And he's got himself a woman worthy of him," Louella continued, her usual bluntness softened by genuine affection. "We're all mighty glad you stumbled into our little corner of the world, Laura Callahan."

The name still sounded new and wonderful to Laura's ears. "So am I, Louella. So am I."

Zeb approached them, looking unusually formal in his suit, but with the same straightforward manner, she had come to appreciate. "May I steal my new daughter for a moment?" he asked Louella.

"Of course, of course," Louella replied, waving them off. "I should check on the food, anyway."

Zeb offered Laura his arm, leading her toward a quieter corner of the hall. "I wanted to give you something," he said, reaching into his pocket. "Been holding onto it for some time, waiting for the right person."

He withdrew a small velvet pouch and placed it in Laura's hand. "This belonged to Boone's mother. She always said it should go to his wife when the time came."

Laura opened the pouch carefully, tipping its contents into her palm. A delicate gold locket gleamed against her skin, its surface etched with a simple floral design.

"It's beautiful," she breathed, running her thumb over the intricate pattern.

"Open it," Zeb encouraged.

Laura did so, revealing a small portrait on one side—a handsome young man she recognized as a younger Zeb—and on the other, a beautiful woman with kind eyes and Boone's smile.

"Mary wore it every day of our married life," Zeb said, a note of quiet reverence in his voice. "Said it kept me close to her heart even when I was out working the far pastures." He cleared his throat. "I know she'd be mighty pleased to see you wearing it now."

Tears pricked Laura's eyes as she understood the significance of the gift. "I'm honored, Zeb. Truly."

"Your family now," he said simply. "Have been since before today, if I'm being honest. The ceremony just made it official."

Laura impulsively leaned forward to kiss his weathered cheek. "Thank you for welcoming me so completely."

Zeb looked momentarily flustered by the gesture, but pleased. "Well now, you're making an old man blush." He offered his handkerchief when he noticed her tears. "No crying at your own wedding feast. It's bad luck."

She laughed, dabbing at her eyes. "I think that's rain on your wedding day, not tears."

"Same principle," he insisted with a wink. "Now, would you like me to help you with that locket?"

Laura nodded, turning so he could fasten the delicate chain around her neck. The locket settled just below her collarbones, a comforting weight against her skin.

"Perfect," Zeb declared. "Now you truly look like a Callahan woman."

Boone appeared at their side, his eyes immediately drawn to the locket. Recognition flashed across his face, followed by a complex mixture of emotions—surprise, tenderness, approval.

"Ma's locket," he said.

Zeb nodded. "Thought it was time it saw the light of day again. On the right person."

Boone's gaze met his father's, an unspoken understanding passing between them. "Thank you, Pa."

"Don't thank me," Zeb replied gruffly. "Your mother made me promise years ago." He clapped his son on the shoulder. "She'd have loved Laura, you know. Would've said you chose well."

"I did," Boone agreed, his eyes returning to Laura's face with undisguised adoration.

Zeb cleared his throat. "Well, I'll leave you two alone. Got to make sure Matt doesn't tell too many embarrassing stories about you, son."

As Zeb moved away, Boone reached out to touch the locket gently. "It suits you."

"Your father said your mother wore it every day," Laura said, watching his face as he studied the heirloom.

Boone nodded. "For as long as I can remember. When she passed, Pa couldn't bear to look at it, so he put it away." His thumb brushed over the gold surface. "Seeing it on you... it's right, somehow. Like the past and future connecting."

Laura placed her hand over his. "I'll treasure it, Boone. And the family legacy it represents."

The music shifted to a slower tune, and Boone's arms encircled her waist. "May I have another dance with my wife?"

"You may have as many as you like," she replied, settling naturally into his embrace. "For the rest of our lives."

They moved together to the gentle melody, lost in each other despite the crowded room. Laura was acutely aware of Boone's strong hand at the small of her back, the solid warmth of his chest beneath her palm, the tender way his eyes never left her face.

"I keep thinking I'll wake up," he confessed. "That this is all some dream, and I'll find myself alone again in that cold house."

Laura reached up to touch his face, the rasp of his evening stubble against her fingertips confirming his solid reality. "Not a dream. I'm real, and I'm yours, and I'm not going anywhere."

"Promise?" he asked, the single word revealing a vulnerability few ever saw in the strong, capable rancher.

"With all my heart," she answered firmly. "This is only the beginning, Boone. The first day of our life together."

He bent to kiss her, right there in the middle of the dance floor, heedless of the onlookers and good-natured whistles that followed. "The first of many," he murmured against her lips.

As the evening progressed, the celebration showed no signs of winding down. More food appeared, more music played, and the dancing continued with enthusiastic abandon. Laura found herself passed from partner to partner—a dance with Matt, who made her laugh with his exaggerated gallantry; a turn with Sheriff Hayes, surprisingly light on his feet for such a solid man; even a brief, stately circuit with Reverend Tanner, who told her how pleased he was to see God's hand at work in her and Boone's union.

Through it all, her eyes continually sought and found Boone, as his did her. No matter who they were talking with or dancing alongside, they remained tethered by an invisible connection that nothing could sever.

Eventually, as the winter evening deepened outside, Zeb approached them with a conspiratorial smile. "The boys and I have prepared a little surprise for you two," he announced. "Your getaway awaits whenever you're ready."

Laura glanced at Boone, noting the questioning lift of his eyebrow. Neither of them had planned any kind of wedding trip—with winter in full force and the ranch needing attention, they had agreed to postpone such luxuries until spring.

"What have you done, Pa?" Boone asked, equal parts suspicious and amused.

"Nothing extravagant," Zeb assured them. "Just thought you might appreciate a bit of privacy for your first few days as husband and wife."

He led them to the door of the town hall and opened it with a flourish. Outside, a wagon waited, decorated with evergreen boughs and ribbons. Matt stood beside it, grinning broadly. The horses hitched and ready.

"What's this?" Laura asked, genuinely perplexed.

"Your chariot to the Richardson cabin," Matt explained. "It's all fixed up and waiting for you—warm fire, food provisions, everything you might need for a few days of... well, being newlyweds." He winked, unabashed.

Laura felt heat rise in her cheeks, but Boone was already turning to his father with appreciation clear on his face.

"The old hunting cabin? You fixed it up for us?"

Zeb nodded. "Been working on it for days. Nothing fancy, mind you, but it's snug and private. About an hour's ride from here, just far enough to feel away from it all, but close enough if you're needed."

The thoughtfulness of the gesture touched Laura deeply. She had assumed they would simply return to the ranch tonight, beginning their married life in Boone's—now their—bedroom. The idea of a few days alone, away from the responsibilities of the ranch and the well-meaning but constant presence of others, was unexpectedly appealing.

"What about the ranch?" Boone asked, though it was clear he was already warming to the idea.

"Matt and I can handle things for a few days," Zeb said firmly. "Lord knows you've earned some time away. Both of you."

Boone looked at Laura, a question in his eyes. "What do you think?"

"I think it sounds wonderful," she admitted, excitement building within her at the prospect of uninterrupted time with her new husband.

A cheer went up from those who had gathered to witness the exchange, and suddenly, they were surrounded again, this time by friends offering good-natured farewells and bits of married advice that ranged from practical to downright embarrassing.

In a whirlwind of hugs and handshakes, Laura found herself wrapped in her winter cloak and lifted into the wagon by Boone's strong hands. He climbed up beside her, taking the reins from Matt with a grateful nod.

"Everything you need is packed in the back," Matt told them.

"Thanks, Matt," Boone said, genuine affection in his voice. "For everything."

Matt waved dismissively. "Get going before someone decides to follow you with more advice or gifts."

With a final wave to the assembled well-wishers, Boone clicked to the horses, and the wagon began to move. Behind them, someone started throwing rice, the small grains pattering against Laura's cloak and catching in her hair.

"Safe journey!" "God bless!" "Be happy!" The calls followed them down the street, fading as they left the town behind and headed into the quiet countryside.

The night was clear and cold, stars scattered like diamonds across the vast Montana sky. Laura huddled close to Boone's side, sharing warmth and marveling at the unexpected turn their evening had taken.

"Are you warm enough?" he asked, wrapping one arm around her while managing the reins with his other hand.

"Perfect," she assured him, nestling against his solid strength. "I can't believe they arranged all this without either of us knowing."

Boone chuckled, the sound rumbling pleasantly against her ear where it pressed to his chest. "Pa can be surprisingly sly when he puts his mind to it. And Matt can keep a secret when it matters."

They rode in comfortable silence for a while, the only sounds the steady clip-clop of hooves on the packed snow and the occasional creak of the wagon. The moon had risen, casting the landscape in silvery light, the snow-covered fields stretching away to distant hills.

"It's beautiful," Laura murmured, gazing out at the pristine wilderness. "Like the whole world has been made new just for us."

Boone's arm tightened around her. "That's how it feels," he agreed softly. "Like everything before was just preparation for this—for us."

The simple honesty of his words warmed Laura more thoroughly than any fire could have. She tilted her face up to his, finding his lips in a kiss that spoke volumes about her agreement.

When they parted, Boone's smile was visible even in the dim light. "Keep that up, Mrs. Callahan, and we might not make it to the cabin."

Laura laughed, the sound bright in the night air. "Then you'd better drive faster, Mr. Callahan."

He did just that, urging the horses to a brisker pace while still being mindful of the snow-covered road. Laura settled against him again, content to watch the moonlit landscape slide by, knowing that wherever they were headed, they were going there together.

The cabin appeared after perhaps an hour's journey, tucked against a stand of pine trees at the base of a gentle slope. Smoke curled from the chimney, and warm light spilled from the windows—evidence that someone had indeed gone ahead to prepare for their arrival.

Boone drew the wagon to a halt before the small porch, setting the brake before turning to face Laura fully. "Wait here," he instructed, jumping down and coming around to her side.

Before she could protest, he had lifted her bodily from the seat, cradling her in his arms as if she weighed nothing.

"Boone!" she exclaimed, laughing despite herself. "I can walk!"

"Not across this threshold, you can't," he insisted, carrying her up the steps to the cabin door. "It's tradition."

Somehow, he managed to open the door while still holding her securely, then paused in the doorway. The interior of the cabin was simple but welcoming—a main room with a fireplace where flames danced merrily, a small table set with a cloth and candles, and a bedroom visible through a partially open door.

"Welcome home, Mrs. Callahan," Boone said softly, carrying her across the threshold and into their temporary haven. "At least for the next few days."

He set her gently on her feet, but kept his arms loosely around her waist, seeming reluctant to let her go even that far. Laura didn't mind. She wound her arms around his neck, drinking in the sight of his beloved face in the firelight.

"Home is wherever you are," she told him simply. "This cabin, the ranch, anywhere at all."

The truth of it resonated in her very soul. After years of wandering, of having no permanent place in the world, she had found her true home—not in a building or a town, but in the heart of the man before her.

"I love you, Laura Callahan," he said softly, the words a sacred vow in the stillness.

"And I love you, Boone Callahan," she answered, her heart so full it felt it might overflow. "With everything I am."

Leave A Review

If you enjoyed this book, please consider leaving an honest review on Amazon.

Visit Our Website:

www.vivianbelle.com

Visit Our Amazon Author Page

Find Us On Social Media:

Facebook

Facebook Author Page

Instagram

www.ingramcontent.com/pod-product-compliance
Lightning Source LLC
Chambersburg PA
CBHW011849300726
48970CB00009B/2716

9 781966 093169